MINEFIELD ENFORCERS BOOK 1

LEANN MASON

Illusionary by LeAnn Mason

Published by LeAnn Mason, LLC 14083 OK-51 #301, Coweta, OK
74429

www.leannmason.com

For more information on reproducing sections of this book or sales of
this book, go to www.leannmason.com or email at:
leann@leannmason.com

Illusionary/LeAnn Mason– First Printing/2018

ISBN: 9781980534709

Cover by: Crimson Phoenix Creations

Edited by: Tina's Edit Service

For everyone instrumental in making this work possible.
You all rock. You know who you are.

CONTENTS

ACKNOWLEDGEMENTS

EIGHTEEN YEARS EARLIER

Dr. Connor Dae

HE SAW IT HAPPENING, inside this artificial hometown. The separation was beginning—no, more like spreading. Like a disease. Division by differences. Segregation. He watched, saddened, as yet another Primal family moved away from his quaint neighborhood.

Connor had a habit of tunneling his fingers desperately within his thick locks when he was troubled, making it the reason he kept his auburn hair cropped short. He snatched his hand from the prickly mass.

The Enhanced–genetically superior humans evolved from a believed result of long-term medical intervention on their ancestors with various continual drug therapies such as antipsychotics or radiation exposure–had already been forced out of the general human population.

But now, those in their invisible cage disguised as a community were taking up the call and further shrinking their world. Sage—those with heightened brain activity, and Primal—those with superior physicality, were no longer united in being different from Non-Enhanced humans.

Now, they, too, were dividing. The physically superior versus the mentally. Soon it would be groups of one or the other, not mixed— making him an outcast by default.

Connor Dae was the son of Lynn and Castor Dae. His mother a Primal and father Sage. His parents were among the initial to be identified and rehomed to Minefield, the first generation of Enhanced. Rehomed? Incarcerated was probably a better term.

Minefield, USA, was a small town in the middle of nowhere north Texas, isolated from the rest of the human population by design. Enhanced humans were deemed such a wildcard by those in power around the world that holding areas were created for the anomalies to be shunted. Each was far enough from the general population that if deemed a threat and needed "large scale elimination," it could be done without risking collateral damage.

Connor snorted at the thought. Though, seriously, since when had a thing like collateral damage stopped a bombing when the powers that be deemed it necessary. Shaking his head and running fingers up the bridge of his nose, he pushed his glasses away and rubbed his eyes to dispel the thought.

One generation. That's all it had taken, a quarter of a century or so, for the Enhanced to turn on one another. Connor shook his head again, disheartened. Hybrids would be a thing of the past if this continued. Couldn't the others see that by joining their gene pool, they could help eliminate their shortcomings? Both divisions of the Enhanced had a flaw. They were opposite of each other: Primals were mentally unstable; Sage— physically weak.

Connor's medically analytical brain told him the best way to combat these flaws was to mingle genes with those who were strong in areas where one was weak.

Maybe it was because they were not seeing marked improvement within his generation, or they wanted more, faster. Instant gratification seemed the way of things. How did you combat that thinking?

What would happen to his little girl, the one his beloved Alana was carrying in her belly? What world, isolated though it was, would she endure? He feared for the future if this mindset continued along the path he was seeing. As a doctor, how could he stand idly by? What could he do for the Enhanced, for his family?

The wheels in his mind furiously turned as he pulled on his jacket, the weather starting to turn from the sweltering, sticky heat of summer, to the brisk mornings he loved. Connor stepped onto the front porch of his humble home and turned back to lock the door. Closing his eyes, he took a deep breath of clean, crisp morning air, the tangy scent of fresh cut grass and dew clinging to the shortened blades.

Connor ambled slowly to his old sedan which the Non-Enhanced had deemed him worthy of, if only due to his profession. The vehicle wasn't anything special, in fact, to the outside world it was woefully inadequate. But he was grateful, and lucky, to have it. The door creaked loudly when Connor opened it, making him wince. Sometimes he forgot that he was stronger than pure Sage, and some objects protested his efforts.

Never on the job though. As an Emergency Physician, Connor Dae was impeccable, and the main reason he held any respect.

He hoped that respect would aid him in finding a way to help others see the detriment in dividing themselves. The Enhanced needed solidarity as the world came to terms with their existence. The question Connor pondered on the short drive to the hospital was, *how?* Would his daughter be the catalyst for change as he hoped, or had he doomed her to a life which held no happy ending? Had Connor made a mistake in tinkering with genetics? Would this new divided Minefield be a safe haven, or an inescapable prison?

CHAPTER 1

"OOF!" I GASPED AS I fell backward, my feet flying up from under me. A second gasp escaped when my back crashed on the soft grass. The impact so jarring, one of my earbuds popped free of its nearly permanent home in my ear.

From my flattened position, I stared at the sky and white puffy clouds breezing along merrily. After gulping air and making sure all parts were still functioning, I used my elbows to prop myself up as I looked around for the reason I was no longer vertical. A few paces in front of me, a football rocked slightly as it settled on the plush grass. A burst of raucous laughter drew my attention to a group of Primal males all roaring, slapping each other on the back and doubling over with mirth.

"Just like a Sage to walk through an ongoing game without knowing," a particularly large Primal guffawed, his friends agreeing. Their muscles

5

bulged, bare torsos gleaming with sweat as they continued to berate my obliviousness.

To be fair, they were right about me not paying attention. I was too absorbed in the invigorating melody of the large stringed instruments wafting from my earbuds. I'd been twitching my fingers with phantom strings and had not been in tune with my surroundings.

I was lucky to not be nearly as fragile as a pure Sage, who would be headed to the ER, most likely with something broken. Dad would probably be the one looking into their injuries. I didn't have that breakability about me. Don't get me wrong, that freaking hurt like a mother, but I would only bruise. No internal injuries for me!

I was a bit more, shall we say…resilient than the average Sage here in Minefield. But then, that was because I wasn't only Sage, and *that* fact made me a larger target for abuse.

Living in a town mainly comprised of Enhanced humans, I saw fantastic things every day. A Sage was always using their telekinesis, or a Primal demonstrating their strength for all to see, much like this group. To us, *Enhanced* referred to people who had developed "abilities" beyond the average human.

Sage possessed a mental gift. My *enhancement* was telepathy, but it was so far from a gift that I considered it a burden. My lack of mental barriers had never been much more than an additional way to separate me from my peers. I often wished I had gained a more mainstream ability such as telekinesis or eidetic memory. Being a professed Primal would've been awesome as well, but that part of my identity was squelched, suppressed. Unexplored.

Primal Enhanced were physically superior to the other divisions, and their gifts added to that divide. Not only were they physically bigger, stronger, and faster, but their abilities were cooler. I mean, how awesome would it be to see in the dark or be so fast that you blurred in people's vision? My Primal ability was pretty cool though. Too bad it only came into play when I was injured, and that no one knew about it. Yeah, that little piece of the Nathalee-Dae-puzzle wasn't given to anyone. What they did know about, landed me in the Sage camp.

I was a telepath.

I read people's thoughts, which all too often were not flattering for anyone. The person thinking unfavorable opinions usually painted themselves in a bad light, making it the biggest reason people didn't want me around. They didn't like that I knew their words and actions were a lie. Sages prided themselves on their stoic, objective nature, and they hated that I could see through the mask. Primals were usually pretty straight forward, or at least what little I'd seen of them.

So, my time was spent alone unless I was with Jade. I usually observed from afar, lost in my music, not worrying about others' thoughts interfering with my own.

I watched Sages play games like the Non-Enhanced humans did, but with teams using thought to propel items instead of arms or legs, seeing as another Sage trait was physical limitation. Sometimes those limits were as benign as being shorter and thinner. Other times, they were more debilitating.

This was the main contention between Sage and Primal Enhanced— each lacked what the other had in spades.

Except me.

Once I'd recovered my breath, certainly not my pride, I stood and dusted myself off with as much dignity I could muster. As I patted down my clothes and tried to keep myself from aching, I popped my earbud in and continued my journey home. As I came upon the picturesque grounds of the equestrian center, however, I decided I needed some pony time.

Veering toward the drive, I took in everything as the music pulsed in my ears, further lightening my mood. I forgot the ache in my midsection, which was surely bruised but mending quickly, and breathed deeply as I passed under the entry gate's overhanging sign which simply read "Minefield Equestrian." I dragged my feet through the dirt and gravel, kicking up clouds of dust in my wake.

Everything about this place called to me, and I removed my earbuds and tucked them into my pocket. I paused at a small turnout area divided into several individual parts, most containing a horse. The occupants threw their heads from side to side, almost appearing to say no as they pranced back and forth with their neighbors. Then they'd stop and attempt a quick bite at the horse across the fence before pulling back, squealing, and kicking out with their legs.

I loved it.

I barked a quick laugh at their antics before pushing away from the railing and heading into the barn proper. Off to my left, I noticed the large man I often ogled from afar. He looked to be hosing down a horse tied to a post. The horse danced an Irish jig, tapping with his hooves across the mat in his futile attempts to keep its face from the deluge.

I'd seen the man at the barn countless times, though, never actually encountered him. I didn't know his name. I didn't know his age. I didn't know his eye color, or how he felt about the weather. I didn't know anything about him other than what I could see from a distance. I think this was why he intrigued me. I hadn't yet been plagued by his internal diatribe. One thing I was certain of: he was not Sage. He was way too tall and wide, too sculpted and athletic. He could be an NE, but he seemed too smooth, too graceful. I shrugged. It didn't matter, really.

I had no idea if he even knew I came here, or who I was in general. He had no notion of my particular brand of crazy, or I his. My time here was spent roaming the barn aisle and nuzzling with the horses, taking in their scents and reveling in the absence of voices in my head.

I sat against the stall door of a horse named Jasper, my legs extended in front of me and crossed at the ankles. I leaned my head against the warm wood and closed my eyes. At this point in the day, my spot was in a beam of sunshine—warming me to my bones. Breathing deeply, I savored the musty, stale air carrying a variety of aromas. Some were pleasant, like the spicy, woodsy scent of pine shavings used in the stalls, or the smells of the animals, which were earthy and tinged with salty sweat. The bouquet of fresh excrement was *not* my favorite, but was ever present and added to the overall feel of this place. My peace.

Jasper whinnied and nuzzled the top of my head in greeting. I returned his affections by reaching up and holding his nose to my forehead. The whiskers on his chin tickled my skin, making me giggle and pull away. Jasper was my favorite animal here. Not only was he a gorgeous copper color with a strikingly blond mane and tail, but he had big, kind brown eyes that seemed to look into my soul. We understood each other without me peeking into his mind, and I loved him for it.

I opened my eyes to a blazing pink and orange sky, the sunlight burning my retinas with its intensity. My backside ached from sitting on the packed dirt for so long and my muscles were stiff, which made me realize the warmth had lulled me into a nap, and not the momentary closure I expected my eyes to accept.

I groaned as I pushed off the ground and stretched. Facing Jasper's stall, the sun's scorching rays behind me, I came back to the present as my stomach roared its verbal protest at the time between meals. I needed to eat. My metabolism was definitely faster than the average bear and I had to continually stuff my gob.

She stayed a while today.

I turned to see who was around and spotted the attractive man two stalls down, putting him several yards away as he walked to the far end of the barn. I couldn't pull my eyes from his strong back as he filled the wheelbarrow with forage for his charges. I'd never heard him speak before, probably because I was usually long gone by this time in the evening. Already back home to assure my parents, my dad really, that no one had taken extra notice of me.

She seems to like Jasper, I heard him say and then chuckle. I couldn't help but smile in reaction to his mirth. I wondered why he found that funny. Jasper was a fine horse, maybe a little impatient. We had that in common. The man had a nice voice, deep and melodic. Soothing. I half expected it to be clumsy and stilted, as every Sage I talked to, or heard, seemed to think Primals and Non-Enhanced were almost a lesser being. Something not nearly as evolved as Sages.

The man wheeled the feed down the dirt aisle, stopping every so often to fork hay into a stall where the horse would immediately pull a mouthful away and chew blissfully. I now realized that the barn was fully occupied with its four-hooved occupants.

When he was about ten feet away, I plucked the courage to speak. "Hello." *Nice, Nathalee, real smooth.*

He grabbed another piece and approached Jasper's stall. I saw myself through his eyes. He was not guarding his mind, and I was curious. I stood awkwardly with my hands at my sides, my blue-green eyes wide, blondish hair a riotous mess that escaped the confines of my ponytail. My mouth, slightly open as if in a stupor, was a nice touch.

This close, I noticed he was a few years my senior. He definitely had a mature vibe about him. I'd guess early twenties. His eyes were a vibrant blue, made more striking by his dark hair and the stubble lining his jaw. He quirked his mouth in a half-smile that crinkled the corner of his eye, and inclined his head slightly.

We stood gawking at each other until Jasper, having decided he'd waited long enough for his dinner, pawed at his stall door, making an awful racket. The moment dispelled, mystery man continued on to Jasper's stall to deliver food. I pulled myself a little straighter and cleared my throat.

"I'm Nathalee. I've seen you here working with the horses. Are you a trainer?" The man glanced at me as he headed back to the cart but didn't say anything. *Not very social then. That was usually my role.*

"What's your name?" Again, nothing. I followed behind him, starting to get annoyed. Geez, was this how people felt around me? No, I didn't ignore them if they spoke directly to me. I just tried to avoid close quarters with crowds. Stomping along, I didn't care I kicked up clouds of choking dust sprinkled liberally with powdered horse manure.

He was tall, over six feet to my five foot, seven inches. I wasn't used to looking up when addressing anyone. Most Sages were under six-feet tall, especially the females— around five feet, four inches on a good day. *Mark another tally for not being like most Sages.*

His dark hair was sweaty and curled around his nape. Every so often, he would toss his head, dispelling a lock from his eyes, seeing as his hands were occupied. He was beautiful. Too bad he was rude.

She's following me.

"Yeah, I'm following you. You didn't answer me like social norms dictate when asked a direct question," I huffed at him and threw my arms up in defeat, letting them slam to my sides. Spinning on my heel, I strode toward the door at the far end of the aisle, intent on leaving. I'd already been out too late.

I kicked a clump of hay he must have dropped and cursed him under my breath. Another flaw in my Sage persona: a temper. Most had an even temperament, at least outwardly. Visually, they didn't really waver to either happy or mad, or anything really. Stoic is how I would describe their overt behavior. Primals, on the other hand…

I continued my tirade until I was stopped in my tracks as a hand closed around mine. I looked down at my fingers, clasped securely in Mystery Man's larger ones.

His was rough, calloused from long days caring for the horses, I assumed, and I marveled at the feel of it. When he tugged softly, I shifted my eyes to his blazing blues with a silver ring around the pupil. They held me captive with their intensity, making me feel as though I could step into the stormy sea reflected there. He wore a contrite expression and opened his mouth as if to speak, only to close it and shrug, not releasing my hand.

I don't know how to tell her I can't tell her my name.

"Why can't you tell me your name?" I asked, wondering if he was not permitted to speak with Sages at the facility or elsewhere.

I can't speak. He sounded exasperated, his eyes sad.

"You can't speak? Like you're not allowed? That's ridiculous!" I pulled my hand away and crossed my arms over my chest. They were safer there. I was safer with them there where I wouldn't marvel at the heat I felt when we touched.

His shocked countenance pulled me from my mental tirade. "What?"

He had dropped his hands to his sides and stood gawking at me with surprised blue eyes and a gaping mouth, looking much as I had earlier.

Can you hear me? he asked mentally in a tentative voice filled with awe and...hope. I loved his voice even if he was rude. I contemplated my answer. Obviously he was unaware of who I was or what my abilities were. It softened me toward him slightly.

I nodded.

He blew out a breath he seemed to have been holding and his shoulders dropped, almost as if in relief. *You can hear me.*

A statement this time. He smiled. A small, crooked line that seemed to belong on his face but hardly had the luxury of being there. I smiled in return, feeling a dimple emerge, and nodded. "Yes. I'm Sage and a telepath." I figured he'd puzzled it out, so no point pretending I couldn't hear, and that statement was the easiest explanation of me.

He reached out his hand and voiced clearly, *My name is Holden,* then smiled. It was big, it was bright—it was beautiful. Then and there, I decided my goal when around him was to bring that smile out anytime I could. I reached for his extended hand. "I'm Nathalee."

13

He mentally chuckled, *I remember.*

I blushed. I had been so caught up in him that I repeated information. *Mental face palm! Time to make your exit, Graceful.*

"Well, Holden, it was nice to meet you." At the end of my diatribe, I noticed our hands were still clasped. Clearing my throat, I dropped my head, feeling heat rush upward as I pulled out of his grasp.

"I, uh, need to get going." I hitched a thumb over my shoulder in the opposite direction and took a step back. I was still blushing. He noticed but was gracious enough not to draw attention to it.

I see you most afternoons. Do you live nearby?

"Yeah. Um, I work at the campus for Doctor Parmore after classes. This is on my way home."

Forgive my intrusion. I am incredibly unaccustomed to holding conversations. Now it was Holden's turn to flush, the tips of his ears becoming red. His eyes averted mine, lowered toward his dirt-scuffed boots. He sighed.

He had a very good vocabulary for someone who didn't use it.

"There is nothing to forgive. You did nothing that has caused me offense. I'm not used to holding conversation much, either, as most people don't want me anywhere near them." I shrugged, feigning nonchalance.

I'm sure that's not true, he said, ducking in an attempt to catch my eye.

Bitterness crept in. "It is." I laughed derisively. "People want to maintain the illusion. They don't want someone around who can unravel them. Call them out on their crap." I had to remind myself that I didn't care. *Calm, Nat.* I looked at Holden, noticing his unbelieving expression, and decided I needed to end the conversation and regroup.

"Again, it was nice to meet you, but I really do need to leave. I'm late, and my parents will worry." I turned on my heel once more and resumed walking to the far end of the barn without waiting for a reply, afraid I would get lost in conversation again. As I reached the entryway, I heard Holden.

Goodbye, Nathalee.

Then I was gone, out the doors and into the ever-darkening night.

CHAPTER 2

AS I WALKED TO the small house I called home, I thought about our segregation from the Non-Enhanced human population. We, here in the created town of Minefield, called those who populated the rest of the world, *Non-Enhanced*, "NE" for short. I called them ninnies, get it? N-Es? As you see, I'm brilliantly witty.

Anyway, NEs are your average, every day, run-of-the-mill humans. The majority appeared to be incredibly afraid of the possibilities of Enhanced humans. Their fear created the basis for our culling from the general population. I compared our situation to being incarcerated. We were deemed "unfit" to mingle within the ranks of the rest of the world. Now, we had our own set of rules and were completely isolated except for the oversight of an outside governing body, which ultimately dictated our entire lives.

For all intents and purposes, we were imprisoned in Minefield.

I pulled out my headphones, picking an upbeat tune, and allowed myself to get lost. The thumping bass line and all too-true lyrics about being an adrenaline junkie crooned as I watched life being lived around me. With music, it was almost like a movie soundtrack and I began watching my surroundings in such a light.

A Primal man had lifted the rear of a car in order to retrieve something which had been trapped under a wheel, then proceeded to unceremoniously drop the vehicle once he had his item. The car thudded, then squeaked as it hit the ground and settled back into place, bouncing a few times before coming to rest. The Primal ability of strength was obviously gifted to him.

Wish I had adrenaline in my veins.

The track changed as I noticed a couple walking down the street, hand in hand. Their dog's leash taut but not being held, floating in front of them. A normal display of telekinesis though I couldn't tell which of them held it in place. There was no telling whether one was an NE.

Some NEs lived in the town. The ones who chose to stay with their families when they were forced to relocate to the Enhanced segregated areas generations ago. Some still came through our gates, though now, they did so with no connection to those inside. It was like a novelty, or a challenge. In fact, the numbers of NEs entering Minefield had been steadily growing in the recent years, and they were fully aware they could never leave.

Insanity.

I had both Sage and Primal characteristics, but I leaned toward the ninnies in appearance. I was unique, and I was hiding the full scope. My father worried constantly that my special Primal ability would be

unearthed. He worried what would come of the knowledge. The
Enhanced were already under intense scrutiny and regulation, feared for
their specialties. I could only imagine what they'd think of someone with a
unique specialty. Though Enhanced humans were only a small percentage
of the overall population, the ninnies worried themselves to death with
"what if."

What if we used our abilities to sway people, governments? What if
our abilities became too much to handle? What if we were dangerous?
People often forgot that anyone could be dangerous. Everyone had the
potential to cause harm whether intentional or not. Non-Enhanced had
just as much aptitude for mayhem as we did, but still, we were the only
ones subject to complete segregation—aside from prisoners.

As I continued to walk, I thought back through my life and tried to
find instances in which I spoke with a Primal because Holden wasn't the
only one I was around. I searched memories but couldn't recall anything
concrete. Nothing personal. I certainly had no friends that were Primal,
and my Nana had died when I was quite small.

I had only one real friend, Jade, who was a Sage, not too much of a
surprise. I felt ashamed to think that maybe I avoided them, maybe some
unconscious effort to stay with what I was comfortable with—just like the
ninnies did with the Enhanced. Then I remembered Holden's reaction
when I heard his voice, his words, and scoffed. I couldn't believe they
lacked understanding. Even if that's what Sages liked to believe.

In fact, I could argue that Sages were lacking or underdeveloped
when it came to relationships between people; in emotion. They seemed
to live in black and white, never straying from the lines. Variation was
deemed lesser and frowned upon. Only the desirable traits were cultivated

and brought along, allowed to flourish. They'd been trying for years to mold me into their vision of what a Sage Enhanced should be. To my knowledge, no one had developed gifts of both Sage and Primal, and I was not anxious to see how they moved forward with that little piece of information about me, should it ever be revealed.

Most Sage seem to have evolved to be telekinetic, likely to help balance the fact that their bodies could not do heavy lifting so to speak, so the mind picked up the slack. Other abilities were less prevalent, telepathy for example. I was the only telepath who heard more than snippets or fleeting images without physical contact, at least, to my limited knowledge.

I heard anyone within range, at least to some degree, and voices got louder or sharper when someone focused their thoughts on me. Though extreme emotion was rarely seen from Sage Enhanced, I heard it in their minds. In fact, stoicism could be a clue as to whether someone was Non-Enhanced human or a Sage. That didn't mean emotion was absent necessarily, just that it was hidden beneath the surface. For this reason, both telepaths and empaths were avoided or made to feel inferior.

If no one had the ability to contradict what one said with their mouth, then it must be truth though I'm sure Primals could detect it as well. They were much more in tune with body language and such nuances…or so I'd heard from Dad. My Nana was that way, what little I knew of her.

I blinked and looked around the nearly dark pathway, aware that I had been lost in my contemplation. The street lamps were on and emitting soft yellow halos of light at regular intervals, like they were my guide, keeping me safe. I knew I was late for dinner and hated worrying my parents, at least my dad, so I hurried my steps as I crossed the street and headed down the last block.

I removed one earbud, so I would have a leg up should anyone approach, but still mouthed the words. My steps matched the beat, head bobbing in tune. The sun had almost completely set, and I didn't wish to be caught out roaming after dark.

My mother was convinced that sanity fled with the light of day. *"You just never know what Primal miscreants come out in the latter hours, Nathalee,"* she'd say. Of course, bad behavior and misdeeds were synonymous with "Primal" to my mother.

At last, I turned the corner to my home and tripped up the path lined with bright blue and purple pansies, onto the front steps. I took a moment to regain my balance, something I struggled with regularly, and immediately smelled my mother's spaghetti and meatballs, causing my mouth to water. I stopped at the door and just breathed it in.

I scented the browned meat, the richness of the herbs and tomato sauce. And garlic. *Yum.* My mother's internal monologue was unruffled, as usual. I hadn't expected any difference, really. I stepped on the worn welcome mat and scraped my dirt laden shoes, gathering breath in preparation for my apology, and pushed open the door like a woman prepared to meet the gallows…or worse, a freaked out parental.

My pent up breath was promptly and thoroughly torn from me in a whoosh as I was gripped in a surprisingly strong embrace. My father wrapped himself around me, one arm around my head, the other across my shoulders as his cheek rested against my crown, squishing me quite effectively against his chest. *Freaked out parental it was.*

"You're all right," he assured himself.

I wrapped my arms around his back and held. I knew he worried about me, knew he was convinced harm would come to me one day because I was different. Because he couldn't sway people into realizing that we should all *just get along*. My being late had planted the seed that today was that day.

I was eighteen, soon to be pushed out of the nest and into my own life. He couldn't worry about me like this whenever I deviated from the routine, but I still felt horrible. I squeezed my eyes shut and berated myself for my carelessness. How could I have worried him like that? Why didn't I let them know I was running behind? I had my phone. Well, honestly, Holden had me all discombobulated and my good sense had flown the coop.

"I'm sorry, Dad," I mumbled into his chest. "I dozed off at the barn and didn't wake up until Holden came in to feed the horses."

My father gripped my shoulders with large hands and drew me away from his body so he could look at my face. Dad was another anomaly of a Sage. Like me, he was above average height and built like an athlete, a product of his being a true Primal and Sage hybrid. He did not however, receive any Primal enhancements. Because he had the mental gift of shielding, he was identified as a Sage. He ran more toward NE strength though maybe like someone who frequented a gym. From physical appearances, we both resembled the ninnies, somewhere between the Enhanced extremes. He was nearly always in scrubs from work, usually green to indicate surgeon.

"Holden?" Puzzled, Dad's brow wrinkled in confusion. "Who is Holden?"

Still holding me away from his now rigid body, bright hazel eyes roamed my person from behind stylish glasses, trying to fish out details.

"Holden is the guy who works at the barn," I said as I shrugged a shoulder. The effect was minimal, still confined under a large hand and I was sure it hadn't worked. My father narrowed his gaze and flicked his probing gaze between my widened bluish-green irises. "I think he's Primal," I whispered. My father's eyes widened a fraction before he schooled his features.

"Primal?" he asked hesitantly. I nodded as he stepped back, dropped his hands, and looked over my shoulder toward the kitchen doorway behind me. "Did he notice you?" He began to pace, looking decidedly agitated. I watched him move the length of the small living room as I answered.

"Yes. He noticed that I was still there past my usual time and seemed curious about it." I continued to watch my father pace but bounced my attention to my mother who stood stock still in front of the kitchen island, her back to us and our conversation.

The scrumptious dinner abandoned for the details I now shared. I returned my attention toward my nervous father, chewing on a fingernail to accompany the agitation of his legs. He turned on his heel and headed the other direction. I was sure a trail would be worn in the carpet if he kept it up. His hand left his teeth to run roughly through his short, auburn hair.

"I introduced myself...and he didn't." I quirked my mouth at the remembered conversation.

"I can't speak."

"You can hear me."

Dad growled, "Did he hurt you?"

"No!" I was offended on Holden's behalf; it seemed the stigma of being Primal didn't allow for deviation, which was funny considering our own lineage. My *father's* lineage, and his thoughts on cohesion.

"He was apologetic. Told me he is unable to speak." That little nugget caused my father's steps to falter, his large frame swaying as he dug his heels into the plush beige carpet in his attempt to stay upright. *That was an interesting reaction.*

He asked if Holden was not allowed to speak to patrons and began his movements once again. I, as Holden had to me, corrected him. "He physically *can't* speak."

"Oh." My father looked at a loss for words, his eyes large and owlish as he blinked behind his black rimmed spectacles. I sat and enjoyed the moment, soaking in the sight of the mighty Connor Dae shocked into silence. Soon enough, his brow wrinkled, and he cocked his head to the side, like he had just had an epiphany. *Interesting.*

Through this whole recounting, I heard nothing from his mind. Dad was the only person I had met who had a full-time mental shield. It was impressive, and it never wavered, unless he wanted it to. He was one of the few people I could stand to be around for long though I was sure if his shields dropped for any length of time that would change. His worry for me was constant, and I was sure his mind circled with it.

Also, my father was a true genius and studied genomes when he wasn't on rotation at the emergency section of the hospital. He focused on how genes had changed since the original genetic deviations; the first cases which noted enhanced abilities. The startling trend was traced back to survivors of extreme mental or physical ailments. Those whose mind or body had been viciously ravaged and survived mainly due to medical intervention.

The examples he gave most often when explaining were a cancer patient and a schizophrenic. If someone had either of these disorders, their lives were inexorably tied to medical advances in treatments. These treatments caused genetic mutations in a high number of progeny of such afflicted. He studied DNA from as many generations, and abilities, as he could.

"I've never heard of a Primal who was mute. Do you know if he was born that way? Was he injured in some way—at some point?" Something was off in the way he lilted the question, like he was fishing for something.

He was right, though, that's what made a Primal such, physical superiority, near perfection, in fact. Sure, there were some with scars or limps or even missing appendages, but to be born with a flaw and still possess Primal enhancements was unheard of. My father mumbled about coincidences or something, and continued his creepy blank stare. I knew he was digesting and assimilating this new information as he stared past me into the kitchen. This would go on forever if I didn't bring him back on point. With the ongoing quiet, I registered that I didn't hear my mother anymore.

I used her absence to bring my father out of his musings.

"Dad, where's Mom?"

My father ran his hands roughly through his hair again and fell onto the ugly floral-patterned couch he had been pacing in front of.

"Your mother? Oh, she was going to use one of her gadgets to locate you after starting dinner." He waved his hand dismissively then froze, his eyes widening as realization dawned. "Did she not see you come in? I can tell her to call off the search," he launched off the couch and charged ahead, down the hall toward the office which housed my mother's "gadgets," and therefore, usually my mother. She must have gone to put her locator back once she'd seen me.

I shook my head and as I took a seat on the couch, I heard my mother's insistent voice both with my ears and in my mind. A moment later they emerged from the hall where my father had disappeared only moments before.

"I told you she would make it home, Connor," she said, smiling indulgently at her husband. Mother was a beautiful woman who reminded me of what a Sage embodied. She stood a mere five feet, three inches tall and her frame was narrow, wispy. Her long, honey-blonde hair was pulled into a ponytail low on her neck, and eyes the color of the sky on a cloudless day twinkled at me with humor as she reached up to cup my father's face in her palms. She had an unwavering faith in knowledge and technology, accompanying the belief that Sages held the keys to making the world whole again.

I wasn't so sure.

Like others, my mother was also a bit leery around me. She didn't like that I could "hear" her. She often wandered off to fiddle with her gizmos. I tried not to let it get to me, rationalizing that her *Sageness* made her feel that way.

"Nathalee, would you mind putting together a salad to go with the pasta?" Mom said. I meandered to the refrigerator and gathered the ingredients for a nice, "well-rounded" salad.

Dad wouldn't eat one that didn't have half the produce section in it, so I knew to load up. Almost immediately, my mother's internal monologue started, though this time, she was visualizing the best way to solve a short that kept occurring in one of her locators. I tuned her out, which was much easier when I didn't understand the subject matter.

I circled back to remember Holden, yet again, as I began chopping the various veggies I planned to put into the greens. I couldn't get him out of my head. It wasn't like I hadn't been around guys before, it's just that Holden seemed so different from the boys I normally interacted with.

Sage men could be attractive, but usually in a sort of geeky way. They were very buttoned up, and—I don't know—cold? Distant? Holden didn't seem to be either. And let's face it, he was also gorgeous. The last part I had known in theory but seeing him up close? He was breathtaking. I swear his eyes could burn holes through whatever held their focus, and his strength was sure to be unmatched by Sages whether or not he was Primal. But by the flowing, graceful, nearly prowling gait he affected, my money bet he was.

A sharp pain lanced my finger, forcing my attention back to my task. I noticed the cutting board now sported a small, but growing, pool of crimson which flowed from a decent slice in my thumb. *Way to go, high five!* This was exactly why you didn't do such things while holding sharp objects, especially if as accident prone as I seemed to be.

I whipped my lacerated flesh toward the sink and grabbed the towel sitting neatly on the edge. My mother was still wrapped up in her musings, so I turned on the faucet to let cool water run over the abused digit. After a few moments, I pulled my hand from the water and took a look. It was already done bleeding, and if I watched, I would notice the flesh knitting back together. This was my greatest secret, the thing that would get me locked away and poked and prodded into oblivion.

I could heal myself.

CHAPTER 3

IT WASN'T AN INSTANT thing, not unless the injury was almost non-existent to begin with, a paper cut for instance. Anyway, not instant, but rapid. My body mended sprains within hours, fractured bones in days. My early childhood escapades clued us into those timeframes and became the referred to incidents when my dad needed to remind me as to just why I could not play like I wanted.

We had to keep my activities very sedate so I didn't reveal this fact. That in itself wasn't too unusual, though many Sages avoided physically strenuous situations as well. Most of their bodies didn't hold up well under stress, especially for longer periods. So to keep my Primal enhancement secret, we played up the Sage portion of my genetics, claiming that other than my height and possibly a bit of strength, I was all Sage.

I resented the fact that I couldn't explore my physicality outside of our home any longer. I wanted to *do* more. Be something *more* than a clerk. I hated that Enhanced were treated as lepers in the global scheme, hidden away and watched. Constantly monitored, and severely limited.

There were cameras, sensors and guards placed at the entrances to Enhanced "communities." It was like a checkpoint, one tipped in razor wire atop a tall, thick barrier. Everyone was stopped and questioned. Documented. Only officially acknowledged and sanctioned exits were allowed and were always temporary. The Non-Enhanced who chose now to enter our gates were documented so that ninnies could be notified of their defectors.

Any others were turned around and forced to return to the confines of the town. This was the only allowed point of entry and exit. The wall encompassed the entire Enhanced community. The government had pulled military forces from foreign lands to be our babysitters.

I'm sure they watched us elsewhere, having many more cameras and spies within our ranks.

"Nathalee?" My mother's face swam into my line of sight, her eyes narrowed in suspicion as she stepped in front of me. This was apparently not the first time she'd said my name. Her internal scrutiny made me stand taller. I didn't like that she thought me "flighty."

"Sorry, Mother, what did you say?" I smiled, trying to relieve the tension.

"I asked if you had finished the salad and could take it to the table." She lifted her eyebrows questioningly while pursing her lips. For a beautiful woman, I rarely saw it. She was too often scowling at me.

I looked toward the cutting board still sporting a half-chopped carrot, and my blood. "Um, yeah. Just let me get the carrot in and I'll bring it right out." I hastily cleaned the blood from the cutting board and mixed the salad so I saw a bit of each component before heading into the dining area. The large table was situated before the bay window and allowed for natural light in this portion of the house during daytime hours.

I sat and bowed my head alongside my parents as my father said a prayer of thanks then dug into the meal with fervor. I silently hoped the rest of the evening was uneventful so I could escape into my room and relax without further elaborating upon my day. I sat and nodded along with mild interest as Dad recounted his thoughts about a higher than normal incident of accidental or rage instigated injuries.

People were coming to the emergency room with major trauma and explanations that didn't add up. Mother was quite interested in his many stories, like it was a riddle she could solve with enough time, but I tuned them out. I finished my meal, cleaned my plates and headed to my room. The moment I crossed the threshold, I connected my music and let myself be lost in the melodies.

Music was my savior. My "go to" for shutting out the world and allowing only my own thoughts to enter my head. Tonight, I wanted something relatable. I'd had a good day, so I picked a song about the best day of life and prepared to be absorbed in harmonies, chords, and bars. Some loud and brassy, some quiet and gentle. All calming.

The next morning came too early, like all mornings. I hated the routine of blearily searching for clothes, food, and making myself presentable before scrambling out the door to make the walk.

The campus was the worst. Not only did I have to deal with inane conversations between idle teens, but I also had to listen to whatever they were obsessing about in their minds. Tack on the fact that my intelligence was a dim light bulb in a sea of chandeliers, and my educational experiences sucked. I had been relegated to classes which most Sage Enhanced students had long ago surpassed. I was ecstatic to have finished my required educational duration a mere two weeks prior. I only wished I didn't have to go back to the campus for my job.

Today was test day for those Dr. Parmore was taking on for summer sessions. These days were easier than lecture days. Less was required of me as there were no materials needed to have been gathered and/or distributed amongst the students. Though people's shields tended to be nonfunctional as they concentrated on their problems, I was no longer required to be in their presence without the necessary tools to overcome the chatter. While it was possible to create mental shields, it took immense concentration or an innate ability to shield without effort. For this reason, most didn't shield their mind often, or well.

So again, school sucked. I had gotten headaches from the mental bombardment. It was just too much coming at me at once and my mind revolted in the form of physical pain. *Awesome, right?* Insistent pulsing behind my eyes and throbbing at the back of my head, it was like everything came in and then tried to pound its way out with no regard for my wellbeing.

Too many people in confined areas made tuning them out difficult. Enter my need for music. Not being allowed to use earbuds in class had been a huge hindrance. That was one plus to my new station in life: I could usually spend much of my time with earbuds in while I worked. It's not like anyone wanted to talk to me, anyway. I had limited success.

After collecting the completed test papers, I trudged to lunch feeling much more relaxed. The campus was large, but seeing as it was where all Minefield children came for schooling, it needed to be. Add in the desire to separate Sages from others, and it sprawled across several blocks and resembled a rundown university campus in a poor city, or so I had gathered from the internet.

The buildings were separate and each housed certain subjects: Harper Hall for mathematics, Thompson Hall for sciences, and so on. I could usually avoid mass mental bombardment during my food runs thanks to this fact. That is until I came upon the commons. Here it was simply impossible to avoid people as there were always at least a few groups. My standard practice was to get in and get out quickly, or make sure I had my earbuds and music to drown out the chatter.

It always seemed like there were twice as many people around when you could hear thoughts because most people thought something different from what they said. If they kept the same track in both, they expanded and dwelled mentally. It was the internal voice that drove me crazy. That mental voice was unfiltered, and truth was dangerous and forever sought.

For the first sixteen years of my life, I was able to tolerate being around groups of people quite easily. In fact, I had many friends. Our enhancements seemed to culminate around one's sixteenth year, though abilities had been seen both earlier as well as slightly later.

So basically, there was no norm.

The most prevalent aptitude within the Sage populace was telekinesis: the faculty to move objects with thought. It was a competence which tended to show itself early. Telepathy was a much smaller group, and skill varied widely. Early in my adolescence, I had a sense of what someone was feeling, a mental "tone" if you will. It wasn't until I was able to actually hear their thoughts in detail that my friend pool suddenly dried up.

The plus to this development was that I didn't have to decipher what was actually voiced via mouth…and respond accordingly. All too often, I had found myself responding to thought.

Do you think anyone will notice if I padded my bra?

Nat is such a prude, I mean, kissing? That's it. Won't let me under her shirt, let alone in her pants. That particular tidbit earned my then boyfriend Toby, a vicious bite during said kissing. Then for good measure, I punched him in the nose. It broke. *Perfect.*

I learned two things that fateful day. One, my temper was worse than normal, which was concerning. Second, that I had more strength than other Sages possessed. This gift of brawn, which I seemed to gain overnight, was physical, further separating me from my peers. They weren't sure if I had clout, or good aim and a temper. In their defense, both were true. Luckily my strength wasn't so much that I couldn't hide the scope of it. It was more in the realm of *really* fit ninnies. Needless to say, there was enough "fodder" of my differences to occupy Sage mouths, and minds, for a long time.

The "friend well" ran dry after too many of those encounters and news of my breaking Toby's nose, coupled with falling behind in classes, kind of sealed the deal. From then on, I was feared for both my mental *and* physical ability. I was now truly an outcast, adrift. This outsider status only made being in others' company that much more unbearable. They couldn't hide it from me and gave up trying, turning instead to openly jeering at me when given the opportunity.

Only Jade stayed by my side, and I hers. *Speak of the little blonde devil.*

Jade sauntered toward where I stood looking over the options of today's rations, trying to find something to satisfy my craving for protein. Jade was small, standing at an even five feet, very slight of build and with severe asthma. Her long hair shone like spun gold and her large eyes were the color of—you guessed it—jade. Her asthma was enough to keep her from most physical activity, so she spent as much time as she could sunbathing. I often found her in the quad, tucked against the trunk of a large oak tree, reading. We had that in common—the desire to be alone and soothed by nature. I usually took my peace at the barn just off campus.

Jade threw me a knowing smirk as she grabbed an apple. Juice sprayed as she bit out a huge chunk, and with it, the sweet aroma of the fruit. It now resembled Pac Man. Reaching to extricate one earbud, she asked, "Test day?" raising her eyebrows in tandem with her question as she batted her eyelashes in feigned innocence. She was already aware of my mild mood. Jade's ability was shunned almost as completely as mine. She was an empath.

She had the ability to feel what others did. She explained it once as her "energy moves to coincide with those around her." It wasn't a sight, sound, or hearing culmination. It was touch. Her energy "buzzed" to match others, and was effective in telling her how they felt, often making her emotions match. Luckily for her, it was a short-range talent. She usually needed to be within a couple of feet of her subject.

I tossed a grape at her and returned the smirk. "Shut up."

I picked chicken strips to add to my tray and continued toward the exit as Jade kept pace beside me, though with her short legs, she really had to work at it. I slowed a bit so I didn't cause an asthma attack. Once we were through the doors and under the sun, I led us toward the least populated area I could find, which turned out, pleasantly, to be under the trees.

I put my back against the trunk of a large oak and slid to sit at its base as I brought my lunch tray to rest across my knees. Jade crossed her feet and lowered herself to sit crisscross applesauce—a silly saying of Dad's—facing me.

As we finished our meals, we each leaned back to soak up the glorious heat from the sun's rays. With us sitting in a treed area, it was chilly. The sun's warming embrace not quite reaching my limbs. I was still able to relax enough that the sound of Jade's voice startled me and I jerked upright, knocking the tray from my lap. I flopped my hands between my legs, widening my eyes a few times in an attempt to focus.

Luckily, it took only a moment to get my bearings, but that didn't stop Jade from throwing her head back and cackling like a loon, her golden hair glinting in the sunlight. I glowered at her, hiding a smirk when she started coughing a bit. She had laughed so hard, she pushed herself into an asthma attack. *Serves her right, the witch!* Jade had an emergency inhaler on her at all times for occasions like this, which happened often, though she never let it slow her down, or convince her to give up her dreams.

Jade's outcast status was one reason I adored her. She, like me, would love to try something new. Something that would make her feel accomplished and like she overcame her shortcomings. Something a Sage

35

didn't do, happy as they were within their molds. We were still working on what feat would achieve this without sending her parents into absolute hysterics, and neither of us to the hospital. Or the grave.

CHAPTER 4

BILL AND JUDY DANFORTH were the type who would have loved to wrap their little girl in bubble wrap and put her on a shelf, away from wandering hands. To be fair, the Danforths had a hard time carrying to term. Jade was the only child of five conceptions. They didn't understand that their nervousness, the constant hovering and gasps of worry, only made Jade more determined.

She was hot to handle and actually showed emotion unlike many Sages, though maybe both of us got our tempers from being exposed to so much of the internal strife of others. It was constant. The relentless barrage of thought and feeling, it wore you down. Made a person twitchy and irritable. So we had tempers, and sarcasm bled from our mouths like a seeping wound.

Now recovered, Jade spoke earnestly. "Have you found something for us yet, Nat?"

Our conversations invariably circled back to this as-yet-unknown-activity which would make us stand a little taller, hold our chins a bit higher, make us proud of ourselves and our lives. Jade was brilliant, unlike myself, so she had promising recruitment offers. Her gift could be used in many professions, as could mine, however people were usually afraid of us getting past their proffered personas and didn't want to offer the chance.

"No," I picked blades of grass and released them, airborne, in an effort to alleviate my frustration. "There are plenty of things we could do that would be risky, but they serve no higher purpose, other than excitement." I looked at her sideways, not wanting to say the rest. *Your asthma could kill you if we go too far.* I went back to killing grass, but she caught my emotions anyway and sighed. Jade wanted so badly to pretend her body wouldn't fail her. That she could push through, but I wouldn't take that chance. I couldn't lose her.

I steered the conversation in a different direction in hopes of clearing our melancholy. "Saw the guy at the barn yesterday."

Jade half smirked and huffed out a laugh as she took up my grass murdering distraction, allowing the redirect. "What was he doing this time?"

"Giving a beast a bath." I waggled my eyebrows. "He was all wet, too, seemed like the horse wasn't too keen to have its face washed."

Jade's eyes lit with interest and she leaned toward me, eager to hear more. Her internal voice let me know she *really* wished she could go to the barn with me. "Could you see through his shirt?"

I chuckled. "No. He was wearing a dark color." I could tell he was built though. And the way his hair dripped and his face glistened–

Jade laughed and threw a handful of grass at me. "I don't need to feel that!"

Heat crawled up my neck at her playful reprimand. "Ugh, I know why people don't like being around me, can't keep anything to myself," I muttered. "I talked to him." I blushed and fiddled with more blades of grass. Jade knew that in all the time I'd been visiting the barn and had seen Holden, we had never actually met.

My phone chose that moment to begin its double beep alarm, letting me know I had five minutes before Dr. Parmore would throw a hissy fit if I wasn't back for her to throw needless tasks my way.

I pushed to stand, tray in hand, and walked to throw it away on my path to my designated holding pen. Jade waved goodbye and headed toward her own room across the quad as I cut across opposite, climbing the steps that would take me inside.

I needed to find my calling, though not being recruited made that harder. No one trusted a telepath.

I entered the lecture hall and took a seat behind the lectern, so I was close enough to be on call should the instructor need me. The room began to fill though seats in the back never were. There weren't enough students for that, and the instructor's voice didn't carry. Truthfully, I had no idea why these halls were used. Most rooms had more than enough space for each class. I think it made the professors feel more important if they used them.

Sages were not a prolific race. Being that our bodies were not free of maladies, reproduction was often difficult. For the Sage women who were able to conceive, pregnancy was hard. Our bodies did not accept the extra weight and needs without consequence. Add to that the fact that infant mortality was high, and you got an idea as to why Sage Enhanced numbers did not rival that of either Primals or NEs.

I looked at my phone again and blew out a breath. Fifty-seven minutes to go.

This particular class had Tori, my old boyfriend's new girlfriend. Needless to say, she didn't like me, which I found totally acceptable because the feeling was more than mutual. She was, however, a gifted telekinetic, which allowed her to continually make me want to scream her secrets to the world.

Tori would use this time to both annoy and humiliate me. She was successful in constantly sending my pencil off my desk, and when I went to pick it up, she would move my desk and chair. She tried suspending it in the air, out of reach, but the professor called on her, making her realize it took too much concentration and caused her to lose favor. Totally unacceptable. Now, was the instructor put off with her childish behavior toward me? No, I wasn't favored enough to be respected. That didn't seem to change with the departure from being in classes.

When I was physically in the room with Dr. Parmore on these occasions, I couldn't get fully lost in my melodic therapy, only able to insert one earbud. After all, I was supposed to be at the professor's beck and call and it didn't bode well if I couldn't hear such *calls*.

So, like I said, I wanted to out her. I didn't though, mainly because she learned to do her version of a mental shield. She hummed in her head. She had no talent in the humming department. I could never decode what she was supposed to be reciting. It just sounded like gibberish.

I listened to music *all the time* and I didn't discriminate in genre, so I tended to at least recognize what I heard. Not with Tori's humming. Not possible, which again made me think it was just randomness. The upside to this would sometimes come when the instructor would call on her to answer, and she had been expending so much energy and thought on her atrocious way of keeping things from me that she couldn't answer correctly. At least not initially, Tori was like other Sages in that she was brilliant in many areas. *I can't catch a break.*

I looked at my phone again and groaned. Still another thirty-five minutes. As I closed my eyes and leaned toward the wall behind me, my pen chose to escape to the floor. Freaking Tori.

Thirty-four minutes.

I headed to the barn the moment Dr. Parmore released me from captivity. Saying that I was more than a little disappointed that my school involvement hadn't ended weeks ago, would be like stating that the ocean was deep—about the biggest understatement you could make.

I likened my learning career to skipping blindfolded across Main Street at peak hours. There was no way to walk away unscathed. It was what would happen after graduation where things got a bit fuzzy.

I would not be furthering my education, unlike most Sages my age. I was unlikely to land any of the occupations normally sought by those of higher intelligence, such as doctors, lawyers, engineers, and a myriad of others. I certainly couldn't teach. All those positions would be unbearable with my telepathic abilities. Couple that with the remaining schooling and there was just no way. Truth be told, I had wanted to experience something physical after I graduated. Not that I was being sought.

As I rounded the corner leading to the front gate of the barn, Holden came into view. He was in the enclosed area atop a beautiful black horse named Raven, if I remembered correctly. They were walking, Holden looked to be barely holding the reins, yet he didn't look worried and Raven seemed to still be obeying him. *Crazy!*

I was mesmerized.

I wanted that. I wanted to be the one sitting astride a thousand pound animal secure in my ability to control the situation. I was sure many Sages also had this wish. Control was a big thing to them. I was also sure none of them would act on it. The danger to their person was too great, and most were too analytical to disregard that fact, which meant I had to decide just how badly I wanted it.

Did I want to give people another reason to think I was different? Did I want to give people an idea that I might not be as breakable as I seem? Would it really be so bad if it were found out? Would I really be targeted? I couldn't fathom how it could end well if I were envied on all fronts, which made me want to keep my secret shoved down deep, away from the smallest tendrils of inquiring light.

Buried. Hidden. Locked in the deep recesses of myself that no one else saw.

Suddenly a masculine hand waved in front of my face, meaning I had zoned out. I blinked a couple of times and saw that Holden had stopped Raven in front of me. I was staring at his jean clad leg, the fabric clinging tightly to the flesh beneath.

Holden was all hard muscle and lean lines covered in clothing that molded to his body like a glove. I bet there was no fat on his body to speak of, and not in the stick thin Sage way, more like honed. After

42

lingering at his shoulders, which were as broad as the horse he sat astride, I jerked my attention to his face, heat rushing my cheeks. He wore a half smile, which seemed more shy than smug, as he allowed my perusal without interference.

Never had anyone look at me like that, he said through our mental link.

"I don't believe that," I blurted before I thought better of it, the bright flush returning to my cheeks. *Geez, Nathalee, the guy doesn't need you gushing over him. Get it in check, Dae!* I cleared my throat and tried again. "I'm sure you've been admired before, Holden."

It was his turn to blush. He ducked his head and ran a hand through Raven's mane, his other still holding the straps lightly. *People don't see me. They definitely don't take the time to get a good look, especially once they realize I'm defective.* His voice seemed a little sad and matched the tightness around his eyes as he looked at me. For a moment, there was vulnerability in their stormy depths, but it was gone in an instant, replaced by indifference.

People's disregard hurt him, but he refused to show it. I felt for him, though my own disregard was for the opposite reason. People knew what I could do, and it scared them, so they went out of their way to avoid me. I understood Holden's pain, as well as his shield of apathy, though our situations were not the same, the outcome was. Both of us lingered on the outskirts, on the fringe.

Outsiders.

In that, we were the same. It didn't matter that he was Primal and I Sage, we both knew the pain of loneliness. I refused to wallow in self-pity and I could tell Holden felt the same. Another reason to come by the barn after school. Holden needed someone to *see* him, let alone hear him.

"How are you able to control him when you barely have hold of the reins?" It seemed I was just spewing randomness in Holden's direction today. I shook my head and kicked at the grass beneath my feet to avoid his penetrating stare.

Raven's very responsive. He works and listens very well to my body as a whole. Again, he pulled his hand down through the horse's coarse mane.

"What do you mean?" I had seen horses ridden before, but to me it seemed the straps were the best means of control.

A horse can be taught to pay attention to any number of indicators that his rider provides for instruction. He clasped his hands over the straps again and laid them at the base of Raven's neck, in front of the saddle. *For instance, I use my left leg to tell him to move right.* He then proceeded to nudge Raven's side with his left foot. The horse took a step to the right and Holden stopped the pressure.

I was fascinated, wanted to know more, wanted to *participate.*

I must have looked like a kid waking up with the roosters on Christmas morning. I was bouncing on my toes, my hands gripping the fence between us, a huge smile and wide eyes lit my face.

He laughed.

I loved that sound, loved that I was the only one to hear it. "Tell me more."

He laughed again.

Now, he was smiling like a fool, as well, though he reined in his mirth as he continued. *Weight can give direction in a number of ways,* he intoned. *If I lean left, he will move so his body is back under my weight.* Again, he demonstrated leaning left which was toward me and the fence, Raven stepped to the left. Holden nudged Raven into a walk then demonstrated how sitting back in the saddle, toward Raven's rear, would make him stop.

As things progress, we begin to combine cues. Give the horse a more complicated set of instructions to follow. He brought Raven around to the fence, this time his right side closest. I watched as he kicked his right foot out of the stirrup and leaned to the left. He braced his hands on the front and rear of the saddle and dropped to the ground, landing lightly on his feet in the deeper dirt of the riding area, making a puff of a dust cloud around his legs and up under Raven's belly.

"Will you teach me?" Gasping, I covered my mouth with my hands. Geez, I just could not shut up today. "I'm sorry, forget I asked."

Holden looked confused. His inner voice seemed at a loss for a moment as well. *You want to learn how to ride a horse? Like, you want to get up there?* He pointed at Raven. *You're Sage. Won't that be too dangerous?* He wore a perplexed expression as he asked this, his brows drawn together making little creases between them, his mouth turned down in a slight frown.

I bristled. I was no wilting flower. I wasn't deterred by the fact I could be hurt, that the animal was massive with a mind of its own. I stood straighter and squared my shoulders. I heard his continued confusion and narrowed my eyes at him.

I wanted to convey my outrage. He thought I couldn't do it. I tuned into his mental dialogue and deflated a bit. He wasn't looking down on me. He knew Sages tended to be fragile and didn't want to be responsible for an injury that could arise.

"You are not responsible for me. If I choose to pursue this, I will do so at my own risk." Then I thought about the fact that not all horses were created equal and amended my statement. "As long as you do your utmost to ensure my safety." I threw out a hand to halt his response. "I'm aware there is an inherent risk in this endeavor. All I ask of you is to do your best to minimize said risk."

I nodded then as I crossed my arms, satisfied with this thought. I could do this. Within reason, I could learn to do this. I held out my right hand toward Holden, and looked him in the eye, trying to convey to him the security in my decision.

His vibrant gaze was assessing, bouncing back and forth between my eyes like a table tennis match, searching for the conviction my words conveyed. He found it.

Reaching out, he clasped my hand. His was work roughened with many calluses along the base of his fingers and so different from my own, from many Sages. *I will do all in my power to make sure you are safe, Nathalee.* Then he turned toward the barn, pulling Raven along behind him. *See you tomorrow,* he said just before he was too far for my ability to pick up. He didn't look back.

I blew out the breath I seemed to be holding and slumped a bit. How did I let this happen? How was I going to explain it? What would happen if anyone found out? Would it really be so bad? All my confidence from mere moments ago was quickly fading, leaving in its place an acute case of anxiety.

I turned on my heel and hurried away from the barn. Hurried away from Holden, from the horses, from temptation. I never wanted to get closer to anyone, especially not a male. Guys were usually way more into themselves than I wanted to endure.

Tomorrow, I would begin learning to ride horses, and I would be taught by a Primal. Who would have thought? Anticipation trickled

46

through my veins as I reached home. How did I tell my parents? Did I tell them? Maybe a good night's sleep would bring light to the situation.

CHAPTER 5

I WOKE THE NEXT morning having solved nothing of my internal struggle, other than reinforcing my conviction to learn from Holden. I was too intrigued to forego this opportunity, both to learn something I thought to forever be barred from, and learning under the tutelage of someone like Holden. It was too tempting.

I rubbed the sleep from my eyes and began the horrible task of getting out of bed at six a.m. *Ugh, work. Who needs it?* Well, in fact, I did. I'd probably be doing mundane clerical work or something similar for like…ever.

The world was a new animal since the Enhanced emerged. The *powers that be* worldwide came up with the system currently in place, which was basically like an internship. Work for housing and get a stipend for food stuffs and other necessities.

Extras or "upgrades" such as handmade items or technology were bartered with either goods or services, unless you were the fortunate few who were somehow put to use by the ninnies on the outside at one time or another. I was not, in fact, in one of those lucky families, though, my father was often consulted by the town council. I rolled out of bed and settled myself to the idea of heading back to the campus.

Being that I was not a brilliant Sage but a mediocre one, my job was that as well. I was a "teaching assistant" for Dr. Parmore at the campus. "Teaching assistant" was polite for the truth; I was her grunt. I was tasked with pulling together the materials she wanted in class and inputting all data into both her computer and the campus system. It was boring, tedious work, but it allowed me to be antisocial and keep a clear head throughout the day. As a bonus, I could put in earbuds and get lost in my music, so *score*!

Dr. Parmore was a biologist who specialized in genomes, so her students were all in various stages of their studies in becoming a wide range of medical professionals. They were almost all Sage Enhanced. Their ages ranged from sixteen to early twenties, depending on how involved their profession would be and how far into that curriculum the student was.

Most Sages completed schooling by eighteen, though a good portion of the curriculum followed classes which others didn't see until elected education. If further education was needed, they were shuttled into specialized schooling which could be coupled with their learning job, like a true internship.

Many had gifts which would aid in the workplace in some form. Telekinetics could do a wide range of things depending on how strong their gift was. Empaths went into medical fields. Charmers tended toward public figures and law. Eidetic leaned toward sciences and engineering. The question was what did telepaths do?

As of right now, they gathered materials and entered data. *Fist pump.*

"Nathalee, will you please follow me to my office?" I stopped amassing my things from the desktop and looked up sharply upon hearing the professor address me.

This can't be good.

I nodded hesitantly. After quickly putting my things in my bag, I zipped it up and flung it over my head and across my body. Holding the nylon strap in a death grip, I trudged toward the lectern at which Dr. Parmore stood with her notes pressed against her chest. Her tortoise shell glasses rested low on her nose as she had both hands occupied with papers and was unable to right them. She stood stoic, no indication as to what this visit would be about. *Maybe I was a bit testy in my latest correspondence on her behalf...*

As I approached, Dr. Parmore turned abruptly and began the short journey to her office. We walked in silence, the only overt sound being our shoes squeaking on the linoleum flooring, especially when we turned down the adjacent hall. I really hated that sound. *Squeak, squeak, squeak.*

I'm not sure what he would want with her, she's Sage. Surely she cannot aid him.

The woman's thought brought my attention sharply from my own irritation back to her. "Who?" I asked, interest piqued.

"Hmm?" My boss was still lost in her contemplation of my impending introduction as she turned her head toward me slightly. Her muddy brown eyes flicked to mine briefly before she looked ahead again, dismissing my question.

We stopped in front of Dr. Parmore's office. It boasted a heavy door, solid wood with a placard reading the doctor's name. I decided to ask again. "Doct—"

She fiddled, searching her pockets for keys. Her answer did not come verbally. *Commander James here for her. Why?* Clearly, Dr. Parmore was not the one calling this meeting and was just as baffled as I was. At least she knew who I would be speaking with, making her more knowledgeable about the situation than I. All I picked up from inside the room was a masculine mental list. Observations of the office.

Just then the door opened from the other side, startling both the good doctor and myself. An internal shriek permeated my own wince. Dr. Parmore clutched her papers to her chest once more, and huffed, irritated that she was not prepared for this situation.

The man standing in the doorway was a sight to behold. Well over six feet tall with an abundance of lean muscle covering every surface of his body, the kind that spoke of strength, but also speed and agility. His face was all angles, his eyes a striking reddish brown. Above those russet orbs were surprisingly sculpted brows and closely cropped brown hair.

I brought my attention back to his and noticed his small smirk. For an older man, he was quite a looker. It was about this time I registered the fact that I was internally hearing singing. *He has a good voice.*

My brows pinched as I realized that *all* I could hear from this man was singing, which meant it was his version of blocking my ability. Well, now I knew he was aware of said ability. I smiled tremulously, wiping suddenly sweating palms down my jean clad thighs, nervous as to what this visit could be about.

Attempting to regain control, Dr. Parmore cleared her throat and motioned in my direction. "Commander James, this is Nathalee Dae, as you requested." The man looked away from me briefly to acknowledge her introduction, which he did by dipping his chin once in Dr. Parmore's direction. He then extended his right hand toward me.

"Nice to meet you, Nathalee. I'm Commander James, as Dr. Parmore has noted." I took a step forward and reached out to grasp his hand. It closed over mine sternly for a brief moment before he released it to cross his arms over his broad chest and lean back on his heels.

Everything about this man said discipline and authority. His attire was dark and tactical, full of pockets for storage and retrieval, and snug so as to not impede movement. *Damn, he really is attractive.* Commander James looked toward Dr. Parmore again and asked, "Doctor, would you give Miss Dae and me a moment please?"

My boss looked affronted and confirmed this with her internal outrage. After sputtering and turning a deep shade of red, which seemed to be due to anger and not embarrassment, she quickly turned and exited the office pulling the door shut behind her and muttering about not being privy to the information given within the confines of her own office.

Once I could no longer hear her inner tirade, I gave my attention to the commander. His thoughts were now cataloging what he noted about me. *Tall, more solid than many Sages, assessing—*

"What can I do for you, Commander?" I decided to get the ball rolling on this party and try to figure out what the commander could possibly want from me. He was obviously Primal, his physique too perfect for him not to be. So what could he want? He couldn't know *that* about

52

me, so what could he need? I watched him, trying to puzzle it out, and came up blank.

"I've been approved to put together a team which pairs both Primal and Sage together in order to best accommodate what needs to be done to ensure that criminals are culled from the general populace most effectively. I've come in hopes of adding you, Miss Dae, as a member of this initial team."

He still stood with his arms across his chest, only now his chin was dipped in order to convey this speech while looking at my eyes and his weight was evenly across his feet. He looked to be measuring me, my grit. The speech seemed rehearsed. The words didn't seem to fit with the man. Too polished. The wheels were spinning in my head as I took this in. I shuffled a few steps into the office and took a seat in the plastic chair to the right, nearest me, hoping I wouldn't feel quite so awkward once seated.

Stalling, I swept my gaze over the sparse space. Dr. Parmore was not one to clutter with sentimentality so there wasn't much to the room. "What is it you think I will be helpful with? How can a Sage assist in enforcement? We can't stand up to the physical riggers you Primals can endure." I snorted. "Not even by half, some even less." I hated that Sages had such setbacks physically, though in truth, some could lessen their frailty a bit with time and effort. They didn't, though.

"True," he nodded. "You cannot keep up with us physically, but you far outpace us mentally. We are, as a whole, too reactive, too... *volatile,* and not attentive enough to be effective in some things." He scratched his chin, then returned his arm to his chest as he continued. "We are looking for a few Sages who have mental abilities that would be helpful in gathering information in criminal matters." He paused, the cumbersome words once again falling from his mouth.

Uncrossing his arms and walking toward the side of the desk, he lowered to the chair next to me, though I wasn't sure how good of an idea it was. The chair looked to be straining under his weight. "Your telepathy could tell us these things."

Wait, what?

I hadn't ever thought of my telepathy as being a good thing. I always thought it would be better to be like others who were telekinetic or had an eidetic memory. I mean, wouldn't it be so much cooler to be able to move objects without touching them, or never having to study?

Instead, I knew that Tommy was frustrated with his inability to "seal the deal" with Julia. But if what the commander said was true, and I could be a factor in delivering justice?

That would definitely be grabbing life by the horns.

"You're aware it's not selective? I have no control over the things I 'hear' when I'm around others?" I twisted my hands in my lap after using air quotes for "hear." This was what I disliked most about my ability— there was no choice; no "off" position. It made all involved uncomfortable. There were plenty of times no one wanted anyone to know what they thought; thus why things were not verbalized. With me around, privacy went out the window.

"We are aware of the repercussions of what I am asking. There are a few of you whose abilities are always 'on', as you say." He paused, narrowing his intriguing eyes at me slightly, then continued, "Can you hear me now?"

I lifted an eyebrow at him and took a moment to assess. I shook my head once. I couldn't. He was shielding, but how long, and how often would he be able to? I got an answer a few moments later, as what I could only describe as a bubble bursting, sounded in my head, along with the commander's brusque "Damn!" I chuckled and looked up at him. His mouth twisted up slightly to one side in a self depricating smile. *Sorry.*

I huffed a laugh at his mental apology and returned his grin. I think I could stand to be around *him* but... "Is that bubble shielding something you are going to be instructing others how to do?"

He sat back in his ridiculously under-built chair and let out a breath he seemed to have been holding as he nodded, stretching out his long legs in front of him. I thought it odd that this man, who was obviously used to being obeyed, seemed so relaxed here, with me. That was not something I was used to. It was...nice.

"Yes, it is something we will all have to work on. Though, we will accept measures that you take, within reason, to keep yourself from being overwhelmed. Or just for everyone's comfort level." He cringed, both mentally and physically.

"That's your way of saying that you don't mind if I wear headphones and tune everyone out?" I raised my brow again and mirrored his pose. Well, *attempted* to. When I went to stretch my own legs, they knocked into the desk we were perched in front of. The pressure of hitting the solid surface caused me to unbalance a bit in my seat.

My eyes widened in dawning horror as my attempt at feigned nonchalance went awry. I shouldn't have been surprised. It was the way of things around me. *Oh, the shame!* I felt the blush creep up my neck and toward my ears as I pushed my chair backward in a haphazard attempt to recover. The legs made an awful screeching sound, causing us both to wince.

It didn't help that in no form could I be considered graceful. I'd yet to meet a Sage who was. In the end, I ended up flailing backward and pinwheeling my arms in my oh-so-brilliant attempt to keep upright as the chair leaned precariously on two legs. I felt the balance shift toward the floor and cringed, anticipating the impending crash landing. *Geronimo!*

The commander's grunt was the only indication of his intent that I received. Faster than I had ever seen anyone move, he was out of his chair and grabbing my shoulders to right me. *Thank God.* I was still reeling from his rescue as I looked at him. "Th— thank you, Commander James," I stammered, easing out of his hold and running my hand across my face to displace the mop of hair that had plastered itself in various places in my disastrous attempts at being cool. Once the commander was convinced I was stable, he, too, stepped back putting a bit of distance between us and cleared his throat, though his features still conveyed concern.

"What do you say, Miss Dae? Are you interested in the position?"

I opened my mouth with a reply when a thought occurred. I had no idea how he knew about me. I mean, it's not a secret as to my ability, but who would have brought me to the attention of the commander, I had no clue. "How did you come to the conclusion that I, specifically, would be beneficial to your agency, Commander?"

The big man once again crossed his arms over his chest and rocked back on his heels, contemplating me silently for a moment. Like he was deciding what to tell me. But I caught it. His mind pictured a man. A tall man with wide shoulders, messy dark hair, and piercing blue eyes.

Holden.

"How do you know Holden?" I demanded, my mind turning circles. How did Holden know this man? Why did he mention me to him? My internal rant was cut short when the commander threw up his hands in exasperation. I pointed at my temple. "Telepathic remember? You may want to work on the whole shielding thing more, Commander." I put a hand on hip and cocked my eyebrow, it seemed the thing was always loaded.

"He, uh, works for me," he hedged. His mind flashing with a sequence of unguarded images, baby to adult. The tones were that of pride and love. I was looking at Holden's family. I would bet money that the imposing man, whose full intensity was currently trained on me, was Holden's father.

Perfect.

The meeting concluded after I said I would consider his proposal. As I turned to leave, the commander gave me a small com device, stating it was to contact him with my decision. I hastily left the office, and subsequently the campus to head home.

Once again, my thoughts in tumult, I scarcely recalled the journey. Twisting the key in the lock, I pushed open the front door of my home. I looped my key on a hook hanging on the wall of the entry and continued toward my bedroom.

I was tired and achy and decided a bath would be heavenly. I began disrobing before I reached my destination, getting down to my undergarments by the time I reached the tub and turned the water on. I turned on the speaker I kept on the counter and attached my music player before I divested myself of my remaining clothes and slipped into the warm, sudsy water.

I was so grateful that I had access to music. It was my sanctuary; my bliss. It allowed me to focus on something other than people and their rampant thoughts. Allowed me to escape into my *own* head. It didn't matter what type of beat, or delivery... I could always find a song to relate to any mood. The lyrics could speak for me; the instruments could make my worries fly away as if they were balloons in a summer breeze.

Sitting in the bath long enough to prune, I released the water, dried, and dressed in my nightclothes, a T-shirt and cotton shorts. I meandered toward the kitchen and scrounged for something to eat. Tonight was "date night" for the parental units, so I was fending for myself.

After inhaling a turkey club sandwich, I rinsed my dishes and wandered back to my room.

My bed was extremely welcoming as I crawled under the plush covers and settled myself against the fluffy pillow. It was one of the few things, other than my music, that was like a retreat. I loved my sleep, therefore this haven needed to be a reflection of this. Within moments of my head contacting the pillow, I was slipping into oblivion and wondering if my telepathy could in fact, be an asset as Commander James had implied. I also had a fleeting recollection that I was supposed to do something that day, but the details escaped into the night.

CHAPTER 6

"OH CRAP!" I AWOKE with a jolt, fully recalling the thought I fell asleep to the night before. I was supposed to meet Holden at the barn for my first "lesson" yesterday, but the meeting with Commander James, who was an unknown member of Holden's family, I had completely forgotten. Not that I would have been a functional learning sponge after that encounter, but still, I needed to atone.

After another riveting day of compilation and typing, I eagerly headed toward the barn. I needed to apologize to Holden for bailing on our horsie time yesterday, and I needed to do that in person as we hadn't given any other means of contact.

Lost in the instrumental version of a rock song and daydreaming about ponies and attractive Primals, I was slammed with a sharp pain in my left shoulder, jolting me from my reverie. I brought my hand up to rub the area which was now throbbing and searched for the cause. My eyes dropped to the cracked sidewalk.

At my feet, amid the spider web of cracks and weeds trying to gain purchase was a large rock, like the kind used for landscaping in the Sage part of town. My eyes pinned to the rock, noting inconsequential details. It was an unusual shade of rose rather than a flat, boring brown and it looked weathered by time. Finally, my eyes continued to scan for the offender. Obviously one of my many admirers had been around, though they weren't now. I wish I could say that such occurrences were unusual, but I'd be lying. It seemed like an initiation for Sage teens to take their shot at me.

Getting lost in music was proving to be a very effective means of blocking mental voices. So much so, I had no idea who had cast the first stone. Mentally shrugging, I continued on my way to the barn and my first lesson in horseback riding. *I still can't believe I'm doing this!*

My first lesson ended up being about horses and practicality, as opposed to actual riding. Holden waved off my groveling as he once again brought out Raven, saying that he was here either way so it didn't have much effect on his day. He walked Raven into the aisle, attaching his halter, which I always called a "head harness," to each side of the aisle with long straps. Holden informed me this was termed "cross tying."

Then he proceeded to tell me about each item in a box he had sitting in the dirt off to the side of the aisle, picking out one dirty and hairy item at a time to impress upon me. Once I was able to tell him what each held item was, and how it was used, he allowed me to approach Raven. Cue dramatic eye roll. Maybe he *was* upset about being stood up yesterday.

The horse eyed me warily as I approached his head and held my hand out palm up as Holden instructed. He dropped his nose into my open hand and blew out a rush of air. I brought my hand up to press at his jaw. *He's so soft...*

Going on some long dormant instinct, one which Sages usually didn't possess, I brought my other hand up to the far side of his head and stepped closer. Once my chest was almost pressed to Raven's bristly head, I bent to his nose and blew, softly. Raven breathed out, and I blew again. He breathed in and blew out, and again I puffed softly at him. I was transfixed by this moment. Lost in getting to know Raven, in letting him get to know me.

Beautiful.

Until the moment I heard Holden's awed proclamation, I had forgotten he was there, lost as I was to the moment. I couldn't tell you why I blew in Raven's nose, only that it felt right to do so. I backed up and looked at the horse. He was no longer wary, each muscle seemingly more relaxed and his head hung low, his tufted midnight ears twitching between Holden's position and myself.

He looked almost like a mangy dog, his coat was still long and thick in places like his ears, jaw and belly. The weather was not yet warm enough for him to release his hold on the extra barrier.

How did you know to do that? Holden was relaxed, leaning against a stall on the left side of the aisle. His corded arms crossed along his broad chest, the right knee bent, allowing his foot to rest against the stall. There was an intrigued glint in his mercury stare. Wait a minute, silver? Weren't his eyes blue? His eyes were definitely blue, I had obsessed about them enough since our first meeting.

What? Nathalee? You all right?

His worried thoughts and expression didn't break me from my confusion. No, that feat occurred as I watched his eyes flip to the beautiful azure I had noted previously. And I mean it was like an ink stain, one moment liquid silver eyes peered at me and the next vivid blue began bleeding from the pupil outward until bright blue eyes stared back at me, the silver now contained in a narrow ring around the pupil. There was no mistaking the change. *Unless you are going crazy and seeing things. I mean, you did just blow air into a horse's face!*

I shook myself and stepped back to regain my composure. If it happened again I would ask, until then, I would pretend it hadn't happened. Wonder if I was seeing things. "Sorry, kinda spaced for a moment." I gave what I hoped was a reassuring smile and nodded like a bobblehead, which probably didn't help my case.

I needed to get us back on track. Raven was no longer wary of me, but Holden now seemed to be. I bent over the box and grabbed the little oval rubber piece that had little nubs on one side, and a strap to slide your hand into on the other. I now knew it was called a "curry comb." *Look at me learning all kinds of stuff today.* I stepped toward Raven to brush his coat in circular motions, letting loose an alarming amount of hair and dirt as I worked. With this action, Holden seemed to come back to himself and continued with the lesson.

We spent thirty minutes grooming Raven, using every item Holden taught me, and discussing the anatomy of a horse. At the conclusion, Raven was blissfully asleep, and my arms ached. It took more pressure and sustained arm lifting than I was used to. Raven stood, rear leg cocked and resting, lower lip hanging loose enough to expose his yellowed teeth and pink tongue to the world.

I gave him a pat, startling him awake and making him move weight back onto his rear leg, raising his head in alert. Holden happened to be in the way when Raven's head jerked and took a good knock to the shoulder. It didn't faze him, of course, and he gave the beast an understanding slap on the neck which reverberated around the otherwise empty and uncharacteristically quiet barn area.

Holden was a good and patient teacher who I really didn't mind hearing internally, especially if that was the only way for me to hear a voice from him. Though I noted he did make some rudimentary sounds, like coughing, and clicks with his tongue. I did not, however, feel up to asking about it. *Another day. One in which you have not already behaved weirdly.* I laughed at myself quietly. Like that would ever happen. While I ruminated about Holden's quiet manner, I remembered how Commander James had come to know about me.

Holden.

Did I want to bring it up? *No.* This moment, this place, was too sacred to muddy with possibly unwelcome inquiries. At least for now.

Having made my decision, I gathered all the brushes into the box while Holden saddled Raven. "Am I riding today too?" I couldn't help the slight waver on the last word. I was nervous. Nervous about so many things, only one of which was that I had never sat on a live, thousand-plus pound animal, which had a mind of its own and could very easily hurt me. Or sit back and watch as I hurt myself.

Holden answered me while he threw the pad over Raven's back in preparation for the saddle. *No, I want you to know and trust them, and yourself, before we move forward.* He hesitated, both hands on the pad adorning Raven's midnight hide and bowed his head. *There are inherent risks.* He closed his eyes. No, he *squeezed* his eyes shut; as if in pain. Then he opened them and stared brazenly into mine.

His eyes blazed a tumultuous blue with the same conviction as his words. *I want you as prepared as possible. Knowing him, knowing signs, and being comfortable, before I set you up there.*

He huffed out a breath and turned to face me, dropping his hands to his sides. His eyes flipped to that same liquid silver color and he took a step in my direction, ducking under the tie and scuffing his toes in the dirt aisle. His look turned pleading as he said, *I don't want you to get hurt.* He seemed distressed by that idea.

I *could* tell him that I healed quickly... but that knowledge was dangerous, and although I *wanted* to trust Holden, I wasn't quite naive enough to think I could, yet. I stuttered to speak as heat flooded my face. *Wow, that stare could make you forget your own name.*

I mumbled some sort of incoherent acknowledgement and ducked my head, willing the blush to recede as I kicked my foot through the dirt. "Ah, well, I guess I will see you for our next lesson." I spun on my heel and focused on making a smooth escape. Holden's intensity had thrown me. It seemed as though he dreaded the idea of me injuring myself, but that he thought it inevitable. In all fairness, he was probably right.

See you tomorrow, Nat.

I looked over my shoulder and smiled. I couldn't really see him from my new vantage, the sun's rays saturating the barn behind him, the streaks reaching like grasping tentacles into the interior. Holden was silhouetted, like an apparition. That second of distraction was enough to cause me not to notice that I was too close to the left barn door, and for me to smash my shoulder into it just as I faced forward. My *left* shoulder, the one already smarting and most likely bruised from the rock that struck me on my way into the barn. It was only fitting that I also incurred injury upon my exit.

I stumbled back and braced my hands on either side of the open door in order to orient myself, Holden rushing to my side.

You all right? Again his concern was palpable. Maybe he was just worried about getting blamed in the event of my injury. Primals were second class citizens in many ways and Sage regarded them as mindless brutes all too often, so Holden's apprehension was founded. If that was in fact what worried him.

I felt his hand land on my right shoulder and let out a shaky breath. He turned me around gently and looked me over, obviously expecting me to be crippled from the impact. I wouldn't stand to be treated as though I were made of glass. I wasn't easily broken.

I would not break, especially not from stupidly smacking into a door, and I would show him. I stood straighter, squared myself and lifted my chin as I heard his internal catalog of my body. I pulled out of his reach, because although I wanted his touch more than I would admit, I did not want his worry or his pity. I was strong, both in mind *and* body and I would prove it to him. Even if it meant getting hurt.

CHAPTER 7

WHAT I DID AFTER I left Holden and the barn may have been reckless, but it didn't stop me. I trudged toward my home, kicking stones and cursing attractive, mute Primals more vocally than would be considered polite, once again cementing my status as the town crazy girl.

Just once, I wished I could tell someone *my* secrets, wished I trusted someone enough not to turn their back on me, or worse yet: tell others. This line of thinking invariably led my thoughts back to Holden. My mind traitorously whispered that maybe Holden was that person. He certainly wouldn't *tell* anyone—at least not verbally. There were plenty of other means of communication. I wanted to trust him, just like I wanted to trust Jade, but my fear of the fallout kept me from doing so.

I tore angrily through my bag looking for the com device Commander James had given me. My hand curled around the small disk, and I pulled it free from the debris littering my overused bag. It looked like a keychain, something ornamental. It was elongated, black with a spot of blue.

I looked closer and found that the blue was in the shape of a stylized shield, much like what I had seen enforcement agents wear in the pictures of people outside our community. As I rubbed my thumb over the emblem, it lit up, emitting a tone in a reoccurring wave. *This thing seems like something Mom would think up.* I'd seen similar technology. It was almost like a two-way radio but highly condensed and concealable. It made me slightly giddy to realize that very few had probably ever seen what I now held in my possession and I wondered who their tech guru was.

After three tones, a gruff voice greeted me, "Miss Dae, good to hear from you." Commander James's deep voice reached my ears, successful in bringing me out of my excitement like a splash of water to the face.

I cleared my throat of the lump that seemed to have suddenly overtaken me, "Hello, Commander," being all I managed to utter. Silence reigned for several seconds after my stilted greeting, like he was waiting for me to say more. I didn't.

"Nathalee, you seem nervous. Are you sure of whatever you want to say to me?"

His softly delivered inquiry finally broke my haze. I had stopped walking once the commander picked up the transmission. I paused a moment to see where I was and sat on the curb of the sidewalk, feet in the roadway, elbows resting on my knees as others continued on oblivious to my life dramatically altering. I blew out a heavy breath and prepared to change my path.

"I am interested in becoming a member of your team."

I heard him release his own heavy breath at my words. "I'm very glad to hear that Nathalee, truly." His words were light, but his tone heavy. It seemed the commander had things on his mind. "Would you be able to come to my current setup to speak further? There are things about this squad and its potential agents, which I do not wish for just anyone to observe."

The last half of his dialogue was almost growled and made me shiver. I would not want to be the cause of that tone...or have it aimed in my direction. It was a dangerous sound. A warning.

Was I crazy? I would be putting myself in direct, continual interaction with this man, and many other Primal Enhanced, all with this same ability to eviscerate me within moments. Not even my healing would save me if I got in front of a raging Primal. I'd seen them go at each other like animals when an argument was not easily resolved. I shivered, my mouth dry again. "Uhh, where is the department?"

"We're in a dual purpose location. A brick building just to the west of the gardens, sign says 'Sam's'. You know it?"

I probably shouldn't have been having this conversation on the com unit out here on the curb once he mentioned that the location was secret. I quickly gave him affirmation and set our meeting for the following day after school. We disconnected and I tossed the device into my bag, watching as it slowly sank from sight. Now came the truly hard part, outing my intentions to my parents. My mouth went dry. *Please let this go well.*

With that wishful prayer, I once again headed home.

Informing my parents of my recruitment would need to be handled delicately. My mother was not the problem. No, the problem would be in convincing my father that I could function coherently when not under his supervision. Getting my father to release me from his bear hug of worry and allowing me to just…be.

I once again climbed the few steps up the porch to arrive at the front door. Today the heavy decorative wooden door stood open and the glass storm door kept out all unwanted nuisances while allowing for the beauty of the day to be seen and appreciated.

I blew out a deep breath and continued forward. *Here goes nothing.* What were the chances Dad would not only tell me no but also attempt to keep me under constant watch? *For your safety,* he'll say. *It's too dangerous.*

"Hey, Nat, how was work?" My Dad's inquiry popped the bubble on my inner rant and stopped me cold. I wasn't ready to talk about my new direction, so I took the time to answer his question. I came to a halt in the living room, taking in the hominess that had been created there.

My eyes stopped at a photographic print. A favorite of mine, it depicted an island beach scene, though it also made me sad because it reminded me that I would most likely never see anything like it in person. "Same as usual, Dad." I scuffed the toe of my old black boots across the carpet, casting my eyes down to watch the mutilation. If I looked at my father, he would know something was up and I wanted to ease him into the news.

I needed to make him see this was a good thing, a way that I could help those who've been wronged in some way, or better yet, to prevent harm. *Yeah, that's what I'll say. Appeal to the healer in him.* Comfortable now in my approach, I broached the topic I needed to discuss. "So I, uh...I'm being recruited," I stammered.

With that delivery, I looked at my father and saw his eyes light up, only to dim. His mouth, which had tried to lift into a smile, now twitched to a frown. "It's not coming from Davidson, is it? You can't work for the council, It's too public, too...seedy. Always trying to spin information, your telepathy would constantly be telling you something different from what your ears heard." He was wearing a hole in the carpet again. I needed to stop his runaway thought train. Pull that cord and bring it to a halt.

"No, Dad, I think Mr. Davidson got the message last time we'd met," I sniggered, remembering how the slimy older man had approached me. Again, he had poured on the charm and insisted that the best move for my future was to come on as part of his team. Council members were the ones appointed to speak to the Non-Enhanced government leaders and other necessary players in the outside world. They held *a lot* of sway within the community.

Really, they did whatever was in *their* best interests and to hell with everyone else. The ninnies didn't care though. They didn't want to know what happened within our walls unless it helped or hurt them directly.

To those pulling the strings, many of Minefield's inhabitants were not important enough to worry about. Davidson had tried to appeal to me as though money and favors earned were all I could ask for out of life. His inner monologue however, told the truth. The man wanted to use me to bury those who opposed him, and he wanted me in his bed.

Never. On either count. So I reminded him of just what my ability entailed. I recounted his previous thoughts aloud, and for all to hear. He hadn't liked that and had turned a very unhealthy shade of red, cursing at me. That is until he realized that others were around to witness the show, and Sages do not let anyone know how things affect them, especially council members. Davidson was also an eidetic, so he would never forget what I had done. I probably should remember that for the future.

That is why my gift left me as an outsider. I didn't buy their crap, and if they pissed me off, I would call them on it. Loudly. Publicly. Really, I'm amazed I'd survived this long. Sages are a prickly, self-important people. And Primals were the opposite, showing all emotion. If I ever pissed one off enough to flip their switch, which is what we called it when instinct and aggression took over their reasoning and function, I would be obliterated, torn limb from limb. Not survivable.

"That's good," Dad said. "Wish I could have seen it." He barked a quick laugh, crossing his arms on his chest as he turned to face me. My father wasn't on the council, but he was often consulted on medical issues and relevant numbers of various occurrences, "Okay, so go on," he twirled his hand in a "please continue" motion, "Who's recruiting you?"

Here goes... "Commander James."

"Commander James?" He looked confused. "Commander James is high in enforcement. I treat his Primals often." The last was said with his chin lowered to his chest, making his glare more effective. It was his way of saying that these people got hurt. A lot. "What does he expect you to do? What does he expect *any* Sage to be able to do in enforcement?" Oh, he was getting all wound up again.

"Relax, Dad. Take a breath." I demonstrated the deep breathing I hoped he'd adopt so his face would return to its normal pallor, then continued. "It's a new branch. One which combines Sage and Primal talents. The Primals are the force, and the Sages will be the investigators.

At least, that's what I gather from the commander. I have a meeting with him tomorrow afternoon to learn more details on the program, and what would be expected of me." I spoke in a rush to get it all out. I was sure some, or most of my explanation was almost unintelligible, but my father was smart. He'd catch it.

He blinked. Repeatedly. "Investigations, huh?" A far-off stare stole his features and I knew he was no longer present in thought. I wondered how often this occurred at work. How many patients or nurses had experienced this very picture, and thought him losing his mind? Perhaps he was, he did it often. He blinked again and was back. "Is it dangerous?"

"I really don't know any specifics yet, and that is why I informed the commander that while I was interested, I would not be thrown headlong into his world without proper information." The more I thought about it, though, the more this life path seemed right.

I had seen some awful things and the result of others' cruelty since I was a child, especially as my father was a sought-out doctor. This world wasn't as civilized as it once was, with no oversight and most everyone having extreme abilities, brutality reigned.

"I'm coming with you," my father said and nodded, like that decided the matter.

"Coming with me? What do you mean?" For the life of me, I could not fathom what he would be accompanying me to. Work? *Could he really be that overbearing?* I was beginning to sweat. The thought of my father dropping everything so he could hover over me was freaking me out. I was visualizing him shadowing my every move and speaking for me, putting me in a protective bubble just like Jade's parents wanted to do to her. *Breathe, Nat, just breathe.*

"Tomorrow. The explanation from the commander." Dad was looking at me with concern brimming in his bright eyes, a little wrinkle set between his brows. If I didn't rein it in, my fears would be realized. I took a couple deep breaths and backed away from the mental ledge. "Yeah, okay. Can you take the time away from the hospital?" Maybe that reminder would get me out of having him as a chaperone.

Dad walked over to me, wrapped me up in his trademark bear hug and mumbled how he'd always have time for his baby girl, then kissed the top of my head and ambled off toward the kitchen. No doubt to put the finishing touches on the meal.

Well, that actually went easier than I thought. Then I remembered he was accompanying me to my meeting. *Well, crap.*

CHAPTER 8

I TOSSED AND TURNED all night, and then proceeded to space out the entire day at the campus. Tori had a field day with that and Jade gave up trying to get my attention. All I could think about was heading to Commander James's "covert location" and learning about this team I was to join.

I was nervous about seeing others who would be on the task force. Would I once again be shunned and avoided? I had a glimmer of hope that maybe this was where I was meant to be, what I was meant to be doing, and therefore would find acceptance within its confines. This infinitesimal sliver of possibility had me bouncing off the walls.

As I exited the hall and came out into the open air, I took a moment to close my eyes, tilting my face to the sun, and just breathing, decompressing. I let the innumerable voices slip from my mind. I needed to keep my head through this session, not give the impression of a whack job telepath with no social skills, even if that's exactly what I was. I

74

snorted my disbelief, opened my eyes, and oriented myself so I could see where I was going. I really didn't want to trip over anything in my distracted state.

Just as I was stepping forward, starting my journey, as it were, my father slid up next to me and bumped my shoulder. That small bump brought me back to myself, and narrowly away from a light post. Now I remembered that my father would also be in on the special moment of my potential future. My enthusiasm dimmed. Dad would ask a million questions about safety and put a huge spotlight on me. *So much for not being a freak show at this shindig.*

The walk was short and quiet, neither of us polluting our ears with chatter. The route took us from the campus which was just on the other side of downtown, across the entrance to the gardens and toward more industrial type buildings on the way out toward the fields.

As we walked, I looked for the brick building Commander James had described. I found it about a block past where we currently stood. It looked like a gym, like a fighter's training area. *Well, that's sure to keep the Sages away.* I watched as a rough looking Primal approached from the southern walk. He was dressed like he wanted freedom of motion and weight. His clothes, wispy and shiny in the sunlight, swished with each step. He was *huge*! I began to panic a bit, remembering that Sages were not the only members of this team. *Can I handle Primals?*

Large hands grasped my shoulders, turning me. My father's eyes bore into me, he was slightly stooped so he could look at me squarely. It made me squirm. I looked at the cracked concrete to avoid his stare. I was one hundred percent sure that my dad would read my fear and march me back home, away from the danger this situation presented. My apprehension slipped away with the thought of failure to move forward. This was what I wanted. I needed to move out of my comfort zone, though let's face it, that zone was miniscule.

"Nat, you can do this. You can do things no one else can."

My eyes snapped up to meet my father's vibrant gaze. I was shocked to my very core at his words, his tone. His expression was open and easily read. He believed in me, believed I was strong enough to handle this path and knew I would succeed.

You are stronger than you know.

Wait. Those were his *thoughts*! I was so shocked, I stood rooted to my current spot, my eyes wide and my jaw unhinged. He had dropped his shields. *Never* had he done this in the open. This new development had me rooted in place, but for a wholly different reason. I had been convinced that every time I heard my father's thoughts, they would be filled with worry and how to avoid outing my uniqueness. This dialogue was so far out of the realm of that. I opened and closed my mouth like a fish, waiting for something coherent to make its way out. Nothing yet.

"Nat, honey. I know I hover and worry. That will never change. You are my little girl, no matter how big you get," He smiled self-deprecatingly. "I know you can handle yourself, and this." He leaned back, standing at full height. "Use your gifts. Maybe you will find people who are trustworthy enough to reveal yourself to. Either way, trust yourself and stay alert. This team is most likely overseen by powerful NEs who will monitor the outcomes."

That was true. I was sure that was who had given the commander "permission" to add Sage to his teams. Here I was, walking into the lion's den, putting myself in a path that could lead to further confinement and scrutiny, and yet I couldn't turn back. Courage clicked into place at his declaration. I would hear what this team entailed, and hopefully after they allayed any doubts I or my father had, I could put all my efforts into rocking this gig.

My father saw my resolve firm and ducked his chin once in acknowledgement, a twinkle in his eye. I took a deep breath and started toward the building. Steps sure, chin high, and father in step beside me.

You can do this, Nat.

A bell chimed as I pulled open the steel entrance door and took a step into a massive space, largely occupied by weights and fighting rings lined with thick ropes, three high. The lighting was sparse and the sounds loud. Metal clanged, hits thudding against both dense bags and flesh. Hard rock screamed from speakers hidden throughout the space, men shouted and grunted in various areas. Even more watched the number of activities currently happening. Along with these intense sights, was the smell.

The stench of stale sweat and tangy blood permeated the air in thick waves, nearly gagging me. That would take some getting used to, but at least the incessant drum beat and scream yelling of the music dulled the mental voices surrounding us.

As the door slammed closed behind me, the men closest to us looked up...and promptly froze. Internal confusion ruled their thoughts. Once their attention had been tuned to me however, the voices came in strong and loud, the music no longer enough.

No one had any idea as to why a young woman would be walking into their space, at least one who wasn't Primal. They figured I was lost, or a pet to the man with me. *Ewww...not sure I even want to know what they meant by that.* I noticed the Primal I spotted outside and decided to put on my big girl panties right there. Start with him. I made sure to project confidence and squared up to him. "Hi, there, I'm looking for Commander James. Do you know where I might find him?" Big smile, batted eyes.

She's cute, but I've no idea why the commander would want to meet her.

I rolled my eyes. "Yeah, I know. I'm Sage so I can't possibly be of use. Yada, yada, yada..." I used hand gestures to imitate yapping mouths and turned on my heel, heading further into the heart of the building. It took me a moment to notice that all activity had now ceased in the gym. There were no sounds, other than the still raging music, though there were plenty of thoughts and the smell did not dissipate.

About halfway through the room, someone cleared their throat, jerking my attention to find one of the men previously engaged in a fight, at the edge of the ring closest to me. His arms flung over the top rope. He was quite large, which seemed almost necessary for entry into this space. He had shaggy blonde hair and stubble lining his broad jaw. Blue eyes scrutinized me narrowly, and intricate tattoos glistened boldly on his sweat riddled torso under the bright lights.

"Who you looking for, doll?" he asked, smirking. My father growled, and the man brought his hands up in a defensive gesture, his bulging muscles bunching, veins popping. He kept the smirk.

"Commander James," I said plainly.

He nodded and pointed in the direction of a door at the back of the space. His internal voice was playful and he chuckled a throaty "Good luck" as I continued toward the indicated door. This gym was quite large, especially if there was more behind this door. I heaved a sigh, looking furtively toward my father. He returned my look and dipped his chin. *You've got this,* he winked.

I huffed out a laugh as my tension lifted slightly and brought my hand up to rap a knuckle on the door. It was almost immediately yanked inward to reveal another fight-ready-built male. He looked at me curiously, cataloging my appearance, but I found no malice in his thoughts.

I managed not to step back at the abruptness of his emergence. I assumed he was Primal Enhanced, his physique was too perfect, his features too symmetrical to be Non-Enhanced, and no one would mistake him for Sage. He had a playful quality to his expression, plenty of laugh lines at the corners of his chocolate eyes and full mouth. That image was confirmed as he kicked up a megawatt smile and thrust his right hand at me. "You must be Nathalee Dae, the telepathic Sage," he boomed at me good naturedly.

I was caught completely off guard with his greeting, and its genuine delivery. "Um, yeah, nice to meet you..." I clasped his hand, my eyebrows raised in question. He continued to smile at me, our hands still clasped. "This is my father, Connor Dae," I said, indicating my dad, hoping to spur a name from him.

"Dane, let Miss Dae and her father into the room please," Commander James's voice floated from behind the enigmatic *Dane.*

"Oh, of course. Sorry, Nathalee, Mr. Dae." He backed away from the entry and waved us forward, still smiling though it dimmed slightly from the chastisement Commander James had delivered. We walked into what appeared to be a conference room. White boards with writing as well as photographs were plastered along three walls, including the section we had entered from.

Some had lines or Xs through them, some were circled. I didn't recognize any of them, but that was to be expected as Minefield was a large town. We were currently about ten thousand strong with room to grow. The long wall to my right was covered with TV and computer monitors with a table running its length, which held various computer paraphernalia. It wasn't clear if all the information was connected or many different things all occupying the same space. As I looked around the room trying to find my voice, my father stepped forward and introduced himself.

"Commander James, good to see you again, sir." That piqued my attention back to my father. The movement catching my feet on the chair I was moving, giving me whiplash. He mentioned he knew who the commander was, that he treated his men often. It was never mentioned that he *knew* the man. I narrowed my gaze at my father's back. What else had he not told me?

"Doctor Dae. Good to see you. These certainly are better circumstances than we normally meet." They shook hands and exchanged a sorrow filled turning of lips acknowledging the poor conditions under which they must normally see one another. My father dipped his chin once and retreated a step, bringing him back to my side, and rested his arms across his chest.

I rolled my eyes. That seemed to be the universal male posture. "Nathalee, glad you accepted my invitation to see what I am trying to build here. This cheery gentleman is Dane. He is one of the enforcers on the team and will be one of the trainers for the inductees." He extended an arm toward Dane as he said this, briefly flicking his eyes away, then back toward my father and me.

I glanced in Dane's direction and saw him puff with pride, but not arrogance. His mental thoughts showed he looked up to the commander and liked being acknowledged. He'd be a good pick for mingling with Sages. He was big, but open, and didn't appear to have a prejudice against us. He seemed like a "water off a duck's back" kinda guy—just rolling with the tide. Amiable, likeable. *Yeah, definitely a good choice.*

"Nathalee? Is there anything in particular I can address for you or your father? Help give you a true representation of what we would expect?" Commander James stood and rounded the large table at the center of the room, only to lean against the side nearest us, crossing his feet at the ankles and arms across chest—the picture of nonchalance. He wasn't trying to guard his thoughts at the moment, so I gleaned that he thought the success of this team depended on my acceptance and ability to mesh the team together.

"You expect a lot of me, Commander." He nodded slowly. "Why do you think I am this person? Why are you hinging this on me?" Thoughts reeled through my mind. How could he base the success of this...*experiment* on me? Could I do this?

I was starting to freak out again.

You got this, breathe. Think. Ask. Once again, my father's voice grounded me. Blowing out a deep breath and looking at the floor, I gathered myself. Prepared to find out what I was signing up for.

"Because I know your father. I know you are a hybrid Enhanced." He indicated my father at my side. "Though that can be figured out easily enough with your height and strength." Here he gave me a meaningful look. "You are telepathic. More so than any other I am aware of. Quite in tune. That alone could make or break cases. You also want to break from the Sage mold and seem to be able to handle new situations." He dared me to say otherwise.

"And how did you learn this? How do you know about my strength?" I didn't think anyone would tell him about the Toby incident, but then, what did I really know?

"You know about the cameras, I think, Nathalee."

Damn ninnies. Always watching, judging. "Okay, how do you expect me to mesh this team? People don't exactly warm up to me. They always feel I'm rifling through their heads and want nothing to do with me." I was at a loss. How could they think a *telepath* would be the glue to this whole thing?

My father had been conspicuously quiet so far. I really thought he would be demanding all sorts of answers to questions I obviously hadn't thought of. "Do you expect Sages to actively participate in cases? Be put in situations we can't physically handle?"

"We will have to evaluate all Sage we bring into the program, but we will do our best to keep you out of situations you are ill equipped for. One of the measures we will implement will be to partner each Sage with a Primal complement to aid in physical ways, though many Sage abilities can be projected and aimed.

"We plan to hone the skills you *do* have in order to aid you in the field. We are also developing weapons which should be effective for Sages to handle if the situation escalates past the point of reason."

Weapons? I'm not sure Sage and weapons were meant to go hand in hand. That seems like it'd be inviting injury…to the operator.

"How do you expect to keep the Primals level? I've heard that tempers and aggression are high, and if that gets aimed at a Sage, it could get very bad, very quickly. Not always for the Sage." As Commander James noted earlier, many Sage abilities could be projected and aimed. If they were recruiting Sages with powerful enhancements, they were capable in their own right.

Of course, my ability was not of that class. It couldn't help me out of a dangerous position. No, apparently for that I would be relying on a Primal partner. I wasn't sure how much faith I had in that plan.

Commander James threw his arms wide and gestured around. "You see where we are? This gym will help to keep my men level. They will be able to get into the ring, lift weights, or hit a bag if their blood gets heated. Hopefully, we will be able to teach the Sage recruits some ways to improve their strength and stamina." At my burgeoning protest, he lifted his hand to stay my words and continued. "I know you won't be able to compete with Primals, but you may be able to surprise them enough to get away or be able to use a weapon if needed."

"So you've thought about the fact that your Sage recruits will be physically inferior to not only your Primal enforcement, but also a number of people, suspects, they will encounter?" My father's question brought everyone's attention to him. He raised his eyebrows, backing up his question.

"Yes, Doctor Dae, we have. We will not be able to address this properly until we are able to evaluate each recruit. Ideally, however, we will be able to shield them from the majority of questionable encounters. It will help that no one is aware of this joint effort, and Sage involvement can be kept quiet and utilized behind closed doors, and in many cases can be done effectively from a distance, if not completely unknowingly to the target. Is that not correct?"

My father got that far off stare again. Thinking about what the commander said about distance being utilized with Sage abilities, at least that's what I assumed as he was back to shielding his mind. While my father thought, Commander James brought his attention back to me. "You do not have to be physically close to, or touching, someone in order to hear their thoughts, correct?"

"No, my range is about twenty feet it seems." Hence the need for headphones. There was potential for *a lot* of people to be within twenty feet of me, and that was too hard to ignore on my own.

"And you can be in another room?" I nodded. "Then we can often use your ability without you ever being physically near, or even for it to be known that you are there and aiding in the investigation at all, which would be ideal. Do you know if certain obstacles are a problem?" At my furrowed look, he clarified. "Cement walls for instance? Steel doors?"

"Oh, ah, I'm not sure actually. I haven't knowingly been in those situations, so I have no way of telling you if I have or haven't had problems." I never thought about testing limits, just minimizing.

"Can we do an experiment?" At my nod, he continued, "Can you hear anyone outside this room?"

As I focused on extending my mental reach, I realized I heard more of a buzz than words or whispers. "I can't make out anything concrete, but I can still..." I did notice a voice. One I would now recognize anywhere, and it was getting louder, more agitated. As I focused on the sound, the door burst open.

Holden stalked in, looking for all the world like an avenging angel. He was dressed head to toe in black, hair in wild disarray and blue eyes thundering. He headed straight for Commander James, gesturing wildly with his hands, making innumerable signs. It didn't throw the commander. Obviously he was well versed in signing and was able to keep up with Holden's tirade.

I however, didn't know sign language and was actually quite grateful for once that I could get a read on the thoughts being thrown around. Interestingly, Dane was blank, his eyes volleying between his boss and Holden.

Apparently, Holden was more than upset that his *uncle* had recruited me into his enforcement team, deeming it too dangerous, while the commander was defending his selection. Seeing as both were thinking out their conversation, I was easily able to follow along. The gist was that Holden told the commander that I could communicate with him in confidence, not to be used to "put her in danger."

When that thought crossed his mind, his eyes bled to mercury again. It seemed something about the thought of me in danger caused a physical reaction in him. *I wonder why that is?* I'd definitely have to push some buttons in the near future…see what happened.

"Holden, I'm sorry but you know how valuable her talent is! *She* is valuable. She can bridge the gap. You know what we are dealing with…" Commander James's voice pleaded the last.

Holden seemed to deflate after that. Hands on his hips, he stared at his feet, lost. Though he was worried about me, his rampage had been more about his uncle using information he received in a confiding conversation as a basis to recruit me into a dangerous position.

Holden had just been excited that I had seen him. He'd noticed me immediately upon my visits to the barn, and the fact that I wanted to be around him *and* able to communicate…a first for him.

He signed again, *All right. All right, but I'm with her. I know her. We understand each other.* His eyes bore into mine as he said this. His irises glowing an ethereal blue, seeming almost to jump with electricity.

Holden, in all his glory, was a sight to behold. Cut lines and stormy expression only drew attention to his other attributes. His stature, his breadth, his grace. Everything about Holden screamed Primal when he was riled. I couldn't look away, and his eyes were all I saw. Our staring was interrupted when my dad decided he had stayed out of it long enough.

"I'm sorry, son, but *who* are you, and *why* are you staring at my daughter?"

Holden's cheeks flamed and he cursed his affliction, giving my father a pained shrug and furrowed brows. I recognized this same body language as what he showed me at our first meeting; sadness and frustration at his inability to readily answer. *But I'm here.* I could be his voice.

"Dad, this is Holden," I smiled a big goofy smile that immediately perplexed the occupants of the room. I looked back at Holden. "I can be your voice when we're together." I hurried to amend at the widening of his eyes. "If you want."

Now I was embarrassed. Would he think I wanted to speak *for* him, like using my words and thoughts, not his? I looked away, skimming my attention across the various information strewn about the room, hoping I hadn't overstepped. I looked back when he spoke. His eyes had lost their intensity and now shone with confounded curiosity.

You want to speak for me? Holden sounded perplexed. *Why?*

"You need to be heard. To be *seen.*" I was sure I had turned an unattractive shade of pink as heat crawled up my neck toward my ears. "I would like to help," I mumbled. I couldn't hold anyone's eyes now. I felt like I was admitting something big, allowing these people to see how I felt. Like they all saw my attraction. *Time to skedaddle...*

"Yeah, well, I'll see you tomorrow, I think." I was more than ready to escape after that awkwardness. "Thank you, Commander James for this introduction. When and how should I contact you to move forward?"

Commander James was still staring at Holden while he replied to my announcement. "Use the com. It's wired to contact me directly. We can set up to proceed with evaluations and new recruits." Finally, he pulled his attention away from Holden and walked toward me. "Thank you for joining the team, Nathalee. I really do believe you will be an immense asset." Holden snorted, anger seeming to seep from his pores.

Time to go!

The commander extended his hand to me. I shook it briefly, he then repeated the gesture with my father and we said our goodbyes. Moments later, Dad and I were headed into the main portion of the gym, toward blessed fresh air.

As we pushed out into the afternoon, I stopped and closed my eyes, falling back against the building and exhaling deeply. *Wow, that was intense. Is that my life now?* Dad bumped my shoulder playfully. "New purpose, here you come." I had to snort a laugh at him. The man had done a one eighty in a matter of twenty-four hours, but he was my rock.

"Yeah, here I come."

CHAPTER 9

WALKING TOWARD THE HOUSE, I reflected on the fact that I hadn't noticed any major mental input from Dane throughout the encounter with Holden. Was he a blank slate or was I just too preoccupied to notice his internal musings? Questions for a different day. Now, I needed a bath. The stink of the gym clung to me and I wanted to be rid of it.

The trip home took us through most of Minefield proper, with us cruising past most everything but the fields. Landmarks we reached evoked strong feelings when I looked at them. The school reminded me of my faults. The spires reaching into the sky like grasping fingers, manicured and polished facade screamed order, rigidity.

Contrastingly, the barn brought to mind the harmony in nature. The railed fencing, horses casually munching on grass or frolicking with one another. The paths all wandered, taking scenic and roundabout ways. The people who visited coveted the atmosphere and peace which the place provided.

Main Street held our most flourishing businesses, especially restaurants and bars. And because I was all about the food, I liked it there…when it wasn't bustling, which wasn't often enough for my taste.

Dad and I walked in silence, both steeped in our own thoughts about the meeting and my future. We passed many people but didn't acknowledge anyone. Whether that was because no one saw my father, or those who did, recognized the thoughtful look on his face and knew it meant he wasn't mentally present, I wasn't sure and didn't care.

Today marked the beginning of a new way of life for me. No more staying on the outskirts, or tuning people out. I would now actively seek to glean information from others. Hopefully, I could hone my ability in smaller areas, not have to scan a large number of innocent and unsuspecting people in order to ferret out the ones we needed…but that was a farfetched dream, I think.

Unless I was only brought in under controlled and contained circumstances, I would need to pry, and be all right with it, or at least *deal* with it. I would also need to know how to defend myself adequately. My strength could help me, but only so much. I was not as strong as full Primals, especially males. I think my tactics here should be surprise and evasion. Hopefully Dane or Holden would be able to give me pointers and training.

Once we reached home, my father and I went our separate ways. He veered toward the kitchen, presumably to speak with my mother about my recruitment into enforcement and what we'd learned so far. I continued down the hall to my bedroom, grabbing comfy clothes to lounge in for the rest of the evening.

I stepped across the hall and into the bathroom, pausing to put my clothes on the counter and turn on my music. Tonight I was in the mood for something catchy and upbeat. Something that made me believe I was now pointed in the right direction, no longer a spiraling compass, but one pointed due north.

A couple bands came readily to mind as I set my playlist. With lively tunes permeating the space, I turned on the shower and got lost in the pulsing melodies until steam filled the room. I stepped under the decadent spray and let the heaviness fall from my limbs.

I woke late Saturday morning having no intention of seeking company. My day was to be filled gophering –from home–for Dr. Parmore. Another day of boredom and feeling sub-par.

There was so much I needed to learn and understand about the law, criminals, rights—what little we had—and procedure. Not to mention how not to draw attention to myself, either with other enforcers or those we were tracking. But I couldn't sidetrack myself with those thoughts, not for a few days yet. Not until I had given the professor time to find a replacement. *She'd be thrilled.*

One more week.

I went looking for lunch after a few hours of tedium. I was starved as my rumbling stomach so kindly reminded me, so I decided on ground beef and gooey cheese laden nachos to keep my tummy from consuming itself. It was highly satisfying. With my cloying appetite appeased for the moment, I decided to locate the parental unit who was home.

I headed toward my mom's gadget room, assuming that to be where I'd find her. My hunch was proven correct as I tuned into my mother's mental signature. She was trying to remedy the short in one of her data chips. I stopped and leaned against the doorway to observe.

Golden hair was piled high atop her head in a hastily applied bun, cheeks flushed and eyes narrowed. I even saw her tongue peeking through pouting lips as she attempted to fit a tiny piece onto the chip. A gifted telekinetic, her specialty ran toward refined, minute movements and placement. Making it perfect for her tiny technology. This in turn made her highly sought after for specialized and custom tech pieces. *I wonder if she made the communication device Commander James gave me...*

The gadget room was organized chaos, especially to someone who had no working knowledge of information systems and engineering. There were neat piles all about the room, covering almost every available surface. Each pile contained items which looked similar but with minor differences, such as color, length or width. To the untrained eye, it was junk or excess. To my mother, it was the missing component, or the corrected length. It made me smile. I loved watching her work, and when she was enthralled in a project, she didn't mind me hearing her.

I think she hoped that maybe some of it would sink in. Unfortunately for her, the things she worked on involved those subjects which I was awful at. I stepped into the room and peered down at her work when she looked to be at a point she wouldn't mind interruption. "Hey, Mom."

She looked up, gave me a slight smile, and leaned back in her chair to rub her eyes. "Hi, Nathalee. How is your day going?"

"All right, doing lecture notes and handouts for Monday's classes," I shrugged. She nodded. I swirled my fingers at her workstation. "Having any luck kicking your short?"

"I think I've fixed the connection." Her eyes lit at that proclamation. I was about to inquire further when my phone chimed, interrupting my follow up. Mom went back to work without a second thought as I ambled into the hallway to check the message.

Jade: I'm bored and my parents are hovering. Wanna meet at the gardens?

Me: Sure. I'll grab us some drinks on the way over.

Jade: Sweet! See you in 20?

Me: Affirmative

"Mom, I'm going to go meet up with Jade at the gardens for a few, do you need anything?" I looked back over my shoulder in time to see her head shake in the negative, a mumbled "No thank you, sweetheart" barely audible. Dad was on shift at the hospital so it would be up to me for dinner, seeing as Mom was in her "zone" and wouldn't notice the time. *I'll grab pizza on the way home.*

I scooped up my messenger bag and threw it across my body as I reached for the door. The gardens weren't much more than a mile from the house and with the coffee shop between here and there, I figured I could walk it. I liked traveling the streets, noticing all the homes and businesses. Most people rode a bike, if not in a car and definitely didn't look at the places they passed. They didn't notice when and where people were absent. I did, and I relished this time to absorb my surroundings without absorbing so many conflicting thoughts.

My walk took me away from the residential area consisting of small but tidy brick homes with minimalist landscaping, all of which were Sage households, and into the business district of town.

Here the pavement was patchy with weeds and everyday debris. The building faces boasted large windows and bright displays for whatever lay inside. Even here, though, there was pride. The ones who owned businesses were fierce in keeping them up and running as best as possible. The little coffee shop that Jade and I adored went by the name "The Corner Bean," and was no exception to this rule.

Run by a Primal couple who had enhanced smell and taste, respectively, their blends were a-maz-ing. There were such masterful hints, undertones, and afternotes in their creations that their business never experienced a lag. This specialty was one which did well for the ninnies and allowed for Minefield to receive monthly supply shipments in exchange for creating blends, which could be sold to the masses.

Most of the money generated could be used to keep Minefield running. Many profitable businesses actually operated this way, which was a double edged sword: giving control to the outside world but also keeping the town from falling into total disrepair from a lack of restorative materials.

Today was no exception in the number of patrons, and I waited ten minutes for our drinks. My chai tea latte was the perfect blend of spice and sweet, and Jade was always well *satisfied* with her coffees. I didn't get that though. I detested coffee. It gave me a bad taste just thinking about drinking it and I chased away a disgusted shiver, continuing past the establishments leading to the gardens.

Sipping on the spicy goodness contained in liquid form, my eye caught on the barn coming up on my left. The white fencing, lush green grass, beige dirt, and iconic red barns always relaxed me. I couldn't help but swing my arms more loosely and walk with longer, more fluid strides as I took it in. It was like the space brought out my inner Primal, making me much more graceful than I ever was elsewhere.

"Oh crap," I muttered as I remembered that I had expected to make it to the barn today for another lesson with Holden. I had completely forgotten, and now I was not only on my way elsewhere, but I realized I had no way to contact Holden to let him know I wouldn't make it. Making a quick decision, which really wasn't hard, I waited for a hole in traffic and bounded across the street as quickly as I could while carrying two piping hot liquids.

I didn't see him in the riding area as I walked along the fence and toward the entrance. There were plenty of horses grazing in their enclosures, and there looked to be noticeably more people moving around on the grounds than I was used to seeing, but none were Holden. I wanted to give him a heads up, to apologize, but I couldn't spend forever looking either. I moved down the dirt lane toward the barn where I had met him previously, still managing to get lost in the atmosphere the place created.

Approaching the open barn doors, I peeked inside. I was greeted by many horse sounds, but no human ones. The horses in residence all made little noises letting me know they were there; neighing, feet stomping to scare off flies, tails swishing and blowing noses came from various areas.

Jasper was here and it was no surprise that he alone made each sound at different moments. I said a quick "Hey, handsome," receiving a whinny in response. Turning away from the barn interior and its familiar scents: dust, animal, sweet hay and woodsy pine, my eyes moved restlessly to scan the surrounding areas but I still didn't see Holden anywhere. Maybe he wasn't here. I shrugged, thinking to myself that at least I had attempted to apologize for bailing on him today, and made my way back to the street.

As I came to the entrance of the green jungle, I pulled up short with the thought that the enforcement training center was just past here. I couldn't see it from this angle, but I couldn't help but look. Continuing into the gardens, I kept to the bricked path and admired the growth. Manicured lawn for lounging and games stretched to the left while a kids' play area unfolded on the right. Past those were the flower gardens, blooming in vibrant shades ranging the color wheel and attracting both bees and butterflies. The entire space ringed in dense foliage.

The path I was on bisected the flower gardens and led to a pristine wood bench situated at the base of a large oak tree. Jade had her legs pushed out in front of her, arms spanned across the back of the bench. Her head was tilted against the tree, eyes closed and lips turned up.

This was Jade's peace, just as the barn was mine. I studied her while she soaked up the serenity, lost to the branches' whispers. Though we heard the reverie of others nearby, no one was overly close. Neither of our abilities were in overdrive here. Jade was dressed simply in jeans and a red long-sleeved top. Her mass of golden hair was pulled over a shoulder to drape down her side. The flip-flops sporting a cartoon kitty with a big red bow completed her casual look.

I figured with both of us in decent moods, she may not have tuned into me yet. I decided to have a bit of fun with her. I crept to close the gap between us, being careful not to step into her beam of light and ruin my fun. Nearly touching her right leg, I leaned forward, almost brushing her ear.

"Boo!"

Jade jumped nearly out of her skin and let off a satisfying squeak of alarm, almost taking out my nose, and our drinks, but I was able to dodge her flailing fist and knee to avoid the hit. Backing up further, I chuckled in amusement while Jade gave me a death glare. *So worth it!* I thrust coffee into her hands, hoping it would earn me points after that stunt. Lord knew I'd need them. Jade was crafty and would come up with some inventive way to return the favor I just bestowed upon her.

"You suck, Nat," she grumbled, sipping her drink, but the tension left her body as soon as she swallowed her first mouthful. "You're lucky you came bearing gifts after that crap," she smirked. The nectar was cradled in both hands close to her face as she sat breathing it in. Jade liked to say just the smell of Corner Bean coffee could get her high, and watching her now, I would be inclined to agree.

"So, what'd the parents do today?"

Jade huffed a long-suffering sigh and thrust out her arm not holding the coffee. "The usual. They keep trying to get me to decide to take the counselor route. They think it's a 'safe' path." Air quotes encased "safe" and she rolled her eyes, conveying contempt of her parents' mantra. They hovered and tried to dictate to Jade how she should live her life, treating her asthma and small stature as weak and frail, as would most.

Jade and I, however, hated being put into those boxes that Sages were generally crowded into. We didn't want to do something just because it was *safe*. Safe was overrated and mundane. We wanted to make a difference somewhere. I had found where I could do that. Could Jade?

As I was finishing my cup of decadence, a wavelike tone began emanating from my messenger bag. Luckily for me, the beverage was too low to slosh over the sides when I started at the sound. Jade pointed at my bag. "You're ringing."

"Very perceptive of you, thanks."

"I try." Jade smiled brightly at me, her self-satisfaction evident.

The banter between us was as familiar as our gifts, and I cherished it. Finally I located the source of the tone and pulled it away from my bag. The enforcer com, its blue shield pulsed with light in time to the tone it sang. Seeing Jade's confused expression, I realized I had yet to tell her about Commander James and my pending job. I vowed to tell her all about it, leaving nothing out...after I answered this thing.

I ran my thumb across the shield, just as I had when I contacted the commander the day before last and spoke when it seemed I had been connected. "Hello?" I shrugged at Jade in an attempt to convey that I was just about as clueless as she was. I mean, I wasn't an enforcer yet, was I?

Commander James's deep voice spilled from its depths, much louder than one would think possible. "Nathalee?"

"Yes, sir?"

"We've had an incident that I believe you may be able to help us get to the bottom of. Would you be willing to come back to the CP and listen to someone for us?"

"CP?" The term was lost on me.

"Command Post. Sorry, I forget that not everyone I speak to understands *Enforcese*."

My brow drew together in confusion yet again, "Enforcese?" *I need to learn lingo, it seems.*

A deep chuckle came over the line as he explained, "Just a term I use to describe things that apply only to being in enforcement. There are many, and they are just easier to use when talking about such issues."

The longer the conversation went on, the more confused Jade's thoughts became. She was almost convinced I was seeing this Commander James privately. That I had a new man in my life and had yet to tell her. She was working herself up to being right pissed at me for not telling her about him. She wasn't right in thinking that I hid him from her...though, she did have a right to be mad at me for not telling her about him at all, and I would accept her ire, later.

"I'm in the gardens now, actually, so I can be there in just a few minutes. I assume the *CP* is where we met previously?" Jade was about to burst. She was so worked up, her eyes were spitting green fire at me in a glare so intense, I was sure that if she could shoot lasers, I would be nothing but ash in front of her.

I smirked as an idea struck. "Commander, do you have an empath on the team?" If he went for this, Jade and I had found what we had been looking for: something bigger than us. A way to be useful, to *do* something meaningful. After the commander answered in the negative, I told him I was bringing Jade with me. At that declaration, and most likely my burgeoning excitement, Jade's thoughts veered toward acceptance. She was happy to be included and finished off her coffee with a triumphant smile.

"Girl, you have no idea what I'm taking you into." It was my turn to dial up the devious smile. Could Jade handle the "command post"?

CHAPTER 10

"WHAT THE–?!" JADE'S EYES bulged comically as they bounced around the brightly lit gym space. "Nathalee, why—" she squeaked when a weighted bar clanked into place on our left, the male working it sitting up and put his arms over his thighs to watch us move further into the space.

Jade glued herself to my side and whisper-screamed in my ear, "What are we doing here?" Her asthma was kicking in, making me think I may have made a mistake. That she'd end up hyperventilating and passing out before we ever saw the commander and whatever he wanted me to look into.

I stopped her with a hand at the elbow and brought her around to face me, looking directly into those too wide eyes. She looked ready to bolt. "Jade, breathe. Just breathe for a minute and I'll explain. It may be better, well *easier* to explain once we leave the training area and the stares from all these Primal males." I raised my eyebrows questioningly and gave

99

her a little half smile. The fact that I was calm seemed to help her. She took a few deep breaths and nodded vigorously at me, her eyes once again focusing. "You good?"

"Yeah, I'm good." Nodding again, she began walking. I steered her toward the door I had entered the day before. It was closed again, so I knocked. This time, Dane's smiling face didn't throw me off, but it did Jade. She stood, rooted in place, staring slack jawed at him. Her thoughts were all sorts of naughty, but she wasn't scared. Not at the moment at least, who knew if that would change when we learned why we were here.

"Hey, Dane, good to see you again."

"Hi, Nathalee." Again, he waved us forward into the room.

"Dane, Commander, this is Jade Danforth." I waved her forward, "Jade is a talented empath. I'm thinking you may want her on the team."

"I'm sure she is quite talented," the commander acknowledged with a small nod at Jade, "Though I don't know why we would need to read emotion when we can read actual *thoughts*?"

I turned to Jade, my expression questioning. She finally walked into the room, her eyes darting between Dane and the commander, assessing. She stopped at my side, glancing at me briefly, then returned to sizing up the Primals.

Finally, having made a decision, she gave me the mental green light to reveal the extent of her ability. I opened my mouth, ready to tell them precisely how useful a true empath could be, but snapped it shut in a lightbulb moment. "Jade, how about you show them what you can do."

Jade looked over at me with a "what the hell?" look as I urged her onward. A moment later a mischievous smirk, one I'm sure mirrored my own, drew across her face. *She's going to enjoy this.* The room stilled as Jade sauntered up to Dane, halting just before she reached where he stood by the computer bank along the right wall. They were locked in an intense stare down.

All of a sudden, Dane's depthless chocolate eyes went impossibly wide, his eyebrows pinched and jaw clenched. Breathing labored and muscles stiff, he swiveled his attention toward Commander James. "I'm terrified! I don't know why or of what, but I am!" His body began to tremble as he brought his attention back to Jade. His hands opened and closed convulsively, his entire body vibrating with tension as he fought the inexplicable urge to flee. Jade broke concentration and stepped back to my side, looking for all she was worth, like the cat that got the canary.

But Dane's mind was elsewhere, still locked in its terrified state. I saw flashes of gruesome images, one after another, until one stayed front and center. A woman, her beautiful face marred with bruises and blood. Eyes like blue pools were open and vacant, shot through with red. Haunting. That's exactly what I was seeing, a haunting memory Dane was reliving. Looking at the commander, I noticed he was watching Jade, unaware of where his enforcer's mind was currently trapped, the nightmare he was stuck in.

I nudged Jade. "He's in a bad place, you have to do something to bring his mind back." I was starting to emulate what Dane was feeling. His thoughts and horror so intense, I couldn't escape it. My breathing sped up to mimic Dane's as did my posture, fists and jaw clenched. Soon, Jade would feel its effects as well.

Jade looked at a loss, not expecting Dane's continued agitation. She was swinging her eyes wildly between Dane and me, her golden locks flying with each turn. "I cut off the terror already," she scrunched her nose, searching for a solution. "I'll send calming juju."

It didn't help. Dane continued to see the woman's unnerving stare, even though his mind and body were calming. It would be extremely confusing later when he thought about this scene. Would his mind and body stay calm as it was now or would he revert to his original emotional state?

"I wish I could say that worked Jade, but he still has the visual."

Before I finished the words, she had marched over to Dane and was standing toe to toe with the big male. She reached up and grabbed either side of his face, yanking him down while standing on the toes of her cartoon emblazoned flip-flops to close the gap between them, as Dane was easily a foot taller than Jade.

The crashing of their lips was enough to startle Dane out of his self-imposed nightmare. Jade was surprised how soft and full his lips were. Once his surprise wore off, however, Dane was a full participant, thinking this may be his only chance to experience her kiss. His dilated eyes bore into hers, mouth opening slightly.

Jade was shocked out of the moment when his tongue grazed her lips. Letting go of his face, she stepped back and out of reach. *I cannot believe I just did that! Just walked up and kissed the man!* she scolded herself. So many mental face-palms ensued that I lost track. She pulled herself together and straightened up, putting on the persona she wore so well. "Uh, sorry. It's the best I could think of to bring you back." Jade was so hotly embarrassed I could almost see the steam escaping her ears.

I cleared my throat and rubbed my now maneuverable hands down my thighs to rid them of sweat. "Anyway, now you know how you may be able to use an empath, or at least Jade, both to incite and calm." I threw her a pointed look, "Though maybe she'll think through her emotions a little better next time…" I raised my eyebrow, asking for confirmation of my statement.

Jade recovered and put a hand on Dane's arm. He was looking at his hand, opening and closing it compulsively as a means to ignore the room's occupants and avoid our eyes, as well as any questions that may be aimed at him.

"I'm sorry, Dane. I just thought making you feel something that was out of the norm for you would demonstrate my ability to override one's emotions. I didn't mean any true harm." Jade looked lost, biting her lip, upset at what she caused.

Commander James, who had been looking at Dane with a concerned, almost fatherly expression, now turned his attention back to Jade. He decided to avoid the previous situation in hopes of allowing everyone to save face. "Yes, I now see how having an empath, at least one such as you, on the team could be…useful." Pause for emphasis. "But carefully."

Squaring up, he gave us the full picture of scary Primal commander clad in a dark shirt and khaki pants with a myriad of pockets. His boots surprised me—not full leather or canvas but a mesh which looked both durable and breathable. Depthless cinnamon eyes blazed at Jade with an intensity which screamed to be obeyed; or else. "You will not use that portion of your ability without being expressly told to do so, do you understand? I will not tolerate anything malicious going on within the team."

Jade nodded like a bobblehead. "I've only done it a handful of times and only on my parents–until today." She went on hastily, "I was only trying to demonstrate. I wouldn't abuse it." She rolled her eyes before continuing. "And if you knew my parents, you'd understand why I would use it on them."

She was rambling as confusion surfaced, both on her face and in her mind. "Wait, what am I agreeing to? I don't even know who you are and what this 'team' is!" Oh, she was back to seething at me for not telling her all that had happened the last few days. I was in for a tongue lashing, and not the pleasant kind. I flushed again as that thought brought forth the memory of being in both Jade's and Dane's heads during their kiss. *Telepathy sucks.*

"Well, Miss Danforth, we are a branch of Enhanced Enforcement. I am putting together a team of Primals *and* Sages who would work side by side to investigate the more severe or confusing crimes committed within the community. We even have an NE or two on the team."

Seeing her about to protest, he held up a hand to stay her objections and powered on. "I understand that Sages are not physically able to compete with Primals, but you are able to use abilities long range, and may investigate better than Primals.

"As I told Nathalee yesterday, we will need to assess where you are physically and what we can do to strengthen your skills, should you need to leave a situation. Hopefully, most of your interactions will be without duress and under controlled circumstances, but I cannot guarantee all will be that way."

Suddenly, I was jolted to the left, having to take a step in order to stay upright. I grabbed at my right biceps, having just received a wallop from Jade. "Ow!" I narrowed my eyes at her, though I knew why she had done it... and that I deserved it. "I'm sorry! I've been so caught up in figuring out what I was going to do, that I forgot to actually...tell...you. I'm sorry." I knew I repeated myself, but really, what else was I supposed to say?

I refocused on Commander James in an attempt to move attention away from myself and my lack of communication with my bestie. "So, Commander, why am I here today? I assumed you wouldn't need me until after I had some training." I raised my eyebrow in time with the question.

"Ah, well, we have a person in custody who is telling us something that does not agree with our findings. I was hoping you may be able to give us some insight." He stepped to the side, dragging one of the boards plastered with people and information along with him. In the newly open space, a large window was revealed. It took up nearly the entire length of the wall, starting about three and a half feet from the base and extending upward.

In the room was a disheveled man. His hair, falling almost to his shoulders, looked tangled and wet, whether from water, sweat, or blood, I couldn't tell. His clothes in much the same state as his hair, were dirty and torn. They also bore patches of a rust color, which I believed to be blood. He was seated haphazardly in a blue plastic chair, staring blankly at the floor ahead of him. His hands, bruised and bleeding at the knuckles, were limply hanging toward the gray floor behind him, legs fully extended in a V. He was in a heavy state of disbelief.

"What happened?" I stuttered, bringing myself close enough to reach out and touch the glass. I traced lines along the blemishes, wondering just what would possess this man to flip his shit. I had seen the product of violence many times with my father at the hospital, so this man's appearance was not a new sight.

His mental state, however, wasn't something I associated with aggressors. Now that I was focused on him, his mental state was all too clear. He was in heavy self-recrimination, to the point he may try to hurt himself. "He's destroyed. Filled with self-loathing," I turned my head to find Commander James behind me, further from the window. He was tall enough that I didn't impede his view so he didn't feel the need to move closer.

Looking a bit uncertain, he answered. "He was reported viciously beating his neighbor. Two of my most capable enforcers were barely able to pry him off the other man. He had flipped. The man he had beaten was already unconscious, but Jerath here seemed to have no intention of letting up. I'm not certain of the condition of the victim as of this moment, but I need to know what Jerath's motive was."

Commander James scrubbed a hand over his shorn hair and down his face, a move born of frustration. "He was raging about how he saw the man hit his wife while he was fixing the fence between the properties. Many Primals are protective of women and children, Jerath apparently is no exception." The man in question still had not moved or changed his expression during this rundown. He was apparently accepting of his fate—at least at this moment. I didn't know anyone who would go quietly into that good night, when said "good night" was Enhanced Prison.

"I still don't see why you need me." I was confused, this seemed open and shut. "He was seen beating the man. He's obviously guilty." I brought my attention back to Jareth's limp form. The man I saw looked lost, devastated. Why?

"We have his version of a motive, though when we checked the victim's property for a female, we found none. Other witnesses said that the wife works in the fields and is gone every day from sunup to sundown. But our assailant was so sure of what he saw, or so he says."

It clicked into place then, "All right, I get it. You want me to read him, see if his mental and verbal accounts coincide." I pursed my lips in thought and bobbed my head. "Well, right now, he certainly isn't thinking about what set him off, I need someone to push his thoughts in that direction."

Dane stepped forward to volunteer, but Commander James waved him off, saying that he would go in and Dane could be back up if necessary. Dane was not comfortable putting his commander in a precarious situation but nodded his assent all the same. "Jade, can you influence his emotions on this side of the wall?" Her skill may come in handy if Jareth flipped again.

Jade looked nervous. "I'm not sure, actually. I've never tried doing it when I wasn't nearly touching the person." She wanted to say she could but didn't want to overstate things. "I'll go in if we need to subdue him." Dane opened his mouth to protest but was quelled by Jade's stare.

She, *we* rather, didn't want to take the easy road. "If I'm on this team, you have to let me do my thing. Be my backup if needed, but *don't* tell me I can't do it." Her eyes were spitting their green fire at Dane as she waited to see if her point was made. Finally, he nodded once, acknowledging her statement.

I turned back toward Commander James and relayed my concern. "I'm not sure how we'll communicate with you in the room and me not."

"Tap on the glass once you get what you need." With that parting statement, he opened the door and walked into the sterile-looking room where Jerath was still sitting, still staring at nothing. "Jerath," the

107

commander's smooth tones reached me through the panes of glass only slightly muffled. "Jerath, tell me again what happened."

Commander James had stopped a few steps into the room and stood tall, his legs braced and his arms crossed with his chin dipped nearly to his chest. He was in a power position, but his tone was coaxing. His query was met with silence, but Jerath's thoughts flickered.

There was a brief image of a man, seen through a large picture window, his back to us, throw out a powerful fist which caught a woman with short brown hair across her left cheek and sent her spinning to the ground. With the image, Jerath's self-recrimination ebbed. That image, the *thought*, enraged him. Commander James tried again, harsher this time. "Jerath, why did you attack Mr. Barnes?"

Jerath's eyes flicked to meet the commander's as he ground out, "I told you. He hit his woman." There was definitely anger there, and it was rising. It was only with this agitation and the subsequent movements that I noticed that the man's hands were bound. Those two things served to remind me that this man was here for a reason, his present state shouldn't sway me from that knowledge.

"And I told you, there was no female in residence when we searched the premises. No one saw her leave, and the whole block was outside and watching you beat Mr. Barnes. Someone would have seen her leave, had she been there. We've been told that Mrs. Barnes works in the fields as do you all, and is never around at the time you claim to have seen her, though your description of the woman does match. We are checking on her status as we speak."

The longer Commander James went on in his speech as to how Jerath was wrong in what he saw, the more Jerath's anger built. I saw the fight unfold, though it wasn't really much of a fight. Jerath rushed the door when Mr. Barnes answered and yanked him onto the porch, digging his hands into the man's shirt and flinging him to the ground when he denied Jerath's accusation of assaulting his wife.

Mr. Barnes landed in a heap on the ground at the base of the porch steps, dazed and coughing on the dust kicked up when his body hit the ground, but then Jareth was on him. He showed no mercy, even as the man shouted his innocence, Jerath landed blow after blow, and had focused his attention mainly on the man's face.

It was about this time I noticed something. I knocked quickly on the glass to get Commander James's attention, he took the cue and turned to leave. Once he was securely outside the room, he asked my thoughts.

"He definitely thinks he saw a woman take a right hook to the face."

Commander James looked taken back. He must have expected that Jareth was lying in order to explain his actions.

"Here's the interesting part," I paused, flicking my eyes between the three pairs currently fixed on me. "The sequence I watched of the initial assault was different from the sequence of the ensuing fight." Three pairs of eyes, blinked blankly at me. Confusion was the overwhelming result of that statement.

"Ok, let me see how to explain…every person has a mental 'voice' or 'signature,' if you will. Something that is uniquely *them*. A way of speaking, a tone, a sequence…always the same for them, but unique to everyone." That didn't seem to help. How did I accurately explain this to people who had never experienced it?

"It's like this. Jade, you know how you say every emotion has a feel?" She nodded slowly. "Well every 'voice' has a tone, a…frequency. All thoughts resemble each other as that tone for that specific person." Heads nodded now. I was heading in the right direction on the explanation. Let's hope I could keep it up.

"The imagery for the woman's assault is a different 'tone' than Jareth's recount of the fight that resulted." I was excited now, bouncing in place. "We *know* the fight between Jareth and Mr. Barnes occurred, so that is a true account."

Jade jumped in, her eyes alight at the revelation that she understood why I was excited. "The other images cannot be corroborated, and *those* are the images which seem out of place from Jareth's normal mental display!" She lunged forward and hugged me. "Wow, we really can make a difference, can't we?"

"Okay, let me see if I understand what you are saying here," Commander James said, still looking a bit flustered at my explanation. He rubbed at his eyes but soldiered on. "You think his mind has been tampered with?"

"I do."

"The whole initial incident—fabricated."

"Yes."

Dane's attention volleyed between the rest of us. Apparently he wasn't quite there yet. This is why I'd been brought in to help, sometimes Primals just wouldn't follow a path where it led unless it was lit by neon and had an arrow.

"Well, shit. This complicates things, at least morally." Commander James's voice was thick as his mind churned furiously, attempting to explain it.

"Why only morally?" Jade wondered.

110

"I can't release him, even if his motive was somewhat valid. He still beat a man nearly to death. He has to do his time." Those words fell heavily onto my shoulders, pushing me toward the floor. Jareth was going to lose what freedom he had because someone decided to mess with his mind. Well, in part. He *did* flip and nearly kill the guy, which may have been a bit excessive, but he wouldn't have done it if not for the implanted visual of his neighbor striking his wife.

What worried me most about this scenario was that the ninnies could use it to say it proved them right, no matter that they have done such things for millennia. Things like this would brand Enhanced for eternity. Would we ever be allowed to integrate with Non-Enhanced populations? Would things get worse? I wasn't aware of any Sages who could project images, and the fact that the first one I came across was using his ability to cause others fear and pain pissed me the hell off.

"We'll have to inform the director that Jareth will need to go into holding and await his trial, though he may wish to take a deal considering..." the commander looked woeful but resigned. We all knew it would be nearly impossible for Jareth to move forward unscathed, his best bet would be to take a deal if one was offered. "Nathalee," he began, "What can you tell us about the implanted scene?"

Blowing out a breath, I reflected. "The scene was a different 'tone' as I said. Everyone has their own mental signature, a particular way they think things. Not only in terms of phrases, words or images, but also a mental 'voice' for each. I may be able to discover who our perpetrator is by this mental frequency, should I come across it again."

I twisted my mouth into a rueful smile, the truth was while that was probably true, being in a situation in which I would be able to hear this person was a longshot at best. We had no clue who it could be and no idea where to look.

At least, *I* didn't.

"All right, new plan. We need to get you girls into training ASAP and move my existing enforcers to see what we can find out about anyone with such ability." I watched the wheels turn in Commander James's mind, listened to him list out procedures and tasks for various Primals to start the search. "Also, once you are in training full time, we have accommodations for you. When might that be?"

I blinked. "Accommodations?"

"Yes, we are grouping the team together in a dorm-like setting, so everyone is in the same approximate location for call outs and training." He looked at me. "The walls are reinforced, so maybe you'll have some quiet time." There was emphasis on *quiet*. "Until that time, you need to come here and train. We need you functional in the field."

"I thought you wanted me in controlled situations," I smirked at him, pulling a hand to my hip. "You know, keeping us Sages all safe and tucked away."

Dane spoke up then. "I think you're going to be needed in the field, at least on this one." He looked to Commander James for confirmation— and received it. "You are the only one who knows that mental signature, and as of right now, it's our only lead."

Way to put the pressure on a girl. "What am I supposed to do? Walk around town aimlessly and *hope* I stumble across his frequency at some point?"

"No, I'm putting enforcers on it immediately. We'll try to narrow the search. Who knows, maybe we'll get lucky and this guy was obvious and this will be over in no time."

"All right, I need to give my notice to Doctor Parmore. Give me a few days for her to replace me. After that, we're all yours to mold," I gave a sardonic salute and added with a smirk, "Commander." He rolled his eyes at me and walked toward the tech area of the command center. *Wow, he really handles my sarcasm well.* He pawed through the gadgets piled at one end of the tables until he came up with another com, which he handed to Jade.

"This is a direct link, both me to you, and you to me. If we contact either of you before your training officially begins, it means we need your...*expertise*. Hopefully, we will not need to use it. Good luck on your last days in civilian work, and we will see you soon. Thank you for coming," his eyes bore into mine as he continued, "you are already invaluable." I pursed my lips and gave a curt nod, turning to leave the room.

"Bye, Nathalee," Dane boomed. Much softer he added, "It was a pleasure meeting you Jade. Well, mostly. I apologize for my lapse," He mentally chided himself for reverting.

"It was very nice meeting you as well, Dane. Commander James," she dipped her chin in acknowledgment. "I'm sorry, for...earlier," she was berating herself also. I decided to head out and give them the space they needed to get over their respective guilt, and heat.

"C'mon, Jade, I figured I'd grab pizza for dinner. Dad's on call at the hospital today. You interested?"

"Yeah, let me tell my parents." Then she turned to the enforcers. "Again, it was nice meeting you. Thank you very much for the opportunity."

Having said our goodbyes, Jade and I headed back through the gym and into the waning sunlight. Apparently we had been there for a while, as the sun was nearly setting. Pizza, then home. We set off to accomplish just that.

CHAPTER 11

JADE AND I SPENT the evening discussing our thoughts on being a part of the enforcers, and being girly. I took the time to fill her in on all that I hadn't before meeting with Dane and the commander; all that happened before we were aware that there was a Sage who had the ability to implant scenes into another's mind and using this ability in a harmful way.

By phone, Jade told her parents she was going to join the enforcers. I stifled a laugh when her mom fainted from worry. Her dad wasn't much better, and I was sure the discussion wasn't over. I was proven right when Jade came back to my house Sunday afternoon after going home earlier in the day.

She showed up with a suitcase in hand, and I shuffled her into my room, letting my parents know of the development. My mom praised the commander for seeing the worth of Sages in enforcement, and Dad loved the fact that Jade and I could watch each other's back. It would most likely be him we were to see if things didn't go well, so he wanted as much protection as possible. In as many forms as we could get it.

I really wanted to get back to the barn and my lessons with Holden, but I had too much to do in preparation for my last days with the professor.

When Monday rolled around, I was happy that the lecture pertained to world history in some capacity. I had studied the subject heartily as I wanted to know about the world which would consistently go to war, taking innumerable lives, but felt *we* were the threat. I'm not sure how much of our subject matter was censored, or just plain left out, but I wanted to know what I could.

They say knowledge is power. Maybe that was why so little knowledge about us to the world was allowed. The Enhanced were quite the mystery to the general Non-Enhanced population, until recently. Apparently the ninnies forgot that they locked a lot of *really* smart people away together.

Once the internet took off, Sages took full advantage. There were plenty of informational and social media sites that painted the Enhanced as wrongly "imprisoned" and misunderstood people who were just like everyone else, but with added perks. It should come as no surprise that Sages were behind the propaganda.

After gathering tests and escaping the room, I made my way to Dr. Parmore's offices to relay that I would not be with her after the week ended. She spluttered and fidgeted, indignant. I felt bad that my notice was so short, but the position would be filled easily. I could kid myself and think that she actually liked me, but alas her lack of verbal response was closer to non-belief.

When I told her I was going to be a consultant, she tried to get me to tell her where and for whom. I wasn't sure what Commander James wanted me to say, if I wasn't supposed to say I was working for the enforcers, so I didn't. I'd have to ask. After working for a few hours with an especially cross Dr. Parmore, I was able to make my way to the barn. To Holden. *Pssh, don't think like that.*

With my earbuds in, I walked in blissful ignorance of the world around me. Taking my time and soaking up as much of the melodies as possible. Today I was listening to electric classical and it was energizing. The screaming violin and rapid piano put a bounce in my step and I bobbed my head as I made my way along the busy main stretch of town toward the barn.

People congregated in small groups around tables outside The Corner Bean as I stopped in to grab a beverage. The groups were largely comprised of what I assumed to be Primal males off shift from their labor-intensive jobs, all huddled closely but speaking at levels much higher than needed for their close proximity.

I was engrossed in dueling cellos and getting caffeine into my system when I stepped back into the afternoon sunlight and into a scene from a tragic movie. I froze mid-step, looking like an awkward statue. One foot hovering in front of me, and the cup frozen inches from my mouth. I was a funny sight, certainly. But what I was seeing, what had frozen my movements, was far from comical.

I watched in seemingly slow motion as a man cast a horrified look toward the busy street and sprinted like a spooked deer into the roadway.

He'd made it just over halfway when a red rock-crawler sped to the same spot.

The impact was deafening. The screech of tires and noxious smell of burnt rubber couldn't drown out the thuds and crunches of metal meeting flesh. Neither could my earbuds. The struck man was thrown yards, his head impacting the pavement with a loud *crack,* which jolted me into motion. My drink hit the ground, forgotten. I stumbled as my foot finally came to rest on the sidewalk.

Then I was running.

People were congregating around the man lying bloody and broken in the street. The woman who had been driving the Jeep was outside her vehicle standing with hands covering her mouth, her eyes wide in terrified shock. Her thoughts were a screaming mess. She was falling apart with guilt.

I rushed past her and into the throng of onlookers. My jockeying through the crowd nearly dislodged one of my earbuds, which at any other time would have annoyed me into fixing it, but not this time. This time, I ignored it and barreled into the throng.

It appeared no one had medical training, or were too shell shocked to move into action, as they all just stood over the unconscious man with wide eyes, gaping mouths, and stunned disbelief wafting from their minds.

Useless, all of them.

I finished shoving my way through the horde and dropped to my knees beside the critically injured man. The accident had occurred at no more than forty miles per hour, but the vehicle and man had been a perfect storm.

The man was stocky but not overly tall, and the vehicle was perfectly in line with his hips, allowing him to be catapulted. Thick red liquid seeped from the corner of his mouth and a similar puddle was expanding like a red halo atop the dark pavement behind his head. *Blood.* One arm was bent so his hand was almost touching his face, the back of the hand down the arm was shredded from sliding along the street's rough surface.

His hips were no longer level, the right inches lower. It didn't look good, like the impact had crushed it, the accompanying leg rested at an angle too great to be naturally achieved, aiding in my belief of major hip damage.

I reached out and felt along the man's neck for a pulse, trying to keep my frantic heart from escaping my chest and my mind toward aid and away from the shock everyone else seemed to be locked into. Pushing my fingers along his carotid, I sagged with relief. He was alive. The pulse was weak, but steady. He must've been a Primal to withstand injuries such as these.

"Someone call emergency!" I shouted at the large group of "lookie loos." Shocked looks and proverbial crickets were my answer. It wasn't until that moment that I realized I heard an instrumental version of a song centered around death. The melancholy timbre much clearer than the internal dialogue of the onlookers.

Ripping the foreboding music unceremoniously away from my ears, I growled in frustration and rifled through my messenger bag until I came across my phone. Quickly dialing the emergency response number, I waited for the call to be connected. Now that I was no longer shielded by enveloping melodic sounds, the surrounding noises and voices assailed me.

Those in the immediate vicinity were both shrieking and doing the mental equivalent of rocking in the corner, or at the other end of the mental spectrum and were relatively unconcerned. There was surprisingly little street noise, and the traffic seemed to have stopped. No, not stopped, but backed up with cars lining down the street. Soon the honking would start and the quiet presently permeating the air would shatter like a rock through a glass window.

The emergency dispatcher picked up the line just as the first impatient honk rang out. Soon it would be its own awful melody, which I could not drown out with the volume of my music. "Minefield Emergency," a female voice intoned through the connection.

"I'm on Main by The Corner Bean and a man has been struck— launched really, by a car. He's alive but unconscious and with severe injuries to an unknown extent." I tried to remember what types of things should be relayed in emergency situations in order to achieve the best result, but it was hard while also trying to contain my shock. My father always spoke concisely, giving highlights and leaving out anything unnecessary. I think I said my piece fairly well and was told that paramedics had been dispatched and should be at our location soon. I was still wound up, and hearing that help would be here "soon," was not overly comforting.

I sat back on my heels and tossed my phone into the bag to be lost amongst the paper scraps and discarded remains of long-ago eaten snacks once again when the commander's com caught my eye. Pulling it out, I ran my thumb across the shield and waited as the tone rang out. Immediately, Commander James's deep timbre came across, "Natha-"

"There's been a major traffic accident out front of The Corner Bean, a man has been struck by a car…" I exhaled a shaky breath. "It's bad."

"I'll get the closest units to your location to clear the area and speak to witnesses. Has emergency been dispatched?"

"Yes, though I'm not sure how long they'll be." With the words barely out of my mouth, I heard a sound of pure masculine anguish reverberate through my skull. Having so many people around normally made it difficult to discern what came from whom.

This situation however, was so far from normal that I knew the sound would only be made by the man seemingly coming back into consciousness; and with that state of awareness, the accompanying physical agony his body was in.

"He's becoming mentally aware, Commander, and he is in extreme pain." I worried my bottom lip with my teeth as I ended the call and reached out to put a hand on the still seemingly unconscious man's shoulder, hoping to relay that he was being looked after, that he wasn't alone. "Don't try to move." I tried to make myself sound as soothing as possible, but I wasn't sure anything would breach his veil of agony. I slumped, closing my eyes and exhaling a breath I didn't realize I had been holding, my fortitude crumbling as I heard the telltale wail of a siren growing steadily nearer.

A hand found its way to my shoulder and squeezed gently, snapping me out of my respite. I opened my eyes and peered over my shoulder, which was difficult while kneeling on the street if I wanted to keep contact with the man.

The eyes mine found as I turned were once again blazing silver, making me wonder just what triggered the change. Holden's features were

121

no less striking in their stony state. I soaked up the sight of him. His unruly dark hair was more mussed than usual, leaving me to wonder if he ran here from the barn, a crease of unease sat between his brows. Jaw set and lips thinned, Holden crouched at my side. His solid frame looking no smaller for it being closer to the ground.

How are you holding up?

I looked toward the brutalized man sprawled in front of me. The good news was that the blood halo didn't seem to be increasing any longer, though I think that was about the best I could say about his appearance.

The sirens had been getting louder and now sounded as though they were surrounding me. *Finally, real help's here.* Two uniformed medics pushed their way through the still gaping throng to where I knelt by the victim's still form and proceeded to assess the situation.

I took that as permission to finally ease away from my charge and rocked back onto my heels and pushed to my feet. Holden's hand once again found my shoulder, though this time he pulled me backward into his embrace.

Nathalee, he softly probed. One hand swept hair away from my face and the other wrapped around my waist to keep me close. I was lost in the feel of Holden at my back, surrounding me, making me feel safe and more comfortable than I should be considering the degree of injury and blood I had been inches from only moments before.

I closed my eyes once again, this time soaking up as much of the calm that Holden enveloped me in as I was able. Nothing else penetrated my bubble. There was no injured man broken and bleeding mere feet from us, no throng of gossipy onlookers to burst this blissful bubble I currently stood inside. No visual replay of the inevitable disaster playing in an infinite loop in my mind. Just the feel of being utterly surrounded by the male I could not stop thinking about, and I wanted to relish it.

I squeezed my eyes shut as I felt his hands come to my shoulders and slowly spin me so my face nearly brushed his broad chest. He smelled so good. Earthy, with a little spice. The slight tang of sweat clung to his clothes, adding to all that was Holden. I didn't want to open to everything else just yet. I liked my fabricated bubble, even if it was imaginary. Leaning into the hand that appeared against my cheek and tipping my head back, I finally opened my eyes.

Intense blue eyes with a mercury ring blazed back at me, burning with a fire I had never seen in him, never seen in anyone. *I wish our circumstances at the moment were more... favorable for me to explore what we have going on here, Nat.*

The intensity ramped up even more as he thought about said *exploring*, and I felt heat crawl up my neck toward my ears. Again. This man had a talent for making me blush. I didn't want to think about his *talents* at the moment. I allowed a small smile to touch my eyes as I reached my fingertips to caress the line of his chiseled jawline, before stepping purposefully out of his embrace in order to gain my bearings and let the rest of the world rush into my awareness.

The paramedics had succeeded in administering pain medication to the injured male as well as getting him secured for transport and were now wheeling him quickly toward the emergency vehicle. *How long was I in my Holden bubble?*

With the departure of the emergency services, the scene blinked back to normal. All returned to "business as usual," with no residual indication of what tragic events had just taken place. The crowd dispersing and traffic plowing forward once the ambulance sped away. The phrase "out of sight, out of mind" never more apparent than at that moment.

Holden's light touch once again brought my attention to him. *C'mon, I'll walk you home.* His hand traveled from my upper arm down to my hand, which he took in his much larger one as he began to move away. I was stuck in my own thoughts, replaying the sight of the downed man's expression and subsequent sprint into the road. What had caused that reaction in him? Why would he sprint into peak traffic without heed? What was he thinking?

I don't know, Holden said solemnly. I jerked my head toward him at his reply. He continued, *You spoke out loud,* answering the question undoubtedly written on my face. Shrugging slightly, Holden continued resolutely on his path. I pulled him to a stop with leaden feet as I spotted the barn over his shoulder, then tugged him toward it.

We were going the opposite way of my house, but this was better. I wanted a moment of my normal peace after the disaster I just witnessed. I wanted the calm Jasper exuded. Hell, I'd even welcome the smell of excrement, as it was normal, expected even, when visiting this place.

I kept Holden's hand firmly clasped in mine as I dragged him down the aisle, kicking up dirt in our wake. I didn't stop until we stood in front of Jasper's stall. He was there, as he should be, and made a noise of greeting.

I reached up and ran my hand down his face, bringing it around to grasp under his wooly jaw as I leaned into him and inhaled. Closing my eyes, I breathed deeply, letting Jasper's musky scent and the stale, dust-saturated air fill my nose. As the atmosphere of the barn and its occupants filtered entirely through my body, I realized I was acting just as high as I accused Jade of being once coffee hit her veins. Looks like we both had our addictions, but in my currently relaxed state, I could function again; *think* again.

Awareness trickled back and I listened in on Holden as he watched me with Jasper. "I was on my way to you," I told him while still conforming myself to the horse's head.

To me?

"Yeah. Here, I was headed here."

Oh, here. *To the horses.* He seemed to deflate a little as he thought this. Disappointment colored his thoughts, though he tried to seem unaffected. Once again, I was struck by how vulnerable this powerful man seemed in terms of self. How he both loved and loathed that he was overlooked so often.

I didn't like that he thought himself invisible, unseen. "I look forward to coming here." I said, taking a step toward him, relinquishing my hold on Jasper's head but giving him a pat as I stepped away. Another deliberate step and I was toe-to-toe with Holden, looking up into his gorgeous cerulean eyes, close enough to feel heat waft from his muscular body.

I was lost to him and shamelessly listening to his thoughts as he warily eyed me. He was trying to figure out my intent so I reckoned I'd clue him in, because I'm nice like that. Keeping my eyes locked on his, I lifted my hands to cradle his face, relishing the feel of the stubble against my palms. The rough feel of the short hairs against my soft flesh had me licking my lips in anticipation. Holden's eyes dropped to focus on my mouth, his pupils burgeoning.

Please.

At his whispered plea, I assailed. That's the only way to describe how I came at him. I yanked his head toward me and pushed onto my toes, having to bridge the gap to a much larger body. The only thought going through my head was *more.* I needed *more* of Holden.

Parting my lips, I ran my tongue across the seam of his, seeking permission to enter. With a mental growl, Holden opened his mouth and thrust his tongue toward mine, his arms wrapping around my body from shoulders to hips. I shifted my hands to his back and pulled him closer as I bit his lower lip then sucked the sting away, only to wrap my lips around his once again. His mental elation spurring me on.

I basked in the knowledge of how I affected him.

Suddenly my arm and face were covered in wet debris. The spell broken, I pulled away and looked up at Holden. His eyes were still blazing, pupils blown. The color was a lighter blue than normal, almost a turquoise like the beaches of far off tropical islands. At least that's what they resembled from the pictures I'd seen. I'd never been away from Minefield so I had no firsthand knowledge.

No one, aside from the first generation of Enhanced and those who periodically worked for the NEs outside our confines had ever been outside our walls, though not even many of those had seen the tropics.

I was hit with more mucus as Jasper once again voiced his apparent displeasure at the situation by blowing his nose directly onto us. Holden was the first to recover as a mental chuckle sounded.

Jasper's impatience rears its head again, shaking his head Holden wiped his face with his forearm, then stepped past me to rub Jasper's neck affectionately. *Good looking out, buddy,* he looked over Jasper's head to where I stood, still attempting to compose, and rid myself of Jasper's thoughtful additions.

This is not the place, or the time to get carried away. Blowing out a frustrated breath he added, *Unfortunately.*

CHAPTER 12

THE INTERLUDE WITH HOLDEN, and the subsequent wet interruption, broke me from my introspection about the accident. As we began our walk toward my home, I was no longer dwelling on the visual of the man sprinting into oncoming traffic, but I couldn't let the incident go either. The whole scenario bothered me.

"Holden?" I looked at him while still attempting to keep an eye on where I was going to avoid pesky obstacles such as lamp posts and glaring cracks in the sidewalk, which would swallow me whole given the chance, or just give my face an introduction to its surface. "Why would a man sprint into a busy roadway?"

I watched Holden's face as I finished my inquiry. His brows drew together and he pursed his lips in the hottest contemplative look I'd yet seen. *Knock it off, Dae!* I shook my head slightly, hoping to dispel the image from my traitorous mind.

He has to be Primal. The fact that, though his injuries were severe, he was not killed when his head impacted is pretty conclusive. He delivered his thoughts while maintaining the look. I quickly glanced away from the temptation he wrought. Maybe if I didn't look at him, I wouldn't embarrass myself. *Yeah, good luck with that, Nat.*

"I can't figure what would have made him forget, no, *disregard* his surroundings," I mused.

We are not "thinkers" like Sage. We are instinctive; reactive. Something raised his instincts.

"But instinct for what?"

Protect or kill.

He said it so matter of fact. *Protect or kill.* Both could mean death, and almost did today. "Oh my–" I stopped dead in my tracks as the metaphorical lightbulb illuminated over my head. I happened to be in the middle of crossing the street, so Holden wrapped his hand around my upper arm and pulled me into motion, stopping just as we ascended the opposite sidewalk, then stooping to try to read my face.

"There was nothing there," I said in a distracted voice, the wheels in full motion within my head now. I looked back at Holden as he attempted to puzzle me out.

What did you figure out? he questioned. He knew I had made some sort of connection but couldn't come up with my conclusion. I mean, it had never happened before. At least not that we knew.

"There was nothing there. No reason for the man to flip his switch." I stared at nothing, seeing only the replay of the accident. Only this time, I watched objectively. Looked for signs of what I believed. As I replayed the scene again slowly in my mind, I confirmed my belief that there was in fact, nothing that should be a motivator for Primal "protect or kill" instincts. At least, not outwardly.

"I think our manipulator was at it again." The more I replayed the events, the more certain I was. "If it wasn't him, it was someone doing something similar." The more I talked, the more I thought about it, the more excited I became. I was bouncing on my toes and leaning into him by the end. Holden wasn't so sure.

"Think about it, Holden." I raised my eyebrows at him in what I hoped was a meaningful way. "*Why?* Why would those instincts have been triggered on a busy roadway, when *no one* saw anything unusual?" I was almost pleading with him to understand. To tell me I wasn't crazy and making connections where none existed.

The man running headlong into traffic wouldn't be something the surrounding people would have considered unusual? Holden clicked his tongue and lifted his own eyebrows high. I rolled my eyes at his sarcasm.

"Of course, *that* was unusual," I glared at him. The turd, he was laughing at my frustration, that was his goal—to goad me. He smiled, that rare, blinding smile that I loved, and my frustration melted away. I grabbed his arm, which my hand didn't come close to encircling, and spun him so we could continue our walk. I really needed to get home.

"I was there Holden. He and his buddies were all huddled up the street from me and laughing about something they obviously found to be hilarious, as they were *roaring* their mirth." Shaking my head, I recalled just how loud they had been. "Then the man's head snapped toward the street." I paused to take a deep breath, the streets and their occupants not even registering in my state. "The next moment he was running for the street with complete focus." I thought back to that moment, trying to analyze it, see it objectively and realized something new. "There was fear on his face."

Fear?

"Yeah." I nodded. "Fear. He was afraid. Afraid of *something*." I wracked my brain trying to figure it out, but knowing I never would, not without the victim. He was the only one who could tell us what ran through his mind. Well, him and the person who triggered the event.

I was now more determined to weed out this malignant blight on our town. I had seen what he wrought, had seen with my own eyes the effect he had. He needed to be stopped, as he obviously had every intention of continuing his manipulations.

The rest of our walk was spent in silent contemplation on both our behalves. Before I knew it, we had arrived at the walkway leading to my porch steps. Holden stopped and pried my hand from his biceps but didn't release my hand.

Instead he slowly brought the extremity to his lips, his eyes boring into mine. My breath caught as his soft lips pressed to my fingers. At the sound, Holden's clear blue gaze bled into that striking color closely resembling a tropical ocean, a brilliant blue-green as his attention seemed to focus even more intently. I could have stared at him all day, and my face must have shown it as Holden mentally growled. Growled! Apparently I liked that Primal show of approval because I melted a little.

You don't know what you do to me, Nat, he breathed. I stood transfixed as his eyes slowly returned to their vibrant blue hue.

"How—" I sputtered. I started again, though still at a loss as to his perpetual changing. "How do your eyes keep changing color?"

Uhhh…

"Don't do it," I warned. "Don't lie to me." I followed his internal struggle though nothing of it showed on his face. Outwardly, he was completely at ease. Right now, he reminded me too much of the Sage I avoided. Seeing that he was not going to tell me, I turned and headed up the flower lined walk toward the front door, which once again stood open to welcome the beautiful day. The beautiful day that had harbored a gruesome reminder that not everything, *not everyone*, was benign.

It's my ability.

I stopped. Hand out and reaching for the screen handle, I had been ready to leave Holden standing on the sidewalk without remorse. But now? *Now*, I was intrigued. I turned again, this time toward the intense Primal male blocking the walkway. "What do you mean?" I asked slowly. I wanted to go to him, but I was rooted to the ground again. This day had too many intense moments and my body was done, my mind not far behind.

The rest of me folded upon my legs, landing in a heap on the porch as I awaited his explanation. Slowly, oh so slowly, Holden prowled toward me. One agonizing step at a time as he watched me with hooded eyes, ascended the steps and stopped. Bringing his large frame to sit on the top step, his upper body turned toward me, his arms across his knees in a show of ease. Apparently, now that he had decided to share with me, he was not conflicted. He *wanted* me to know.

I'm what we call a chameleon.

I blinked. Then blinked again. He couldn't leave it at that. I had no idea what that meant. "What's a *chameleon*?" I asked skeptically. He better not tell me it was a lizard. I'd punch him, though he wouldn't feel it any more than a horse would a fly. My strength would have no real effect, so I wouldn't waste the effort.

I have the ability to alter my appearance. He watched me, searching my face for a reaction. His eyebrows drew together and his teeth caught at his lower lip. It was distracting under normal circumstances, but at the moment, I would not be deterred.

"Change your appearance *how*, exactly?"

Holden blew out a heavy breath which puffed out his cheeks. *I can change coloring or minute physical details.*

"Really? Can you show me?" That sounded really impressive and was yet another ability I thought I may have traded my telepathy for if it were possible. I found myself inching back toward him, waiting with bated breath for him to...*change.* I found myself mere inches from him, though standing as I was on the top step and he sitting, I lorded over him until he unfolded himself and came to a stand just in front of me.

I couldn't tear my focus from him. His beautiful blue eyes, his full mouth. The strong jaw. As I was mentally cataloging his facial features, they began to morph.

I stood agape as I watched his bright blue eyes bleed to a gem-like green. The full mouth I had been kissing not long before thinned and stretched farther across his face, his cheekbones became sharper. I cocked my head like a curious dog, taking in all the changes of his appearance, then sucked in a sharp breath as I watched his dark hair shorten slightly and gradually change to a strawberry blonde. When freckles began appearing across his cheeks and nose, I couldn't hold back any longer.

Slowly bringing my hand up to his face, I brushed along the planes. This new Holden was no illusion, he was flesh, and he was different. So very different. The man now standing in front of me looked like a movie star I'd seen before, not the Primal male I knew. He closed his eyes and exuded contentment as I explored the changes. "Wow," I murmured, still tracing. As I brought my thumb across his lower lip, he opened his mouth and tucked his lip inward, bringing my finger as well. Then he closed his mouth with the tip of my thumb inside.

I gasped. Eyes the color of the purest emerald were overtaken by onyx as Holden's pupils eclipsed the irises. He took a step up the porch, my finger pulling from his mouth. Suddenly I was looking up into those blown out, intense black eyes and hearing a growl emanate mentally from Holden. My breathing became heavier as I stared. Watching as the Holden I knew came back to the surface, the imposter receding slowly.

Nathalee, he murmured mentally, as he brought a hand to my face, engulfing the entire left side from temple to jaw. *Do you know what it does to me when you look at me like that?* His Primal nature was coming out to play. My reaction to him seemed almost like a drug, like he could live off of it, and wanted to. His mental voice was no more than a whispered suggestion, his muscles were coiled so tightly from the restraint of his touch, he looked like he was made of marble.

I still couldn't tear away. Not my eyes from his, or my face from his hand. I was cemented in place, like I too, was a statue. Staring, just...staring.

The creak and slap of the screen door opening and closing finally broke the spell we were bound by and I turned to find my mother drying her hands with a red dish towel while eyeing us carefully.

Not a hair out of place in her meticulous bun and a freshly laundered outfit giving the impression of togetherness, though I knew it hid the wandering mind underneath. She was never focused on just one thing, unless that one thing was a gadget she was working on, everything else would get bumped to the side in her brain space when a question or answer relevant to her work popped up.

I knew that look. It was calculating. My mother's genius mind was whirling. Her mental thoughts were bursting with curiosity as to the man who *so obviously entrances* her daughter. She was leery as most Sages were of Primals and was waffling about asking Holden in for dinner. Wow, I must have really been *entranced* by Holden's display to not have heard her until now.

Holden, now back to his own physicality, gave her an embarrassed smile and timid wave of his hand. Funny how a little five foot, two inch pixie could make a strapping young Primal male blush to the tips of his ears and mumble internally about getting caught by a girl's mom. I gave a little snort of laughter and quickly clapped a hand over my mouth to halt the offending noise. *My turn for embarrassment!*

Seeing the sheepish expression Holden displayed must have been the tipping point for my mother, because just then her decision solidified. "Holden, is it?" At his nod, she continued with the coolness Sages were known for. "Would you care to join us for dinner?" With how the words were delivered, you would have thought she didn't care whether he chose to join us, but I could hear the truth behind the facade.

If Holden didn't accept, he would never have an ally in my mother. Glancing my way, she caught my raised eyebrow and promptly shut down her thoughts while her shoulders stiffened and she narrowed her eyes at me. This was why she and I would never be close. Most Sage believed their minds were sacred and above reproach, so my being able to see below the surface rankled, especially with there not being an "off" switch, or rather an "on" switch.

It seemed Sage were only at ease around telepaths who were more limited in their abilities. Those limited by touch were the most easily accepted; it was easy to avoid contact. My mother was not the exception. Still, Alana Dae gave indifference the *ol' college try*.

"Nathalee, Jade wanted me to tell you that her parents have calmed slightly and she went home for the time being." I nodded. It made sense that the Danforth's would want as much time with Jade under their roof while it was still her home. I hoped they were able to enjoy the remaining time.

Holden looked at my mother, and appropriately reading the situation, gave a brief nod of acceptance. With a stiff return nod and a mild bump in her regard, my mother opened the screen door and ushered us both into the house.

"I'm almost done with dinner if you want to take a seat." She wiped her hands on the red towel again and headed toward the kitchen, which emitted the heavenly smells of pot roast and potatoes. As my mother's internal dialogue began cataloging what she needed and how to arrange the table, I was set to follow when I realized that I was in need of a shower to cleanse myself of the earlier events. I wasn't sure if I should bring it up to my mother, or what. Did she need to know? Would she care? I mean, he was *just a* Primal. As it stood, I didn't have time for the works, so a change and wipe down would have to do.

"I gotta change," I gestured down at myself in explanation. "Make yourself comfortable, I'll only be a moment." I threw over my shoulder as I hurried down the hall to my room. I rummaged through my dresser until

I found a nice but comfy set of clothes—a gray V-neck tee and stretchy pants—and quickly shucked the clothes I had on in favor of what I'd found.

As I pulled the shirt down my torso, I shuffled across to the bathroom to wipe myself down with a rag and splash my face. I wasn't wearing much makeup and my mascara was waterproof, or so it claimed. I guess we'd find out for sure. I made quick work of cleaning and double checked the mirror before I headed out. Not great, but it could be worse, I guess.

Color was returning to my cheeks and my hair was somewhat orderly after I smoothed water over it, but I looked tired. My blue-green eyes were greener at the moment and a bit red from the stress of the afternoon. *At least the mascara didn't run.*

As I came back into the sitting area, Holden was still standing, his hands clasped behind his back as he wandered the room, taking everything in. He was currently stopped at the fireplace examining a picture on the mantle. This one had my father and me at the gardens laughing, his arm around my shoulder, mine around his waist. I remembered this day.

Dad and I, and even Mom, trucked out to the gardens for a picnic under the trees on the beltway between activity areas. Dad brought a Frisbee and we tried trick throws for an hour, finally ceding defeat and collapsing in laughter and hunger. Mom hadn't participated in the shenanigans but it hadn't surprised me. It was a good day, and just a few months ago. I sighed at the remembered fun. Those days would most likely be few and far between now. Especially with me moving out.

The sigh seemed to alert Holden to my return. Once again, I told Holden to make himself comfortable and gestured toward the sitting area before turning to join my mother in the kitchen. I took two steps before I realized Holden was directly behind me.

I want to help your mother, he said, correctly deciphering the question I was just about to ask. I felt my face soften from the quizzical look it had held the moment before as my mouth tipped into a half smile. I nodded my understanding and continued on my way. As we entered the kitchen area, I announced our intentions to my mother. She wasted no time giving us each bowls and directing us toward the dining table.

I noticed Holden taking in everything around him. It hadn't changed much in my memory, but I found myself wondering what he thought of the room, of the house with its gray-blue walls and how it compared to his.

I knew all the people on my street. I had grown up here, much like my parents had since my father took his job with the hospital. This was his provided housing, but he'd had a lot of work done by grateful Primals. People who didn't have a lot but wanted to do something for a man they respected. Connor Dae had earned the respect of the whole community for the work he did, and those he helped.

The clinking of silverware derailed my now sightless stare out the bay window. Refocusing my eyes on the room in front of me, I shook my head slightly to dispel the fog. I quickly laid the plates between the silverware which had been placed neatly at either side of each seating area. The brightly colored place mats featuring random geometric outlines, all fighting for space, screamed *Alana Dae*. I quirked a small smile thinking how my mother embodied the stereotypes.

The rest of the setup was quick and efficient, just as Mom liked. Holden's thoughts were simply to be helpful to her while Mom's were trying to figure him out. Her curiosity was obviously piqued, which meant this could be an interesting meal. I'd have to stay on top of the conversation to make sure my mother didn't ask questions inappropriate for someone she had just met. With the thoughts swirling around that big brain of hers when she looked toward Holden, I knew I'd have to dictate the conversational tone this dinner set. *So much for an easy evening.*

Once we were all settled at the table, the meal nestled invitingly in the center, we paused for a quick prayer of thanks, which seemed to surprise Holden. At my pinched brows, Holden filled me in, admitting that he hadn't been sure logical thinkers, which my mother *clearly* was, believed in a higher being.

I tried, and failed, to hide the wry smile that spread across my face. This would be an interesting evening. I decided to steer the conversation, circling back to today's ordeal. Shame lit my cheeks as I realized I hadn't worried about the man since Holden had opened up about his Primal ability. I cleared my throat quietly and prepared to tell my mother what I had witnessed, all the while wondering what her reaction would be.

It occurred to me that though this day had marked something new for me, the old still lingered. I still had one more day of work. One more day until I was thrown into the new life I had decided on.

As I opened my mouth to let the events of the afternoon fly, there was a multi-beep tone which emitted from Holden's direction. I snapped my mouth shut and watched as he twisted his wrist to look at a large square affixed to his wrist, much like a watch would be. I was completely absorbed in the curious thoughts ballooning in my head. *How does a man who cannot speak, communicate when not seen?*

Holden tapped the face of the device and swallowed what he had eaten and lifted his napkin to wipe his mouth. He lifted the device for us to see and shot a questioning look toward my mother, effectively asking my mother if he could accept. She nodded and watched with as much fascination as I when Holden scooted away from the table and accepted the link.

The commander's booming voice rang out in greeting for his nephew as he moved back toward the living room. I cocked my head in interest as I heard a responding click from Holden, much like a sound he used to tell Raven to speed up. *Interesting.*

My mother and I wore matching expressions of fascination as we realized Holden was clicking his tongue from behind his teeth in order to reply to Commander James's inquiry. Once again, my mother's mind went into overdrive, now thinking up devices which could aid Holden in speech.

Her thoughts were soon shoved to the rear of mine, as Holden began walking back in our direction and I caught what the call was about. Reality of the day's events came crashing back. The Primal male who had been violently struck by a car earlier in the day, the man I had *seen nearly killed*, was in surgery.

Commander James would like for us to meet him at the hospital soon, to see if we can determine the cause of his untimely sprint.

I nodded. "Mom, is Dad at the hospital tonight? He's working ER, right?" At my questions my mother's brow bunched but she answered in the affirmative.

"What happened?"

So I told her. Recounting the *incident*—I firmly believed it could not be called an accident—and how I watched as the man was struck with enough force that most would have died, she brought her hand to her mouth to cover her gasp. Her eyes were wide and her mind was turning, analyzing.

"No one helped, Mom," I said quietly, remembering with fresh horror how the gawkers just...watched. "I need to get to the hospital." My mother was still lost in her own musings, so I gently shook her by the shoulder hoping to regain her focus for just another moment. When her eyes slowly slid to mine, I asked to borrow the car.

The car was a luxury not all had. Seeing as it was something we needed to get from the ninnies, there were strings attached, as well as a hefty price tag. Dad got one as part of his stipend for ER work. So he could get to the hospital quickly if an emergency arose, though he rode a bike when working normal shift.

My mind, once again wandered, wondering if enforcement was a position which would garner a vehicle. The press of jagged metal into my palm forced me from my musings. I gave my mother a brief hug and headed across the kitchen to the door leading into the garage.

CHAPTER 13

THE TRIP TO THE hospital was uneventful, for which I was thankful. I didn't need any more *events* today. Holden was tense and his thoughts were determinedly focused on searching out this *perp*—a new nifty enforcer word for me—and stopping him from harming more people.

I pulled into an assigned parking space for *Physicians Only*. The hospital, and the ER, in particular, were spaces where not only a large number of people gathered, but people who would have loud and intense mental voices. A place where I had a very hard time shutting people out. Luckily, I remembered to bring my earbuds.

As we emerged from the car, I warned Holden I would be putting them in to drown out the anguish. He nodded in acknowledgement, and with a hand at the small of my back, allowed me to lead the way.

The last rays of sunlight were fading over the horizon, leaving the cloudless sky a blazing orange, reminding me of the day I met Holden, officially anyway. My cheeks flamed with color at the remembered interaction, at his reaction to learning I could hear him.

The warmth of his hand at my back was like a pulse, pulling me to the current moment. Back to the hospital and its fluorescent illuminations spilling into the burgeoning evening. I took a moment to fill my lungs with the last of the crisp, cool air. The air in the hospital would be rife with malady and disinfectant, stifling with its intensity and made all the worse by the heat of many bodies in tight spaces under hot lights. *So breathe deeply while you can, Nat.*

I positioned my earbuds in the appropriate ear and tried to get lost in the beat, the lyrics. This song had a great recurring drum beat though the lyrics were slightly melancholy. Maybe I'd pick a peppier one...

"Ready?"

Holden gave a nod and a small quirked smile graced his lips. *Nat, I've been here before.* I started my music, the familiar beats allowing my muscles to relax. Just that one act, turning on a melody, no matter what tempo or range, allowed me to get lost. Lost in the intent, in the words, which were so carefully thought out. I relaxed further.

The hand at my back once again urged me forward, and after a few strides we breached the doorway, the insistent tone of electric classical buoying my resolve. It was just as cloying as I knew it would be, but the music had its desired effect, both mentally and physically.

Holden was on a mission as he headed directly for intake. We stopped at the glass partition and the small woman behind it. No, not woman, girl. I hadn't seen her before, which meant she was fairly new, though it *had* been months since I'd been here. *Hadn't realized that until just now...*she had thick, unruly chestnut hair which framed a round face with thin lips and round brown eyes, made all the more comically large by the bottle glass thick eyewear she was sporting.

Hoo hoo, Holden chimed as I removed one earbud.

I spluttered a laugh before I could stifle it, and pressed my lips firmly together, raising an eyebrow at Holden as I tried not to let another escape. That gorgeous quirk of lips once again graced his face as his eyes danced with mirth. Apparently I wasn't the only one to draw an owl comparison.

C'mon, darlin', tell the nice girl why we're here. Holden's deep timbre rumbled in my head. I had never seen him playful. It was *so* not the time, but I *loved* it. I would add it to my list of things to bring out in him more often.

"Hi, we received a call from Commander James that a car crash victim was in surgery and to meet with him. Could you point us in the right direction?" I tried my best to be perky and charming, ending the inquiry with a smile and lift of eyebrows. The girl, whose name tag read *Jessica*, continued looking at her computer screen as if we weren't there, scrunching her brow and puckering her thin lips as though working out a tough problem. Her mind was whirling, looking for a name. It was like a litany, and I was going to disrupt it.

I thumped on the glass between us with an open hand. "Excuse me," I began politely. The sound finally broke through her haze, causing her to jump slightly. She settled, then one at a time: straightened her back, straightened her glasses, and straightened her scrub top. Only when finished did she finally look at us.

"Can I help you?" Her eyes widened even more as they roved Holden, though looking at her you couldn't be sure if it was from astonishment or intrigue but I could hear her secret appreciation of him, though she automatically thought him beneath her because it was *obvious* he wasn't Sage. I really hated this divide we'd allowed in our homes but I didn't have time to worry about it at the moment.

"Yes, hi." I cleared my throat as I tried to get back on task. "We were contacted by Commander James about a car crash victim who came in earlier. We were informed that he was in surgery, could you point us either in the direction of the commander or the patient?"

With a small huff, she pushed the glasses, which had once again slipped down, back up her nose, turned her attention to the computer and began typing. *Her glasses must be heavy, what with the whole bottle attached...*

I shook myself slightly to waylay the errant and unkind thought, only to realize she was once again on the task we interrupted, instead of the one I asked for as she mumbled internally about not wanting to have to help Primals. So she knew who my victim was, and was stalling. *Nuh uh.*

I knocked on the partition again, fist closed this time. A falsely polite knock, which did not reveal the threat my words carried. "Oh, Jessica," I singsonged. "Before you decide to blow me off, know that my name is Nathalee Dae." The typing stopped. "Dae, as in *Doctor Connor Dae.*" Pause for dramatic effect, "You might just jeopardize your recruitment..." I let the words hang.

She looked up at me then, wide eyed and once again comically resembling an owl as her mouth formed an O. "So again...car crash victim? The *Primal.*" I emphasized the word just to drive it home. She was in this position to help people, *all people*, not just those she wanted.

Blink. "Um, yeah, let me check for a room number," another push of glasses and a scrunch of brows, "Yeah, his name is Rolph Duggan. He's slated for room three fourteen. Take the elevator—"

"I know my way around the hospital, thank you, Jessica." I waved a hand dismissively in her direction, turning away from the window and heading across the waiting room toward the bank of commercial elevators gleaming like industrial refrigerators under the harsh fluorescent lighting. The squeaking of shoes across the gleaming linoleum flooring with every step, letting me know Holden moved with me. *Geez, being here is a constant assault on the senses,* I couldn't understand how Primals handled it.

There were Primals who worked as orderlies or security to help with the physical aspect of medical care that many Sages couldn't handle. Either their senses weren't heightened—unlikely—or they simply ignored or learned to tune it out. A trick I would most like to work on concerning my telepathy.

Holden bumped my shoulder as we waited for the elevator, a mischievous grin on his face when I looked at him.

That was awesome. It's really hot watching you get all authoritative. There was that playfulness again. Maybe I could be good for Holden. I grinned back at him. We must have looked like we were up to no good as we stood facing the silver doors and grinning like idiots at each other. The grin slowly slipped from Holden's face as his pupils overtook the beautiful blue of his eyes, his look nearly melting me with heat.

The arriving elevator broke the spell we once again found ourselves cocooned in, the doors opened with a cheerful *ding,* allowing us entry to the sterile interior. The ride to the third floor was short but seemed longer as I purposely avoided meeting Holden's gaze. We were here to get information, to help give a man justice for a wrong committed, if I was in fact right in my assessment of the situation.

But that's what we were here to do, *not* get lost in each other's eyes like lovestruck teens. I was not lovestruck. *Keep telling yourself that, Nat.* I tried to focus more on the music still pouring into one ear to distract myself. Words about young love filtered through my consciousness along with the light sounds of a piano's melody… *so not helping.*

My stomach rose and then dropped as the elevator made its arrival on the third floor with another *ding.* We stepped out into the recovery reception area. This was the green floor. All the walls were decorated with a thick green stripe at the top where the walls met the ceiling. Color coding was a quick and efficient way to tell where you were in the hospital. It was often a madhouse, and with so much going on constantly, attendants often ended up in the wrong places.

I'd arrived at the green floor fairly often in my forays to visit my father. It was a quieter and more sedate floor than emergency. *Obviously.* I rolled my eyes at myself. I was just full of insightful thoughts all of a sudden. I made my way toward the nurse behind the circular desk area in the middle of the room, with a true smile across my face as my eyes found the attending nurse.

"May!"

Looking up sharply at the sound of her name, May's face mirrored the genuine happiness mine held. The nurse was dressed in bright pink scrubs, a designation of this floor, and bright white sneakers which squeaked more than my own as we hurried toward one another. Soon I was enveloped in the arms of a tiny whirlwind of enthusiasm.

May was one of the few people I had met in the hospital or otherwise who genuinely didn't care who you were. She was going to make you feel better. I loved her. She embodied Sages in stature, being just over five feet tall with few curves to her name. Wild brown curls were contained with the rubber band which really only succeeded in keeping her face clear of the mass. Her hazel eyes sharp and bright, often with a bit of a so called *twinkle*, her lips were thin but bowed perfectly. She was gorgeous; inside and out. Never mind that she had a limp. Her personality made sure you never noticed the defect.

The older woman pulled back and held me at arm's length to look me over head to toe. The mental catalog reminded me of last week when Holden did the same. I heard Holden chuff internally, which translated to a puff of exhalation verbally. Blushing, I pulled back.

"May, this is Holden." I motioned to the curious male at my back. May looked around me toward Holden, scanning him in much the same way she had me, except this one was clinical; assessing, and not familiar.

"You looking out for my girl here, boy?" Wow, she's got more bite about her than my own mother.

Holden held her gaze and dipped his chin in acknowledgement, as I tried to wave off the insinuation.

"We're working together, I accepted a recruitment." I looked over my shoulder and shot my eyes toward Holden's. Their blue seemed brighter. His answer was a low mental growl which I waved aside, then hedged. "We're feeling things out." I lifted my eyebrows in question, was that good enough for him?

Nodding slowly once, he acquiesced.

When I turned to face May again, she was staring toward the hallway leading to the rooms. A pretty blush rose to accompany her stare as I followed her attention to...Commander James. *Interesting.* It seemed May liked looking at the good commander if nothing else.

He was walking briskly toward our little group, his heavy boots clomping purposefully. His eyes were flitting between the group, before resting on May as he reached our huddle in the middle of the room. His thoughts mirrored May's in appreciation. *Very interesting.* Holden snickered, bringing me out of my meddling.

Other mental voices buzzed in the background but were drowned out by those standing with me. I quickly retrieved the earbud I removed in the lobby, stuffing it harshly into the ear currently void of melodic distraction.

I released a heavy breath as the punchy beat overtook my attention. *Safe and sound, just like the song says.* There was a brief discussion between those surrounding me which I was able to completely ignore, lost as I was to the music. The commander turned on his heel and waved us forward, down the hall and into Room 314, where Rolph currently lay in a medical bed, nearly unconscious.

I didn't enter patient rooms when I visited, only stayed in public areas. Usually the nurse's station, which was one reason I knew May, and spoke to my father when he had time. The room was as you would expect for the most part. Sterile, white monochromatic color scheme throughout. A large window encompassing the far wall, with slatted vertical blinds that would cast dancing shadows across the walls in daylight. This room, however, was also covered in various bouquets of bright color as cheery flowers enveloped most available surfaces.

Rolph was loved. From the number of little bouquets, I would guess by many. I felt my eyes sting at the thought that someone had tried to end a man who held the hearts of so many. I jumped at the tap to my shoulder, lost as I was in my own thoughts. I removed an earbud and turned my attention to the *tapper*– Commander James.

"Rolph," Commander James inquired gently, stepping to the side of the infirmary bed.

I took a deep breath and forced myself to look at the figure on the bed. The man lying atop its surface, took up most available space, though much of his right side was encased in thick white casting, adding to the bulk of the already large male. His midsection, right hip and upper leg were all cast heavily with no option for mobility.

Moving my perusal upward, his right arm was encased in a blue fabric sling, the material extending over his elbow, a strap crossing his chest and around his back, holding the appendage at a forced right angle. He reminded me of the jerk boss in one of the superhero animated movies I remember watching when I was younger; nearly covered head to toe in bandaging and unable to move.

Finally, I allowed myself to look at his face. His neck was in a brace, most likely a nasty case of whiplash incurred as he hit the pavement. Dark brown eyes rimmed with purple bruising followed my appraisal making heat rise up my neck. Mr. Duggan's head was wrapped heavily with gauze, making me remember the spreading pool of blood beneath him.

It wasn't until I heard a woman's distracted voice that I realized the door had opened to admit another into our little party. I jerked my head to the entry as a list was absentmindedly created by the interloper—*Deena and Davis are with my parents, the bed is set up, neighbors are already bringing food...* She sighed heavily, a weary sound. Her words and movement stalled as she stepped further into the room, noticing the now crowded space.

The woman was tall—close to six feet—with broader shoulders than I'd ever noticed on a female. She was trim and muscled, giving her the overall appearance of swimmers I had once seen perform on TV. When her gaze landed on Commander James, they lost their suspicious glint. Instead, lighting with a fire her thoughts mirrored.

"Travis, Rolph would not have just run into traffic!" A deep breath. "*What happened?*" Her mind took up the chant as she moved to the bed, grasping Rolph's left hand—one of the few areas not encased in white plaster—and began rubbing her thumb across the back side as she slowly lowered herself into a chair which sat in sentry next to the bed. I turned toward Holden when her thoughts were broken by anguish.

"Sheena," Commander James began tentatively. His voice also held despair, something I had not previously associated with him. His thoughts revealed that this couple, this *family,* was close to our commander. I cut my eyes to Holden, wondering if he felt the same, and if he did, why had he not mentioned something earlier? He was with me when Rolph lay unconscious and bleeding on the cracked roadway.

Sensing my attention, Holden glanced my way. I raised my eyebrows in a silent *Why didn't you tell me you knew him?* accusation, to which he only lifted one shoulder and said, *You needed me more.* That obviously wasn't true. He'd been the one laying sprawled brokenly on the roadway. I opened my mouth to argue, but Holden had turned his attention toward the remaining occupants of the small room. Seriously, the room couldn't handle any more bodies.

As if God found it funny, at that moment, the door once again opened. This time admitting a mumbling man in green scrubs staring intently at the clipboard he held. The other hand grasped the knob on the still open door. The distracted surgeon was my father. *Perfect.*

CHAPTER 14

"MR. DUGGAN," MY FATHER began distractedly, still looking at the chart in his hands, "the surgery went well and we were able to repair the ilium and pubis of the lateral compression fracture you sustained from impact." After finishing with his reporting of the procedure my father finally looked up and took stock of his surroundings.

The room was becoming too loud with unspoken words, making my fingers twitch. I wanted to escape into my music—if I couldn't escape the hospital entirely—to eliminate the competing voices. It wasn't like a typical verbal conversation where everyone waited their turn to speak. Nope, we all thought over each other's words, and if I had no focus, it sounded like a cocktail party in my own head, though thankfully sometimes on a lower volume so I could drown it out with music.

Once again, my fingers twitched to put the earbud back in, making me feel like an old west gunslinger, itching to pull my weapon. I always felt like a creeper when I heard people struggle with private thoughts.

Thoughts which I had no business knowing. But then wasn't that exactly what I was to do for Commander James? Peek into people's minds to find answers to questions they otherwise may not answer? My brow furrowed with the effort of not grabbing for the magical little music delivery device. The unilateral audio flow I was currently experiencing was not near enough.

Just then, my father's attention landed on me. He knew the struggle. I may not be able to read him, but I *knew* him, and he knew me. He turned to Commander James with a slightly censorious look.

"Commander, do we need to do this now?"

"Don't you think we should get a start on this if we can?" Commander James returned with raised brows. He stood tall, almost rigid, with his feet planted in the stance I was coming to know was like a default hip width apart and flat on the floor. There was no impatient fidgeting from the dear commander, he was too disciplined for that.

"Do you truly think you will get any answers with his current state," my father countered.

"Five minutes."

My father slid his eyes to Mr. Duggan, contemplating, then to the woman who I assumed was Mrs. Duggan. They both returned his curiosity, but not about their mental state, about the situation which caused all of us to be standing here, around the sterile hospital room and talking about them. Both their thoughts were focused, though Rolph's were slightly slower than I assumed to be normal for him. Probably the combination of anesthesia and pain meds.

"They're up for it," I broke in. I flushed pink, heat suffusing my neck and cheeks, as all eyes in the room turned to me. I was now the bull's eye of five sets of peepers, and four mental inquiries—though I knew the number was truly five. I centered my attention on my father who still stood by the door. He nodded, knowing I would be privy to that information.

"All right, five minutes," he returned my stare, "and I'm staying."

My head whipped to the commander for confirmation, as did Holden's. I realized then that Holden had been fairly quiet in the mental cacophony that had been assaulting my senses, and I smiled privately at the thought that he was trying to be unobtrusive. For me.

The commander was standing near the foot of Rolph's bedside when he began. "Rolph, can you tell me what happened? Why did you rush into the street?"

Rolph blinked slowly and focused on the commander in hopes of better assimilating the questions being asked of him. The wheels in his mind began turning faster than he was able to relay verbally, though it was broken and stilted.

"Standing, talking with. Regulars. Past outside seating."

Seeing the difficulties he was having in speech, I jumped in. "He was standing near the edge of the outdoor seating, talking with a group of regulars." I looked directly into Mr. Duggan's eyes as his attention jerked to me. "Don't move your head like that Mr. Duggan," I admonished, "it's bound to hurt." Holden chuckled, the slight movement of his shoulders and chest the only outward signs.

The commander jumped in to explain just as Mr. Duggan tried to voice the question, his furrowed brow giving away his intent. "She's telepathic. She's working with me on a case," he cleared his throat before continuing with, "a case we think may involve you."

Rolph refocused on Commander James. Questions began pinging through the minds of both Mr. and Mrs. Duggan, rapid fire like. It had me rubbing my temple and closing my eyes. I tried focusing solely on Rolph to lessen my struggle.

"Please, don't get quite so worked up," I pleaded. "It really does project well." I gave a humorless twist of my lips that would not pass as a smile and powered on. "Even if you can't verbalize what you want to say, I should be able to get the general idea. I can then relay to the others."

Rolph watched me warily, trying to decide how much he disliked the idea of someone hearing his thoughts. *Get in line, mister.*

"Trust me, Mr. Duggan, I wish I could have had any other ability."

He eyed me skeptically but after a moment, opened his mouth to speak. Everyone within the cramped room ceased their internal chatter to hear.

"Thought," the word came out a near croak, as he battled to recover from anesthesia and trauma. He cleared his throat, readying for his next attempt. I didn't interrupt, though I could see the image flashing in his head. This one would be more difficult to suss out whether it was planted, due to the haze surrounding all his thoughts. So it appeared things could influence the clarity of what I read from people. *Makes sense.*

I needed to remember that and let the others know. I should still be able to tell if the "voice" was his or not, whether the thought was his own. Especially because I already knew what our illusionist "sounded" like.

"Saw my daughter."

"You saw Deena?" Mrs. Duggan said anxiously. She'd previously gripped his left hand and had been idly rubbing then stilled at his words. Wrapping her previously free hand around it a heartbeat later, she brought them to her face to lay her cheek upon the tangled mass. Her thoughts now racing with questions of how that could be, when she knew the child to be with her parents.

"She," *cough*, "she was in the street." His voice cracked with emotion this time.

That one statement got the inhabitants of the room buzzing. Though the reigning thought was simple: *How?* For the Duggans, it was: how could he have seen their daughter in the middle of that crowded street. For the rest of us—the *agents*—it was *how is he doing it?* As the Duggans spoke softly to one another, Holden moved to catch my attention.

We need to have a serious brainstorm about this guy. He turned and signed the same to his uncle who gave his response in the form of a curt nod, then caught my attention as well. Locking eyes, Holden communicated, *Tomorrow, after you finish work,* chuckle, *we will have a sit down to try to find some answers.* He narrowed his eyes a bit and said in a lower, more serious tone. *You'll officially be an agent in training. We need to get that started, ASAP.*

I nodded my assent and tuned back into the Duggans at about the same moment they came back from their own conversation. Mrs. Duggan seemed to have been reassuring her husband that their daughter was in fact not ever downtown, that she was safe.

Both their mental voices seemed more at ease, calmer than when the conversation started. Rolph also seemed more lucid, the effects of the sedatives wearing off, albeit slowly. A lively group of cut flowers caught my attention briefly. The mix of pinks, purple, and white—lovely really— were so cheery, I momentarily forgot they adorned the countertop of a sterile hospital recovery room.

I tried to focus some of my energy on the music flowing from my headphones, one of which still remained plugged in its corresponding ear. The vigorous violin grounding me while the bass pulsed through my body at a steady tempo.

Taking a deep, cleansing breath I once again focused on the now.

"I know, my friend. It may be hard to recall the events between the incident and now, but Rolph, this is important. I need you to remember exactly what you saw that flipped you." He stalled Rolph from speaking by raising his hand in a "wait a moment" gesture I was beginning to realize was almost like a trademark move for him and steamrolled ahead. "I know you saw Deena, but was anything off about her?"

"Yeah! The fact that she was supposedly standing in the middle of a downtown street," Mrs. Duggan said heatedly, clearly exasperated and not understanding why we would be asking these types of questions. She thought her husband had been hallucinating. *Probably a sound conclusion under normal circumstances,* but we all knew that Minefield was nothing near normal, which was what necessitated our involvement in the first place.

Mr. Duggan thought about what he had seen, so I got a peek. His daughter looked to be around six or seven but it could be hard to tell with Primals, they were just so large...*I digress.* Round brown eyes looked to be pleading, shining with yet unshed tears and staring directly at me —so directly at her father—as she stepped out into traffic.

Her light up tennis shoes were flashing, one poised to take another step when I heard Rolph yell to her and dart forward. The image was clearer now. It *did* contain the signature of our unknown subject. His clipped way of forcing an image made me think he was still honing his craft. Maybe that was why he was targeting Primals, less chance of them noticing little inconsistencies and stopping to wonder what they were seeing.

He was *counting* on the Primal reactions. I needed to remember this little lightbulb moment, when the time came to actually sit and discuss a plan of action for this asshole.

"Her clothes were wrong." Mr. Duggan had been analyzing the image of his "daughter" as I had been analyzing the signature, and found the image lacking. Hopefully this would give us some insight. We needed to find this guy and put a stop to his little game.

"Her hair was shorter." Mr. Duggan nodded, confident in his realization that he had, in fact, *not* seen his daughter do such a foolhardy thing. But with this realization came anger, just like the other man Jerath. Another Primal reaction: rage. We should have seen this coming, we should have brought Jade.

"Rolph, man. This wasn't some heedless thing you did," Commander James soothed, "this was done *to* you." That last statement seemed to pull Rolph from the anger at himself so the commander continued. "This is at least the second incident which has brought harm," he gave a small squeeze to Rolph's uninjured shoulder to convey solidarity, "We're convening and will be actively looking for whoever did this to you. I don't suppose you remember anyone of note, anything different about today, anyone that seemed upset with you?"

"Not that comes to mind—" he paused with his own lightbulb moment. "She looked like her picture."

Seeing the perplexed faces of those around him, Rolph expanded his thought.

"The Deena I saw in the street looked *exactly* like Deena in the picture I have behind the counter at the shop." He turned his eyes on his wife. "The school picture from earlier this year." He was much more animated as he looked at each of us in turn. "Down to the hair and clothes." His high of emotions plunged into the depths as he realized that he was hurt because he had brought a picture to his business, and someone had used it against him.

"Stop that," I admonished. "This is no one's fault but the bastard who is *trying* to hurt people. You cannot take his success as your failure." I nearly vibrated with conviction by the end of my speech. Somewhere along the way, I stopped talking about our current predicament and tunneled into my own darkness.

I was sick of feeling like I did something wrong. Like I was a burden with my telepathy. I didn't want this man to feel like that. I didn't want *anyone* to feel like an outsider. Yet, wasn't that what we *all* were? Every last man, woman, and child forced to reside in Minefield and other towns like it. *Outsiders.*

The more I thought about it, the angrier I got. The melodies piping into my eardrums were fuel to my fire, and I raged.

I startled when a hand landed gently on my shoulder, the fire extinguishing in a rush of exhalation.

You are not alone, Nat.

Holden.

You have a gift. A gift that, I for one, am more than grateful you have.

I had turned to look at him and softened at his words. I wanted to throw my arms around him and never let go but figured now was probably not the best time for such things, so I settled for a small smile of appreciation. I could really get used to having him around.

I turned to the commander. "I have what we need."

"Good." The word was clipped and decisive. Commander James wanted our perpetrator caught, and yesterday at that. A flash of something in his mind caught my attention before he quickly masked it with righteous anger for the Duggans. I cocked my head as I studied our good commander. That thought, that one *piece* of thought, could change *everything we knew.*

CHAPTER 15

STUFFING MY DANGLING EARBUD back into my ear, I looked to exit the hospital room as quickly as I could without seeming rude. I just wanted to get out of the mental clog of so much anguish. Luckily, this section was fairly empty and my music was enough to keep the crazy at bay.

Once outside of the room, I leaned against the outer wall in the corridor. I closed my eyes and thought about the fragment of an idea I had gleaned from Commander James and breathed in the idea of freedom. Unfortunately, there was no freedom in what I breathed here. Instead, I was assaulted by the cloying combination of solvents, blood, and fear. Blowing out the insidious air, I pried my eyes open when I felt my father's presence in front of me. I knew his stare without looking. I knew his thoughts without having to hear them.

"Yes, Dad. I was there," I intoned as I once again removed one earbud. *I just want to get lost in my music for a few...*

"Wh—"

"Yes, he was manipulated," I sighed heavily, feeling the weight of this problem come to rest on my shoulders. "I don't know how much I can share," I shook my head slightly and fully opened my eyes to look into the concerned gaze of Dr. Connor Dae. "I'm good," I assured him shakily, as my heart continued to thunder in my chest. Then, again with more conviction. I *would* be all right, but not until we stopped this man.

My dad's eyes mirrored my own conviction. He knew what I was thinking and approved. There was brightness to his eyes now, they shone more green than brown, and were piercing in their intensity.

"Use your gifts to help keep people safe, kiddo." He chucked me lightly on the chin, then turned on his heel and went farther down the hall of patient rooms, disappearing through a door. After watching his escape, I ached to do the same, though I wished to leave the hospital entirely.

I jumped as Holden again laid a hand on my shoulder. He was good at sneaking up on me when I was unprepared and must have exited the Duggan's recovery room while I was distracted watching my father amble onward. What good was this gift if I could still be unaware? *No, Nat, you need to make* yourself *aware.*

I needed to get into training, to understand how I could help the team and what my limitations were. I needed to tread carefully though where my healing was concerned. I bet not everyone would take that one in stride, and being the envy of all sides was a very dangerous circle to be centered in.

You all right?

I nodded over-enthusiastically and pulled a hand through the hair that had detached from my ponytail, currently plastered to the side of my face. I knew the motion was not only futile in expelling the unwanted strands from my face, it was also a nervous tell, which Holden picked up on. I bit my lower lip and stared at Holden's chin in order to find time to formulate a reply.

"I have a lot on my mind right now," totally the truth, "I need to get training so I won't be a burden in the hunt for our bad guy."

We need to focus on how to best evade an aggressor.

"I need to be able to handle myself and be helpful," I seethed. "Don't tell me I have to run away."

Holden scooted right up in my face, ducking and hunching so we were eye to eye. Hands gripping my upper arms forcefully, or rather, with more pressure than he had ever previously bestowed upon my body, kept me from turning away. I stared back defiantly, watching as his crystal blue eyes bled to mercury silver. His worry etched into his thoughts ran rampant.

I lifted my hands inside the circle his arms created and pushed outward, breaking the hold he had on me. His eyes blazed with concerned intensity while mine blazed in fury, but he let me retreat. My temper rose hot and fast, fueled by the feelings of helplessness I had felt previously. I backed up and rose on my toes, jabbing a finger into Holden's muscled chest, which tightened in response to our argument, much like his jaw.

I prepared to let him have both barrels. His eyes were no longer silver, his thoughts no longer on my safety, for once. My head was buzzing with enough of my own emotion-fueled thoughts that I couldn't hear more than a buzz of anything else.

"Don't," *jab* "tell me," *jab* "that I will not be defending myself," *jab* "that you expect me to *run away*." I pretty much growled the last. "I need to learn how to handle not only myself but aggressors. If you won't teach me, I'm quite sure I can find another mentor."

Holden and I were locked in our standoff, neither willing to relinquish their position, when Commander James clanged through the door and into our stare down. His thoughts were able to penetrate my fog as they were presented as a picture, the same scene he had just walked into—Holden and I raging with chests heaving and fists clenching. My hair was once again plastered to my face, and my eyes fevered with intensity, blazing a glittering turquoise. Holden was wondering why I showed so much more emotion than the Sages he'd shadowed or observed before. *Crap.* I needed to lock this down before I made him curious as to how else I was different.

"I'm not sure what has you both so riled up, but it makes your Primal side show, Nat. Simmer down and walk with me."

Holden and I fell into step behind the commander, though we maintained a distance we hadn't until that moment. I seethed but pushed the dangling earbud into its home and proceeded to let the music bring me back from the ledge. *Man, this anger is rough.*

I waved at May on our way to the elevator but didn't acknowledge anyone else. The happy, upbeat tunes proved to be useful in backing me out of my own damaging thoughts, in addition to drowning out unwanted thoughts of others. *This is not the best day of my life, but tomorrow could be.*

The tension which clogged the air in the confines of the elevator, slowly dissipated as the beat infiltrated my anger. I bobbed my head, keeping time. The tension popped like a bubble just as the elevator doors opened, spilling the three of us into the dreariness of the waiting room. I didn't waste time making my move to get out of the hospital, nearly running to the exit.

Pushing out into the night, I stopped once again to breathe in the shadowy breeze. Air free of disinfectant, but heavy with rain. It smelled damp and acrid with tar. The wet smell the asphalt exuded was noxious, and I was thankful the smell was only slightly present. I just wanted to go home and sleep. This had been one hell of a day and I was so ready for it to be over.

I turned toward the hospital entrance and watched Holden and his uncle exit at a much more leisurely pace than I had. I used my brilliant powers of deduction to draw the conclusion that they were in discussion as I watched Holden sign. I was glad they were still far enough from me that my earbuds were effective. I was enjoying the songs too much to go back into reality and participate just yet.

"You have alerted Doctor Parmore to your departure, yes?" Commander James intoned as he and Holden came to a stop in front of me, pulling the music from one ear with a knowing grin. "Existing employment?" the question was punctuated with eyebrows raised in question.

"Ah, yes. I already gave notice," I nodded and played with the dangling headphone, twisting the cord around my fingers. "Hopefully forever," I muttered sullenly.

"Good, then tomorrow after classes will be the official beginning to your time with the EEA." He turned to Holden and continued. "C'mon, let's get you home. You begin teaching tomorrow."

That perked my ire once again and I piped up before they could get too far away. "I don't know that Holden is the best person to see to my training." I didn't have to cut my eyes his way, though I did, to know that he was upset that I felt that way. His mental tirade was joined by the commander's questioning one. "I don't think Holden will teach me all I want to know to be effective. I think he worries about me too much," I cut my eyes to him again and softened my tone, "but I need to be out in the field. I need to be proactive in my pursuit of the people who intend harm. I am stronger, like you said, Commander. I can handle it."

Both men watched me for what seemed like minutes, their wheels turning. Both mulling over my words and finding truth in them. Damn him, he needed to get over it so he could *help* me. "You want me at my best, I should know the ins and outs so I can be the best asset I can, right?" I knew Commander James would back me, I just didn't know if he would force Holden, or if I would be working with someone else.

"Well, it's late," Commander James broke in. "We'll discuss things further tomorrow. The whole team will be there, so you'll get to meet everyone." He grabbed Holden's arm and began dragging him away, toward where I assumed his car would be found. "See you tomorrow, Nathalee."

Goodnight, Nathalee.

I muttered my reply but they were out of earshot. I pulled the key to my father's car out of my pocket and headed in the direction I had parked. The street lamps lit the ground with halos of light well enough that I didn't have to guess where I had left the car. The lot was fairly full even though it was after dark. The emergency portion of the hospital seemed to always have patients—we were good at getting hurt or sick.

Once at the car, I pressed the button to unlock the doors and grabbed at the handle. The dark blue vehicle looked black except where the light touched it as I yanked open the door and bent to get into the seat. I was so preoccupied I almost missed the other voice.

I looked around, searching for the person I knew to be around, but found no one. The darkness would hinder me and aid them if they wanted to stay hidden. I sat in the driver's seat and pulled the door closed. As I turned the key in the ignition, I removed my remaining earphone and rolled down the window slightly, hoping it would boost my "hearing."

What I got was a mental image of myself as I sat in the car, face hidden by wisps of escaping multi-hued hair and hands gripping the wheel. I recognized it. The mental signature was none other than that of our illusionist.

He was here, and he was watching me.

CHAPTER 16

FROM THE PICTURE HE painted, I had a pretty good idea of where he was, but I couldn't see anything. It wasn't an area with abundant lighting and the shadows swallowed up anything not in the intermittent bubbles of florescence. I didn't know if he would be able to follow so I didn't want to go home, didn't want to give him any additional information about me. I couldn't lead him to my mother. Instead, I drove to The Corner Bean.

I idled at the curb, facing the spot where Rolph Duggan had been struck. The street was open and most reminders of the incident removed. I knew the blood would still be there when morning came, even if I couldn't see it now. I turned the key and unbuckled my seatbelt. Preparing to exit the vehicle, I took a moment to scan the area with my gift. I continued out and toward the coffee shop when I didn't hear anything alarming.

Looking both ways, I crossed the street at a jog and approached the door of my favorite place on Main, only to notice the closed sign in the dark window. I really thought The Corner Bean stayed open later into the night, so I walked closer to the posted piece of paper to read it. The air left my body as if I had received a punch to the gut when I comprehended its contents. The small makeshift sign read: *We're sorry for the inconvenience but due to a family emergency, The Corner Bean will be closed until we are able to make arrangements. Thank you for your understanding during this trying time.*

That's when it hit me. Rolph Duggan was one half of the Primal husband and wife pair who had enhanced smell and taste and were able to make the amazing concoctions I considered a staple of my diet. I was sure Jade would agree. The proprietors of The Corner Bean.

Jade. Oh geez, I needed to let her know what had happened today. I pulled out my phone, extremely outdated though it was, and hit the speed dial for Jade as I walked back to the car. Most of Main was still open and older rock music permeated the air from the sports bar down the road, something about wayward sons. Laughter could be heard from within, but not many were on the streets.

Sages usually turned away from noisy, raucous, public displays they felt to be barbaric. Primals on the other hand, they lived for it. Ninnies within the town usually joined in, so the establishments which catered to such usually did a good business.

The phone connected on the third ring, and Jade's sarcastic greeting chimed in my ear.

"Oh, my dearest friend, Nat! To what do I owe this pleasure?" I could just picture her bowing mockingly as she delivered the lines, and a smile graced my face.

"I love you, girl, you know that?"

"Yeah, I know that. So what's up, friend? Why the late-night call?" Man, she was chipper this evening, which was perfect for what I needed. She must have smoothed things out with her parents.

"Have you talked to Commander James at all today?"

"Uh, yeah. He just called a few minutes ago to let me know there's a meeting for the whole team tomorrow." She snickered "Like a meet 'n' greet. Sounds fun, doesn't it? Can you imagine how it's going to be having all of us, Sage, Primal, and NE all in one little conference room?" She was nearly hyperventilating with laughter as she continued. "The Primals are going to puff up like peacocks, the Sages are going to shrink in on themselves until intellect is called upon and the ninnies are going to be feeling like they're the ones entitled to everything."

"Geez, Jade," I wheezed through my laughter, "please elaborate!"

"We are going to be in a world of mental and emotional hurt tomorrow, my friend."

Those words sobered me, and I wiped my eyes of their moisture while leaning my head back against the headrest of the worn seat and closed my eyes. "Yeah, it's going to be rough." I blew out a frustrated breath. "Today was worse though, Jade."

All the lightness in Jade's tone vanished as she asked, "What happened?"

"Our illusionist, the one we realized was the cause of the incident where you met Commander James and Dane?" I rolled my eyes as I heard Jade's sigh at the mention of Dane. She could swoon another time, I needed her to know about today's incident. "Well, it seems he's not done. I was walking to the barn from The Corner Bean—"

"Yum..."

"Yeah, and I watched as a man ran out into traffic and was hit by a car." I paused at Jade's intake of breath.

"Oh my God, Nat! Is everyone all right?" I definitely had her attention now.

"No, but the man's alive. He's Primal which saved his life, though he definitely is going to need a long recovery time. He broke his pelvis and dislocated his right shoulder, had major whiplash and hit his head on the street and slid a good ways."

"But he's alive? And expected to recover, that's good." I knew she would be nodding at her statement.

"I just found out that he is one of the owners of The Corner Bean." I let the sentence hang and was met by silence, "They've closed the coffee shop until they get things settled."

"No." That was a statement. "No, that is not okay. It is not okay that someone is playing games with others' lives, and *definitely* not okay that said game is keeping me *from my coffee!*" Jade was serious about her coffee, obviously.

"I'm sure they'll get it back up and running in no time. There were so many bouquets in his recovery room that I'm positive they'll be able to get things sorted quickly. Many people care about them." I remembered the sheer number of bright bunches covering the sterile room and added, "They're loved."

The drive home was uneventful after hanging up with Jade, though I tooled around town and about every Sage street I knew, just in case I was being followed by my ill-intentioned watcher.

It was late enough when I arrived that my mother was already shut up in her room for the night. I trudged through the house toward my room to grab what I needed to get ready for bed myself, then headed to the bathroom for a much needed shower. I had changed and run a rag over myself when Holden and I had arrived here after the incident, but I needed to be clean. I needed to wash away the dirt and blood I still envisioned on my body and in my hair. As per routine, I found a song I thought would help me unwind and pressed play on the speaker, then started the water flow.

The shower did as I hoped it would and relaxed all the muscles in my body. I probably should have taken some time to look over what Dr. Parmore wanted of me the next day, but I was wrung out. I wouldn't retain anything, as it seemed I never did. I crawled under the covers and prayed I'd find sleep tonight.

Sleep found me easier than expected. I had minimal dreams about broken and bleeding people sprawled out before me, and I awoke refreshed the next morning. I was a little worried that the incident hadn't affected me more. What did that say about me?

The sun shone through my sheer silver curtains into my room, signaling the need to vacate my bed. A bed which I found even more comfort in than normal. I groaned as I threw off the covers and put forth massive amounts of effort to heave myself up and out. Apparently feeling refreshed still didn't make mornings any easier. I trudged slowly to my dresser, and once again, rummaged through the contents until I found something I figured would be good for the day. I paused mid-search as I remembered that today I would be meeting the rest of the mixed-bag making up the commander's new enforcer team.

Who would be on it? Would I know the other Sages? Would we all be able to handle not only being in the same vicinity as each other, but also having to actually *work together?* This could all go massively awry, and quickly. Jade would hopefully be able to help keep everyone on an even keel if needed. *Hopefully* being the key word.

After glancing at the clock by the bed and reading the big green numbers, I realized I had about fifteen minutes to finish getting ready if I wanted to actually make my destination on time. Seeing as it would probably be best not to draw too much attention to myself on the last day, I hurried through my morning routine of making myself presentable, shouldering my bag and starting my music. I grabbed a muffin and water as I rushed out the door and headed toward the campus. Putting the water into my bag and the muffin in my mouth, I pushed the already flowing music to my ears.

Today's walk seemed slower than normal, I once again noticed cars, bikes, and people as we passed each other, but with my tunes surrounding me, I didn't hear much else. I just bopped along, singing, off key, I'm sure, as I made my way closer to the final moments at the schoolhouse, I hoped.

The sun seemed brighter in the sky, its warmth infiltrating my entire being. Today was going to be a good day. That was my thought until I entered the campus and proceeded to be bumped and jostled, some unknowingly and some not, if the sneers were anything to go on, and made my way to the lecture hall.

Tori and her groupies were arriving just as I came to the door and pushed past me, throwing my shoulder into the frame as they knocked me to the side. I glared daggers at her retreating form as she threw a hateful smirk over her shoulder. She flicked her long strawberry blonde hair off her shoulder as she faced the room once again and looked for a place to park that ass of hers.

I made my way to my usual seat within the classroom behind the lectern. I shuffled into position and turned to face the front of the room, taking my bag from my shoulder and preparing to sit. I lost my balance and flailed, my arms pin-wheeling as I began the inevitable descent to the floor, butt first.

The chair I had been maneuvering into was no longer directly behind me...but directly above.

Freaking Tori. I no longer held the slightest remorse for picking her brain. Maybe I'd find something of note while I was in there. *Bring it on.*

Two hours and one massive headache later, I booked it out the auditorium doors and down the halls, most of which were rather quiet today. As predicted, Dr. Parmore had found a replacement for me rather easily so she made a point to let me go early, almost like a firing, and to state that she was quite happy her new aid wouldn't be such a distraction to her students. I pushed my headphones in and opened the science department doors out into the sunlight once again.

Jade was waiting at the base of the stairs. She smiled and waited for me to reach her side. Her thoughts were buzzing with different scenarios of what we could walk into when we met with Commander James and the other team members.

"You're nervous," she chimed, all false cheer.

"So are you," I returned with a cracked smile, which Jade reciprocated. The tension began to wane with just that one action. A smile from my best friend. With her by my side, I could do this. I could do *anything*. "Let's grab lunch on our way over. We'll be a bit less volatile that way." Jade burst out laughing at that. "*We?* No, *you're* the one who lets her inner Primal out to play when hunger strikes."

She took a deep breath and wiped at the moisture escaping her eyes along with her mirth. I gave her a playful shove, not too hard or my strength would hurt my little friend. Man, we needed each other. We would wither and become husks without the lightness and understanding each brought to the other.

We ran across a good number of students emerging from their test rooms, or who were soon to be starting. All groups came to the one campus for higher schooling, though the types of classes were often more divided, and there was virtually no mingling between them. The division was extremely noticeable here and I scanned the groups I saw as we walked.

A younger group of Sages were all laughing as they used telekinetic gifts to upset and confuse Primals in the area. I watched as they moved a Primal girl's hat, which had been lying over her face as she dozed, to repeatedly smack her in the face until she awoke, then moved back to its original position as the girl looked around in confusion. Each time, she became more agitated.

As we passed her, she released an honest hiss of aggression and swung her eyes our direction. Whatever color they were regularly had been entirely engulfed in black. She was about to flip her switch, and it looked like Jade and I were the targets. *Perfect.*

My telepathy was not usually much help in these situations, but I removed one earbud so I could readily hear those around me. Jade and I stopped, preparing for the girl's onslaught. She was livid and having trouble thinking past her anger. Luckily, she narrated what she wanted to do, so I had a heads up. "We are not the ones messing with you." I put my arms up, hands extended with palms facing the girl as I attempted to gentle her. "It would not be in your best interest for you to injure us."

"Why do you mess with me?" Her voice was almost unintelligible, gravelly as it was with anger. "I do nothing to you." She was nearly vibrating. We needed to end this confrontation, and I wasn't sure talking would do it.

"Jade," I spoke softly, hoping to avoid angering the girl further, "you may have to use your persuasion on her." My eyes never left the Primal, and I made sure to not lose track of her thoughts. "We don't want any trouble." The last I projected toward the girl, hoping her mood would ease the longer we held off a confrontation.

I distantly heard the Sage troublemakers snickering at our predicament. At the situation which was created by their hand. *I really am not a fan of the Sage superiority complex.* I breathed a deep sigh as I realized the futility of this conversation, the girl angling for an attack. She began circling us like prey.

I was *not* prey, and I wouldn't let Jade be either. I made sure we turned with her, having grabbed Jade and kept her angled behind me as we assessed the situation. The Primal's thoughts gave her away, and I knew when she'd make her move, though I didn't quite anticipate her speed.

I stepped us back and away from her grabbing hands just in time. As she lunged past us, I jabbed out with my right hand fisted toward where I knew her kidney was, leaving Jade unattached behind me.

I knew even if the force wasn't enough to do any damage, it was a spot to cause more pain than others. As my fist impacted, the girl stumbled to the ground, landing on hands and knees, coughing from the pain. Jade took that moment to lunge past me and put a hand on the girl's nearest shoulder, thus enacting her gift.

"Easy," she cooed. "You're fine. Breathe." Jade bent over and patted her back as she said this. "Get ready for class, relax and be calm. All is well." Then she stepped back, letting her arm fall to her side.

She wrapped her left hand around my wrist and began moving me forward, the conflict clearly over as the Primal girl rose from the ground and headed back to where her things still lay on the grass under the tree, grabbed her hat and backpack and began walking toward the quad. Presumably to class.

Jade hadn't made her do those things, but she calmed her enough that rationality won out and the Primal berated herself for losing control. She looked to be about sixteen, which meant her Primal instincts and abilities were new to her, at least to the full degree of maturation.

Jade was practically dragging me as I watched the girl move away. "Wow," I breathed. "Jade, you are one scary capable empath." I pulled my arm out of her grip and began walking in earnest, now easily able to keep up. Jade didn't look my way but smirked and flipped her wavy golden hair over her shoulder.

"You better remember that."

I definitely would.

"So," she continued blithely, "I was thinking lunch at Constantine's." I was still watching her, and she cut her eyes to me. "Well?"

"Oh. Yeah, sounds good," I said distractedly. I was still in awe of her. She was so tiny, and wielded so much control, it was kind of scary—but cool.

"Perfect. I could really use some tasty fries, and a shake, yum!" Jade was lost in her thoughts of grub for the moment, and I ran with it.

Constantine's fries and shakes were to die for, especially together. *Mmmm.*

CHAPTER 17

AFTER STUFFING OUR FACES with piping hot, crispy crinkle-cut fried goodness, not to mention the cool, sweet, creamy shake deliciousness...but never mind my gluttonous ways. The point is, it was oh so yummy, but maybe not the best decision if we were to begin training today.

We walked on in silence. Well, *verbal silence.* I had my headphones in again hoping to give Jade some semblance of privacy in these last few moments before we were officially training to be enforcers, which was still a surreal thought. Sages as enforcers, never thought I'd see the day Primals agreed to it.

A jaunty country tune pervaded my ears and sang about loving a man just a bit too much as we came to the gardens, the gym just beyond. The end of the school year, there was much more activity within the confines of the gardens. Groups of Sage and Primal flocked to the peaceful area to be social, though, of course, not together. There were definite lines in the sand and it truly confused me. Shouldn't we band together in our exile? Maybe not necessarily *against* anyone, just *together*. Sing Kumbaya or something.

Luckily we were able to continue past without a repeat incident. I was once again narrowing my focus to the sounds of drums, guitars and singing, when I must have caught an uneven edge in the sidewalk and began my headlong descent to the ground.

Jade's startled vision permeated my mind as I watched the pavement come up to greet me with startling speed. My eyes were comically large, full of the knowledge that this fall would not be prevented, my hands out in front; ready and braced for impact. Maybe I was seeing things, but my freckles seemed to be more prominent than usual, as if they too were coming out to meet the ground. The next moment, those hands roughly impacted the concrete surface as did my left knee.

Somehow I had fallen with a left tilt, and only the extremities on that side were now paying the price for my negligence with a slight sting.

"Only you would actually *fall* from stumbling on the sidewalk," Jade chuckled. "Is Commander James aware of this Sage gene you seem to possess?"

"It's not a Sage gene," I countered as I dusted off my hands. "I know plenty of Sages who aren't clumsy." I nodded once as if this rebuttal won the debate.

"Sweetie, it's a physical ailment, albeit a gray area, that can keep you from doing physical things."

I thought for a moment as we continued toward the command post and realized that maybe Jade was right. Was clumsiness a *physical ailment?*

Maybe it was like an inner ear thing, I'd heard of that. *I'm sure Dad knows.* Why did *I* not know?

I shelved that question for a later time as we reached the gym doors. The place didn't seem so ominous anymore, maybe repeated exposure was the key to overcoming fear. I felt like I had heard that somewhere. Shrugging it off, I lugged the heavy steel door open and waited for Jade to enter, following behind her, allowing the door to close with a bang.

Once again, we were the focal point of all eyes in the cavernous space, but only for a moment. Most returned to their original tasks, probably to ensure they were not injured due to their inattention. *Good call.* This was definitely the type of place such things occurred. *Note to self: do not lose focus around here.* Mental note filed away, Jade and I weaved through the gym to the door at the rear. This door was steel as well so I once again heaved it open, sparing Jade the effort it would take her.

I was distracted watching Jade while immersed in my dance-worthy tunes, so it wasn't until I looked up mid-stride of entering the actual command center that I was startled. I hesitantly continued my trek into the room and took out one earbud in order to listen to the room which was currently filled to bursting with six people other than Jade and me. I moved my eyes to the clock flashing red digital numbers which read: 15:55. Military time, but of course. *Guess I need to brush up on that system.*

I returned my attention to the room, and the seven sets of eyes, and minds, now sharply focused on me and my silence. I blushed and gave a small wave to accompany my rueful smile and raised eyebrow. "Greetings, are we late?" I shot another pointed glance to the clock and its glaring numbers, "It's not yet four...right? I mean, I am reading that correctly, aren't I?"

That little remark earned me a number of snickers and one derisive snort. I tuned to focus my attention on the owner, who happened to be the man who was in the ring and directed me to Commander James on my first visit to this Primal haven. The visit in which my father had accompanied me.

The man was much less jovial this go around. He looked at me with nothing short of disdain, as he did Jade, and the other Sage I noticed in the room. This meeting was off to a smashing start.

By the look of things, getting Primals and Sages to work alongside one another would be...difficult. I was getting an overload of internal insults from both sides. I scrunched my eyes closed and rubbed at my temple in an attempt to dispel the headache I could already feel barreling to the forefront.

Can't even handle being in the room now, snort, *No way she'll make it. I'll make sure she doesn't, that none of them do.*

That got my hackles up fast. Slowly, I lowered my hand and opened my eyes. My head still angled toward the floor, I looked up from lowered lashes and glared at the man, though I'm not sure it had the same effect Jade's had on me.

A mental snort was my answer. His body still bunched in restraint, dark tattoos peeking from beneath his too-tight tee, and eyes doing their best to maim us with non-existent death lasers.

Nope, he was not impressed. I cocked my hip and brought my hand to rest on it, taking on an unaffected air—or so I hoped—and looked about the room. The room, which before had seemed quite open, was now filled to the max with people, conference table, and seating as well as computer bank and case notes. The tangled thoughts continued.

Arrogance on both sides would make sure this meeting was full of testosterone. *What a mess.*

Jade and I were the only females present. Other than those I knew, there was also our derisive Primal, the arrogant Sage, and a quiet male who sat at the computer bank, away from everyone. He was concerned, but like me, seemed to be more about cohesiveness than any direct anger. He just wanted to "play with the machines" and would leave the pissing contests to the rest of us. *Interesting.*

The unknown Sage male was about my height and build with wire rimmed glasses that he pushed up his nose so they settled at the apex, amplifying his mud colored eyes. He was dressed in designer jeans and a light blue button-up shirt. The boat shoes and perfectly styled blonde hair were the kickers. This guy was either from a family who did well or he wanted us to think he did. Time would tell. He would think about it at some point, hopefully I would be blissfully unaware when he did.

Normally Sages would have a facade in place for uncomfortable situations, be outwardly unaffected and either seething or trembling internally. This Sage however, wasn't. He was wholly unaffected by the large Primal's aggressive position. It fascinated me.

"Enough, Devlin!" Commander James finally ordered, apparently at his limit of posturing for the moment, his own temper had been building since this Primal, with a chip on his shoulder, had begun his intimidation attempts. "We're all going to work together, so you all—" he paused and met eyes with everyone in the room in turn, effectively showing us all just who was alpha.

No one wanted a piece of the commander. We all knew better. I wasn't sure as to his enhancement, but I had no doubt there was one—

184

and that Commander James wielded it to perfection. The silence that descended was the type to have been accompanied by the sound of crickets.

Satisfied that he had everyone's attention, Commander James pulled out the plastic chair which he had nearly crushed with his grasp and weight as he restrained himself from becoming physical. Maybe he thought it wouldn't go over well to have the head honcho knocking heads within five minutes of team assembly. The thought brought a smile to my face, and that had Jade elbowing me.

She cut me a sideways glance as she tried, and failed, to hide her own smirk. Being able to feel the emotions, or hear the thoughts, of those around us was every so often...comical. *Not often.*

Not now, woman. Don't make me laugh now. We need to show these oafs, all of them, that we belong here just as much as they do. That we are an asset, not a burden. Jade's mental speech was a bit long, but she was right. I needed to focus. I needed to show them I could do this. I needed to succeed. So I wiped clear the smile, and pulled out a chair. The screeching of metal legs pierced my eardrums as it dragged across the linoleum flooring toward my feet.

I had just sat, Jade to my right, when the chair on my other side scraped away from the table. Startled, I looked up into Holden's gorgeous face. His eyes bore into mine briefly before he sat and turned his icy glare to the others at the table. He was still sore with me but wouldn't let anyone take shots at me either. His death glare stayed on Devlin once it landed, slicing and brutal, it promised pain to the larger male.

Devlin just smirked, his thoughts a tangle of superiority and prejudice. This was going to be harder than I thought. He was the picture

185

of arrogance, leaned back in his chair with arms folded over his massive chest. His legs no doubt fully extended under the table, probably crossed at the ankle with feet wagging. I snorted. Devlin's cold eyes shot to mine and narrowed.

Unflattering thoughts were once again thrust my direction. This time I rolled my eyes as Commander James's crisp voice cut across the room.

"Right then, now that we are all present and accounted for," eyes fixed on Jade and me from around the table.

I blushed but stood my ground and met all the accusing eyes. Who knew there was a time for this thing? Time to move on.

"You're all here because you bring something unique and valuable to the team. To the cause we are striving for."

"Which is?" Boat shoes Sage chimed.

The commander's dark eyes fixed on the wispy Sage, making me almost fear for him. This guy could be trouble. This idea of cohesion could be just a pipe dream, snuffed before it was ever realized.

It almost looked that way as of now, with so many ready to explode.

Eyes still locked on the brat, Commander James thought about how to answer, what to say. That was when I caught a flash thought that was world changing. Again. Then it was gone, and Commander James did not seem to be forthcoming as to its existence.

CHAPTER 18

WRENCHING HIS GAZE AWAY from his target, Commander James began again. "Let's all introduce ourselves. Tell us who you are and what your ability is." He turned his attention directly to his left, which happened to be Dane, who like the rest of us, was extremely leery of putting forth any personal information, especially something as potentially sensitive as our ability.

Dane cast a questioning glance at the commander and upon receiving a curt nod of confirmation, took a deep breath and began. "I'm Dane. Primal. My enhancement is my tracking ability."

"*Tracking ability*?" Boat Shoes scoffed.

Oh, he was a piece of work. He and Devlin would be perfect for each other. The thought made me smile again then cringe. That would get ugly, but it would be entertaining. They both deserved what the other could deliver. The rest of us on the other hand? We could do well without their egos.

Dane laced his fingers together on the table in what I knew to be an effort not to strangle the obnoxious Sage. "If you leave something at a scene, I can find you." He was now talking directly to Boat Shoes. *Warning him.* "Once I have your scent, I will *always* hunt you down."

Boat Shoes smiled indulgently at the massive Primal so I guess it didn't stick.

We continued around the table. The techie, named Trent, was very average looking. Average build and height, with casual clothes and forgettable features. He turned out to be Non-Enhanced, the only NE in the room. He was a master hacker and coder and claimed to be able to find anything if computers were involved. This proclamation brought on another round of scoffs and snorts.

Next was Boat Shoes, whose name was actually Steve. *Steve? So plain.* He was telekinetic, though he professed that his specialty was to *halt* movement. When Devlin laughed, Steve froze *him.*

Like total paralysis. Devlin couldn't even spit the vitriol his mind was throwing at Steve, who just sat back and smirked. He seemed to be at ease, but I knew better. I felt the strain on his mind, the concentration and effort it took for him to keep a male as large and intent, shall we say, from movement.

When Devlin was released, both males were nearly panting with exertion. The exercise was a nice reality check for both egos, though it only solidified the malice they felt for one another as they each tried to liquefy the other with the imaginary lasers they shot with their eyeballs.

Jade said her piece next, throwing a wink at Dane when he blushed, remembering her demonstration.

Next, it was my turn. As predicted, no one was happy having a telepath in their midst. The fact that my range was so wide and complete bothered just about everyone. Jade and Holden being the exception.

"We will be working on methods to shield thought," Commander James interjected before the table's occupants revolted. "Miss Dae also has her own methods of granting privacy to those around her, so please, calm down." He was very frustrated with how the meeting was going so far and was beginning to realize how difficult his task of building a cohesive working unit would be. This meeting drove home that we truly were a town divided; not only from the rest of the world, but within our own seclusion.

It was good news for me that Holden's ability to change his appearance, and therefore be undetected, went over just about as well as the rest of ours.

Devlin rounded out the "team" and was the tactical guru, his gift being stealth. An enormous, silent hunter... *perfect.*

After introductions, we all sat quietly fidgeting, casting wary glances at the others in the room. The tension was so thick, it felt like a physical weight pressing on my shoulders. I had to resist the urge to hunch under its imagined weight. Instead, I decided to move the meeting into a productive direction, hopefully.

"Commander James, have we been able to discern any information about this illusionist that seems to have been targeting Primals?" I raised my eyebrows significantly at the Commander, hoping to get this meeting back on track and into useful information territory. I needed to find this guy. Now.

The Commander turned his attention to Trent though as he addressed the room. "Trent is going through available video feeds, searching for anyone who looks out of place at the scene of Duggan's... '*accident*.'"

Yeah, I would hesitate over that phrasing as well. While the outcome was an accident, it also very much *wasn't*. Just because the people hurt, as well as the ones doing the hurting were unaware, didn't mean this incident was wholly accidental. The ball had been set into motion already. They were just pawns.

Sage minds filled with questions. Both Jade and Steve—I'd still call him Boat Shoes—were tripped by that. No surprise that it was Steve who voiced his questions, only he didn't question. Once again disdain was evident in his tone, in his whole blasé attitude.

"How exactly, is one to be 'out of place' as you say?" He used air quotes on "out of place" just to be a dick in his delivery. *Douche.*

Commander James puffed outward at the challenge, raising himself even higher, making his whole body that much *bigger*. I swallowed thickly, suddenly slightly worried that Steve may not leave this room untouched by Primal hands.

Then he noticed the wide eyes of his Primals, the men he knew and trained, read the alarm in their postures. I looked around then, tearing my gaze from the commander's intimidating visage to notice that Dane, Holden—and to my surprise—Devlin all tensed, chairs pushed from the heavy table with their large bodies all perched precariously, and gripping the arms with white knuckled intensity.

They were worried. Worried that their stalwart and stoic commander would snap and break the obnoxious Sage like a twig of the namesake spice which our moniker resembles. Though, maybe not to that description. No, their minds were yelling something to the effect of *'Holy crap! This guy is going to make the commander snap!'*

Apparently that never happened. Commander James was very level headed and tolerant for a Primal, which was good, given his role in our little society. It wouldn't do well for the Enforcement Commander to be a hot head. This situation needed to be de-escalated stat and kept on track. Maybe Steve needed to be removed from consideration. If he would be a hindrance in attitude more than an asset in ability, we needed him gone.

"What Commander James means, *All-Knowing-Sage,*" Trent sneered, "is that I'm looking to see if anyone's reaction either seemed disingenuous or plain unreactive to the fact that a man ran into the main thoroughfare of this little town," dramatic pause, "seemingly without provocation." Trent finished with a flourish of movement. His hands and arms twisting into the air as if to demonstrate his point. His tone turned mockingly questioning as he brought his attention back to Steve. "Do you understand *that* explanation?"

Steve's face was crimson with the recrimination, but he must have seen how close the commander was to the edge, as he just crossed his arms and leaned back in his chair. Dipping his chin to chest, Steve nodded curtly once, and then glared daggers at the conference table. Commander James deflated then, and sat back in his chair, scooting in toward the lip of the table.

"Maybe it would help us all..." another hesitation. But I heard it. I knew he'd finally spill that seedling thought that I had caught, three times now, with the rest of us. "To know *why* we are trying to make this team, this *agency* a success." He swiped a hand over his buzzed hair, rubbing vigorously as he determined how best to proceed. His face unable to hide the conflict he felt. He didn't want to reveal the stakes at this state of team infancy.

I sat quietly. I didn't want to intrude on his moment or bring attention to the fact that I already knew what the end goal was. That I knew *why* we needed to be successful in our endeavors. I didn't need any attention on me at this moment. This was Commander James's show, he needed to decide what information to feed us.

Though I could always get more than anyone *wanted* me to have, I didn't need or want to draw attention to the fact I wasn't limited by the same constraints as the rest of them in these situations. Yeah, that's what made me a loner. No one wanted someone else in their head, though Holden seemed to be the exception.

At the thought of him, I swung my attention imperceptibly to the left. Holden was stone still, his face a mask of placidity, except for his eyes. His vibrant blue eyes held the same question his head did, *are you sure?*

When the commander didn't readily continue, the room erupted in a mental barrage. So many thoughts and questions were being flung about like streamers that I once again felt the headache begin to pulse behind my eyes. I didn't know if I could handle this. If being on this team was going to put me in constant pain, I wasn't sure I'd be of much use, or if I'd even want to.

It would certainly be easier to stick my head in the sand and be happy in our little section of exiled nowhere, but my desire to be of use, to help people, wouldn't let me. Then there were *the stakes*. The carrot dangling in front of the noses of the Enhanced, though none knew it yet.

The melody flowing through my one inserted headphone was slow and dramatic. A pulsing, thumping piece which only amplified the weight of the conversation which hung in the air, a perfect backdrop to the moment as we waited with bated breath and screaming minds.

With a growl, Commander James ripped his hand from his hair and brought it to meet the other on the table, leaning his weight forward and looking at each pair of eyes on him as he began.

"The purpose of this team, this whole experiment, is to see if a few special Enhanced can police the rogues effectively."

Boat Shoes snorted again. This time I didn't restrain my mouth.

"Hey, Boat Shoes," I called. The room looked my way almost in unison, creeping me out a bit.

Steve looked my way with a smug look plastered on his mug, "Boat Shoes?" Those two words escaping his mouth made me decide to air something he wouldn't like.

"Would you prefer Douche-Canoe? I think it's just as accurate a description, much more so than *Steve*," I sneered. "I'm not sure you qualify as top tier in the Enhanced community we have here. The commander may have better luck with a stronger telekinetic."

Steve finally showed a reaction, like I knew he would. His face was once again that overwhelming shade of red as he spluttered and spit. Finally he was able to speak past his anger.

"There *is* no stronger kinetic!" He slapped his hands onto the table, putting enough pressure on them that his fingers began to turn white. He leaned across the wood separating us and hissed, "I am able to *stop momentum*! Do you even comprehend how much power that takes?" He scoffed, "Of course, you don't. I know all about you, *Miss Dae*." A dismissive wave, "You are no true Sage, ending your schooling only just getting through physics."

I was beginning to truly boil at this guy…so I went for it. "But for how long? How…*taxing* is it?" I raised my eyebrows at him. His were bunched in confusion. I powered on, angry enough not to care if I pointed out a weakness. "How much effort did it take to stop Devlin? How long could you hold him? Could you stop multiple objects? People? What's your limit? What would happen if you played at being invincible and held too long to something?" I was finally getting through.

"You have no idea what we could—what *you* could face in the future. You may have been the baddest kinetic in your neighborhood, but we most likely won't be dealing with your familiars. You will need back up.

"It's absolutely necessary to be a cohesive team. To put aside petty differences and *work together* to overcome, or to just identify our targets. You need to realize it's not only *you* being jeopardized." I went on, emphasizing each word but gaining steam as more words tumbled out of my mouth.

"You will endanger each and every one of us, if not the town, if you do not accept your limitations and learn how to circumvent them. Learn how you are vulnerable and work on eliminating that vulnerability. Sometimes, and most likely often, that will mean relying on your partner. A partner that will be one of the three *Primals* around this table.

"You *cannot* take on the world alone and survive. If you are intent on trying, then I think you will find yourself broken and bloody by the end. You are playing with human lives. You are endangering our *freedom*." The last came as a near plea.

I took a breath and blinked, finally noticing the other occupants of the room once again. Everyone was riveted to me, entranced by my tirade. I blushed furiously, realizing I had been so lost in my point that I hadn't noticed I was under a spotlight, though I certainly did now. Slowly, I returned to my seat and ducked my gaze, willing the blush to recede.

The room was still in eerie silence when I returned to myself and looked around the table. Even the mental voices had ceased. Finally a spark of life came from Steve, a slow Cheshire grin spreading across his face. Then the silence was broken, the noise like a gunshot in the silence as Steve brought his hands together in a booming clap. He continued slowly for a few rounds. Then crossed his arms over his meager chest and nodded once, that sly grin still in place.

"Well, all right then, Captain."

I sat stunned into a silence like what had encompassed the room a moment before. He wasn't being completely condescending. He was almost sincere, and it threw me.

"Hey, now, what's this about 'Captain'?"

Commander James rose, and once again leaned on the table. His dark eyes boring into mine made me want to fidget, to look away. I held his gaze. "You, Nathalee, have just proven yourself as a capable and insightful part of this team. I think you have made it so that you will be looked upon as an authority, though you may need to work on your temper almost as much as we do." He moved his finger to include the Primals in the room.

"But I'm not even trained!" I was beginning to panic a touch. I didn't know anything about decision making for other people. They couldn't put me there! My vision began to tunnel and I got a little dizzy. Then I heard Jade's voice in my head.

Breathe, Nat. Take a breath. Calm down. Please. I'm barely hanging on here and I'd prefer to not have to manipulate my bestie's emotions. I took a moment to really look at Jade like I hadn't since we'd stumbled into this mess of a meeting—literally for me.

She was buzzing, hard. Her emotions were all over the place, soaking in so many strong energies for so long was definitely getting to her. She was practically vibrating. I tuned in to the others for a moment, and breathed a sigh of relief that none truly expected, or *wanted* me to lead them.

Seeing Jade in her manic state allowed me to step back and compose myself. I took several slow, deep breaths, unclenching my protesting muscles as I sunk back into my vacated seat. Then other realities began filtering back into my awareness.

Dane was worried about Jade. Commander James was hoping my speech had rallied everyone. Devlin was scrutinizing me, still unconvinced a Sage could be worth anything in the field, while Holden was proud and conveying that I had him as backup. Steve and Trent however, were mulling over a certain phrase I apparently spewed in my heated tirade: *endangering our freedom.*

Had I said that? Crap. I guess I had kind of let the cat out of the bag, a little. Maybe they wouldn't actually ask about it and I wouldn't have taken the choice from the commander.

"So, what was that line about endangering our freedom?"

Trent. Damn. I closed my eyes in defeat.

"Apparently, I was not shielding my thoughts as well as I hoped, but then, that just proves the worth of a telepath." He smiled. My slip was a good thing?

"What Miss Dae is referring to is the heart of the matter. Our stakes. What rides on the success of this team and its effectiveness."

"What are you talking about, Commander?" Dane asked, lost. The big man may have been a great tracker but he definitely needed to be spoon fed words.

"I have been asked to put a team together as a test run. The test? To see if especially gifted Enhanced can be effective in policing those within our society who go rogue, deciding to do harm with their gifts."

"Okay, I get that…but where does the 'freedom' come in?" Steve and the air quotes again.

"If we are proven effective in this task," cue dramatic pause. *Nicely done there commander.* "The powers that be say they are willing to allow us to leave our exile, free to walk among the world."

CHAPTER 19

THAT ONE SENTENCE ACTED like a silencer. The whole room went dead quiet. No one spoke, no one moved, no one *thought*. Then, like responding to the starting bell of a horse race everything kicked back on.

The room exploded in noise and movement. Devlin and Dane shot up from their chairs and began launching booming questions at the commander, while Steve and Trent took a quieter, though no less urgent approach.

Not Jade though. No, she and Holden remained sitting to either side of me. She sat, turned sideways in her metal chair to better gape at me. She was struggling. Once again, I had not told her something of major importance. Her brow was furrowed, her mouth turned down and her mind working overtime. Holden watched and listened to the commotion around the room. Watching, waiting to see if he would be needed to break up anything that escalated.

The whole room faded out of my conscience as I tried to implore Jade about my part in this.

"Jade, I didn't know the whole of it—" I stopped, wondering how to explain that I knew, but I *didn't know*. "I saw a nanosecond of thought from Commander James last night at the hospital, that's it." I pleaded, trying to convey the truth of my position through my eyes, my face, my *emotions*.

Jade sat back in her chair, about as far from me as she could get without physically moving from the seat. Her eyes were still worried, as were her thoughts, but as our silent communication continued, I saw her relax. She looked down at hands which were knotted in her lap, chewing on her bottom lip before taking a heavy breath, finally letting her body sag in relief.

"Okay. I get it. You knew, but you didn't *know*." Deep breath. "And didn't want to say anything to get my hopes up." She nodded, still looking down at her fidgeting hands. Finally she looked up, her eyes now pleading with me. "No more, Nat. No more secrets. We're in this together. Completely."

I brightened and nodded vigorously. I was choking up, but I couldn't lose it now, not here. Not in front of my new team. I needed to be strong so they didn't turn on me. They knew the stakes now though.

We might not like each other, but I didn't think anyone wanted to be the reason that Enhanced had to stay locked away. We all had the same goal now, as if the safety of our town wasn't incentive enough, and we needed to show that we were effective. Enhanced who strayed from the moral path and brought harm could be caught, could be stopped.

"If we're all done gaping and chin-wagging," Commander James said, his deep voice rumbling through the space. I was fairly confident that if the room weren't filled to the brim, that his words would have echoed a good while. It slowly quieted as everyone realized there was more to learn. Everyone was enthralled now. The commander had effectively captivated us all.

Commander James surveyed each of us, drawing out anticipation and putting everyone on edge, except me. The good commander had not yet mastered shielding and was concentrating way too hard on the current conversation to keep from broadcasting his thoughts.

I heard everything loud and clear, but once again, I didn't say anything. It was not my place, and he hadn't pissed me off to the point I didn't care about etiquette or his privacy, so I sat quietly, leaning back in my rickety chair with arms folded across my chest, and just waited.

"Yes, this team is like a test. The ninn–" *cough*, "the Non-Enhanced in power within the country at the moment see that global connectivity has virtually eliminated our exile. The relative secret of the Enhanced. There are now many NEs choosing to live within our walls and even more who take the position that it is civilly criminal to treat us as threats without proof or prior offense."

"Hot damn! I knew we'd break through!" Trent was lit up like a firework. His eyes alight, a huge grin splitting his face. "I knew social media would be our savior. Gain the sympathy of the masses, and the government will fold." He scoffed. "So predictable."

"Well, it worked in our favor, why do you care though?" Steve jeered.

"I'm just as stuck here as you are." Trent continued, his attention back on Commander James. "I'm assuming this is privileged information."

"You would be correct. No one is to learn of this. There would be upheaval. Whether they wanted the opportunity, or feared it, we would have chaos." Commander James began picturing riots and attempts to forcefully leave Minefield, making him grow pensive.

"Commander, you do realize those reactions you are envisioning, they will happen no matter what? There will be no 'single file line' going on." I raised my eyebrows and looked around the table, everyone was now riveted back on me. "We will have our hands full when this comes to fruition, our people don't—*won't*—know how to handle freedom."

I took a deep breath whispering the truth I hadn't thought about as a negative before. "*Everything* will change."

The meeting settled down a bit after that. There was still plenty of excitement, but it was tempered with thoughts of how this would all play out. There were so many variables. The whole thing may have hinged on our success, but that was far from the end of the battle.

Once we had the go ahead to integrate into Non-Enhanced societies, we would then have the monumental task of learning how to live in the world. Learn to live among people who were not like us, people who may fear us. It was the fear I was most worried about, as should we all.

Wars were waged, and genocides attempted out of fear.

Once Commander James was able to bring attention back to the present and our current challenges, he told us to be back at the gym at "zero eight hundred" to begin training. I had forgotten about the military time clock. I really needed to get the conversion down so I wasn't early or, more likely, late for training in the future.

We were told to wear clothes we could easily move in, running shoes, and to bring an overnight bag. Then we were dismissed to go on our merry way for the evening. Holden stood and accompanied Jade and me on our walk back to my house.

The walk began as a rather tense experience. Jade and I more so than Holden. He and his uncle had spoken on the matter previously. Who better to tell than someone who couldn't speak, didn't hurt that he was also family. I had my headphones in, completely lost in my own head and the pulsing beat, at times watching the cars and bikes, the people, as we walked.

People were so open, using their enhancements without thought or trepidation. We knew what to expect here. In the real world, we would be like children experiencing the big city for the first time. It reminded me of that movie where the kid gets left behind when his family goes on vacation.

It would be a new freedom, and like children, we would push boundaries and explore limitations to see what we could get away with. Not everyone would test limits, that was true, but enough would that it might make our integration that much harder. Add in the fact that not everyone would want to leave. Would they have the option to stay?

I was so lost in my thoughts that when my headphones were ripped from my ears, my consuming melody falling away, I jumped sideways straight into Holden. He wrapped his hand around my elbow to steady me as we continued walking. I cast a quick glance at him, giving a small smile of gratitude.

"So what do you think of everything going on now, *Captain?*" Jade asked through a knowing grin while twirling my headphones about her fingers playfully. "You obviously saw this coming," she chided.

"I think that proving ourselves capable of handling one or two rogue Enhanced at a time will not prepare us, or the ninnies for the...*enthusiasm* and ignorance the Enhanced will display once we are freed. Our segregation has made us prisoners. Some of us may not adapt well," I declared solemnly. "What about you, Holden? You knew well before me, and more in depth, I assume," I said, switching my attention his way.

I couldn't say anything. You have to know that.

I nodded. "What do you know about it?"

"What did he say?" Jade asked.

I totally forgot that she couldn't hear him, and that made me flush. I felt the heat radiate from the tips of my ears as I relayed to Jade what Holden had said.

She nodded thoughtfully, and with a look which said she understood his decision.

I shifted back to Holden, "So?"

So, I know basically what we were told today, just...sooner.

"Does your uncle realize the effect this news will have on the general population of Minefield? On other Enhanced communities?"

He knows adjustments will need to be made. He has spoken to the council about steps that need to be taken prior to actual cohabitation, should we make it that far.

Jade cleared her throat, her non-verbal reminder that she was not privy to our conversation. She was also growling at me in her mind. I chuckled at her impatience and relayed what Holden had just said. Once again, she nodded thoughtfully, happy to be in the conversation.

Our chatting continued all the way home. I had to stop thinking of it as *mine*. I would soon be relocating to a frat house, as I had dubbed it, to live with the other members of the team. Another measure taken to ensure cohesion. Didn't they realize it was more likely that the close quarters would end in some form of a showdown? Hadn't they ever watched those reality TV shows? This is the kind of stuff that brought in the big ratings. Come to think of it, I wondered how no one had exploited that little niche market yet.

Best not to explore that thought as I'd hate to see it brought to light.

Holden walked Jade and me past the vibrant flower beds planted at the base of the steps and onto the porch where Jade excused herself and headed into the house. "What's for dinner, Mrs. Dae? It smells fantastic!" I heard my mother answer we were having roasted chicken and potatoes. The smells wafting through the open doorway were once again mouth watering.

I stood awkwardly on the porch facing Holden, not wanting to leave, but not sure what to say. He seemed to be having the same problem, as we continued to stand in silence. His mind was a jumble, though, and I let a chuckle tumble out listening to his mental tennis match. Should he or should he not kiss me? So I took the decision away from him, leaning in and lifting onto tiptoe, I snuck a fast one on him. Just a quick peck to show him my affection.

"I'll see you in the morning," I said as I reached for the screen door and pulled it open, a self-conscious smile on my face as I looked back over my shoulder. He was still standing where I left him, staring after me, with his fingertips pressed to his lips.

Then the screen door slapped closed and I walked into the living room, leaving Holden alone on the porch. After a moment, he turned and headed back down the steps and away from the house. I released the breath I had been holding and fell onto the couch, closing my eyes and laying my head to rest along the back of the furniture. *So much to think about.*

"Hey there, kiddo." My dad sat next to me on the couch as the cushions depressed, causing me to fall to the left and into the newly created indent.

Sprawled into Connor Dae's side, I closed my eyes once again and wrapped my arms around his waist. "I'll miss you, Dad."

"Oh, Nat, we won't be but a ways away," he said as he stroked my hair. "I'm proud of you. You'll be so good at this." I looked up into his smiling face and warm hazel eyes. I needed this. I needed my dad, and I wasn't sure how I would get along without him, so I melted into his side, enjoying his embrace and the comforting silence he afforded me.

CHAPTER 20

MORNING CAME ALL TOO soon, and zero seven hundred...earlier. I felt as though I had just laid my head on my pillow, when I was jolted awake by the blaring screech of the alarm clock pulsing its re-occurring beep bouncing around the confines of my room. Definitely not the sound I preferred to wake to.

I rolled out of bed and began my morning ritual of rushing about, trying to get all that I needed done and get out the door early enough to not be late for my first official training day. Without Jade here to prod me into oblivion, my wake-up routine was back to chaos.

Luckily I wasn't one for fashion, so my wardrobe was filled with semi-appropriate clothing to "train" in. The house was quiet except for the distant tones of my mother's thoughts while she worked in her gadget room.

I hopped across the hall and finished readying: brushing the snarls out of my too long sandy blonde hair and pulling it up into a trademark ponytail. *They're just so practical.* I brushed my teeth and decided to swipe a coat of mascara over my eyelashes in an attempt to look a little more alert. It definitely brightened the blue-green of my eyes but did nothing to dispel the dark bruise like coloration below them. *Oh well, it'll have to do.*

By the time I emerged from the bathroom, I had about four minutes to get my butt out the door. The walk to the facility would take *at least* fifteen minutes and the clock in the kitchen read 7:37. I popped a piece of bread into the toaster and pulled out the butter from the fridge. I swiped honey from the pantry when the toast popped up. I quickly added my toppings and grabbed a bottle of water, shoving my feet into my tennis shoes as I reached the door and pulled it open with one hand.

I squealed and dropped both the bottle of water as well as the toast I had been gripping with my teeth. Holden stood on the porch, a small smirk on his lips and a mischievous twinkle in his eye as he appraised his handiwork of scaring the crap out of me.

Morning. His hands were shoved deeply into jean pockets, his shoulders scrunched almost to his ears as he rocked back on his heels before tipping back forward. He looked so good, standing there all innocent-like on my front porch. Like he wasn't sure of the reception he would receive.

His demeanor was almost childlike, though nothing else about him could be confused for anything other than a virile male. *Ugh, Nat! Pull your head out!* I shook my head to dispel the distracting feelings, though the smoldering look in his vibrant blue eyes showed he knew my thoughts.

His black V-neck shirt was tight and left little to the imagination. Realizing I was once again sidetracked by all that was Holden, I blinked rapidly and looked away from his shirt, into his face. I needed to show that I could have a perfectly controlled conversation with his body—I mean, him. Him. I could hold a conversation with *him*.

"What are you doing here?"

Holden's mirth dimmed at my curt question. *I came by to escort you to training. You know, make sure you made it on time.* The laughter was back in his eyes by the end of his statement. It made me smile, just a little.

I crossed my arms at my chest. "Don't trust me to get there on my own, huh?"

Where's your overnight bag? He raised his eyebrows in question, knowing full well that I had forgotten.

"Damn it." I opened the door and waved him in as I turned on my heel and trudged back to my room, deciding to nosh on the floor toast as I went. The ten second rule applies after all, and in a Sage house, it could be indefinite. I now had about two minutes to leave and know for sure I wouldn't be late. I grabbed my backpack, shoving in a change of clothes, including undies, then ran to the bathroom and gathered essentials. Given my rushed timeframe, I was sure I missed something, but I'd worry about it later. Now, I needed to leave so I could arrive on time.

Turns out "training" meant running the Sages until we puked. At least, that's how it started. Commander James was letting Devlin handle the physical portion of our *assessment*. All the disdain from yesterday was back, and then some. He really hated that we Sages, and even Trent, had just about zero fitness capabilities.

Jade was severely asthmatic, Steve had a heart murmur and Trent, well, Trent was just out of shape. I had no room to talk. I didn't have any major physical ailments which kept me from exercise. No, it was just that I didn't want to broadcast my differences to other Sages. I guess I needed to stop thinking like that.

I wasn't Sage, not fully anyway. I was a hybrid. I could do this training thing. Eventually. So as Jade puffed her inhaler in huge gulps and Steve and Trent panted with me, recovering from their bouts of vomiting, I vowed to do all in my power to transcend the Sage label.

I needed to be more, to be *me*. With everything that entailed, even if I didn't know what that meant yet or that my jellified legs and cramping sides were telling me it was going to be a long, hard road.

I still needed to try to keep my healing abilities under wraps, at least for now. There was just too much animosity within the team, and that little bit of knowledge would only drive the wedge deeper, though, it may give Devlin and Steve some common ground. We would see if I could trust this *team* with my secret if we ever got past the divide of Sage versus Primal and were just Enhanced, or better yet—*human*. So I drew myself up through the pain that rocked my chest and legs, and waited for the next test.

The Sages continued to fail the tests that were presented. Pull ups? Nope. Ten push-ups? Nuh uh. Most of us did manage to hold the plank position for a minute, the first time. While I was strong, I was most definitely not in shape so my capacity was flimsy. Finally, Devlin had enough and threw up his hands in both defeat and disgust. He eyed all of us with barely concealed contempt, his blond hair long since disheveled from all the times he'd pushed his hands through the locks and grabbed hold as if he wanted to rip it out by the roots.

"We're done," he growled at us.

"Thank God." Trent breathed and flopped backward onto the blue squishy mat we were currently sprawled upon in various poses of defeat and recovery. I didn't fail as hard as Jade and Steve, though Trent outpaced me in some areas. I guess I fell in the middle of our pathetic ranks in terms of current ability. I knew I needed to rock this. The faster the better, so I vowed to work on training my body the way I had been taught to always expand my mind. I was strong, but I had no endurance or technique.

Here, in the confines of this sweat and heat filled center for physical excellence, I could truly explore my physical limits like I never could in the open. My parents had decided long ago, with the route our town had taken to separate within itself, that it would be best to not broadcast my differences, to not remind everyone that I was *more*.

But here, in the situation which I willingly put myself, I could bridge the divide. I could be both Sage and Primal. I could be useful, pivotal even. A lynch pin. Maybe we could begin to mend the divide the Enhanced found themselves in.

Someone snapped their fingers in my face. The loud sound, coupled with the gesture performed directly in my sight line was an effective tool for getting attention. Steve stood to my right, smiling like I had just gifted him with ammunition for many jokes to come.

I shoved him away with a little more force than I meant, which had him widening his eyes in surprise. His mind was rife with the realization that Toby's broken nose could easily happen to him if he let his guard down. Then he smiled. The thought of using his gift on me, to keep me from him, made his day. Seems we hadn't become buddy-buddy yet. *Oh well.*

After reporting our abysmal physical prowess to Commander James, we were all shuffled into a large SUV and driven to our temporary living quarters. The drive was short, only a few minutes toward the fields which surrounded Minefield.

There, standing sentinel was a massive white farmhouse, which looked to have been erected well before any of the Enhanced inhabited the area, at least a century in age. Its wraparound porch and divided windows were like a balm to my soul.

I loved it. I could picture myself on the porch in a rocking chair, listening to my music, or even the music of nature, which surrounded this place. If I thought I had liked the gardens, that paled in comparison to my instant affection for this place. I could only hope that being stuck here with six other feuding Enhanced would not dampen my enthusiasm.

Walking inside, we could see it had been updated with modern conveniences we thankfully still had in our little slice of containment: running water, indoor plumbing, and a fully functional kitchen. *Not that I'm a good cook.* Air conditioning wasn't central, but we had window units available.

We would get a stipend for food and necessities and could each claim a room to make our own. The house boasted eight bedrooms, though they were smaller in order to accommodate the number, as well as large sitting and dining areas.

This house was like many that Primal families grew up in. Seeing as they tended to have little problems with conception and birthing, their units needed to be larger to accommodate, so larger buildings that could house many people were erected in areas where Primals were heaviest. The various fields nearby housed many such abodes.

I left the group to wander by myself. Take in the feel of the old home. It was vibrant even in its age. I could imagine how it would look if we took a few steps to restore its neglected appearance. I wandered the long hall on the second floor which housed all eight bedrooms, four to each side. Right now, there was no difference in the rooms themselves, the blank walls, and dusty floors. I rubbed my nose to dispel the musty odor and keep the itchy twitch to a minimum.

But the *view*. Oh the view from the second room on the right. It was breathtaking. It looked out over the grounds, which were a bit wild and untamed in their current state but flanked by large trees. Trees which blocked said view from the other rooms on this side of the house. Seeing as I was the first to take a look, I figured it was safe to call "dibs" on this room.

I wandered closer to the dirt smeared window. It looked to have been a while since the house had anyone within its walls. I wondered how, and when, the commander had come onto this property. It was nothing like anything I had ever been in before.

Next I went in search of the bathrooms. All the while praying there was more than one. Turns out there were two upstairs. One on each end of the long hallway. The washrooms were nothing fancy and definitely not large, but they each had a sink, toilet and shower/tub combo, wasn't that all that mattered? Still, with only two, I could totally see arguments about bathroom time, and order, becoming an issue.

The flooring in the entire house was wood plank, I assumed original, with the exception of the bathrooms, which were vinyl. It was updated but still out of date and in need of some TLC. I would have to start small and hopefully convince the others to follow suit so we could get this place to the glory I pictured in my mind. The regal sentinel of this land. A haven for our rag tag group of feuding hotheads.

One could dream.

There you are. Holden found me in "my room" about twenty minutes later. I found a broom and had set to work, attempting to make my room presentable. The floor was now blissfully dirt and dust free. I didn't find any glass cleaner so I wet a rag in the bathroom and used it to work on the window.

I stood almost pressed to the clear pane as I watched the tall grass and trees outside sway in the wind, which swept through with decent force. I half turned, looking back at the doorway Holden was occupying, and cocked my head at him.

I hadn't "heard" him or anyone else in the mental voice of the others since I claimed my area, which reminded me this house had been modified to withstand Primals, so the walls and flooring most likely had either dampening or reinforced walls and floors, probably both. Heavy on the insulation too.

"Could you give me a hand?" I indicated the window. The frame was stuck and wouldn't open. I'm sure I could have gotten it open, but probably would have broken it in the process. I was hoping Holden could do it with a little more finesse. "I'm not sure I can get it open."

Holden nodded and stepped forward into the room, his strides long and purposeful. In what seemed like an instant, he was standing directly in front of me and I was once again caught up in his stare, in *him*. My heart pounded in my chest as he leaned forward, reaching around me with both arms. Almost like he was coming in for a hug. His eyes never left mine as his muscles tensed, pushing his body into me.

A loud crack from behind startled me from my haze. Holden pushed the window up with both hands, his arms still encasing me, trapping me. He stood there leaning. His eyes began their lightening, working to match the Caribbean Sea I had seen in pictures, holding me captive in a completely non-physical way.

I would still be trapped if he dropped his arms and allowed for me to leave. His thoughts were very enticing as they showed images of him reaching for my face tenderly and kissing the crap out of me. With the lyrical sounds of the insects buzzing from beyond the now open window, I would easily become lost in his kiss.

This your room then? His mental voice rumbled through my body, though it was not spoken, making me shiver. Holden had the most sensual voice I had ever heard, all deep and rough. I smiled to myself that I was the only one privileged with the knowledge of that fact.

He brought his hand to my face and brushed the corner of my mouth. *What is that smile for? It's a bit smug.* His hand slid across my jaw and clasped the back of my neck as his own smile kicked up in the corners.

A thump from the doorway drew my attention. Jade was there, dragging her large "overnight bag" past the door and down the hallway. The thump must have been when she got it to the landing at the top of the stairs. She looked a bit sheepish as she passed my doorway, throwing a mental "sorry" at me.

It was only then that I realized everyone else had now joined us in checking out the second story and discovering sleeping arrangements. No doubt everyone had seen Holden and me, seen the lust in our eyes, at least in mine, as I was the one facing the open doorway.

I hoped Holden's height and breadth hid the extent of our moment from the others. I didn't need another point of contention between us and I pushed out of the circle of Holden's embrace, putting much needed distance between us. Living with this many people would be rough, but being here with the knowledge that Holden was always only yards away...oh, man.

I went about rifling through my bag, pretending I was searching for things, making sure to keep my back to Holden. It would be nice when there was actually some place to *put* my things. Soon, I hoped, I would get proper furnishings and make this place feel more homey. After a few minutes, he wandered down the hall to check out his own area. I couldn't hear more than mental buzzing with the reinforced walls, making me like the place that much more. I assumed everyone else also surveyed the rooms. Most seemed to take it in stride, Steve did not.

Surprise, surprise.

"There's no master!" Steve's appalled voice rang through the entire upper floor and rolled down the stairs. With my window now open, I'm sure the neighbors would have heard had there been any. The nearly feminine shrieking continued as Steve ranted about his expectations in accommodations. I once again wondered what his family did. Why he seemed to have more than any of us were accustomed to.

Maybe we should regroup with the others? Apparently Holden had wandered back my way.

"Nah, I hear enough from here. In fact, I think I'll go downstairs now. I'm kinda hungry, you interested?" I raised my eyebrows and walked past him. Now that we were a respectable distance from one another, my heart was back to its normal, stable pace as I cleared the doorway and hooked left, clomping heavily as I headed toward the stairs. I certainly wouldn't win any awards for stealth.

As I descended, the mental voices of the rest of the team diminished to nothing. All but Holden's, who was keeping pace with me a few strides behind. I blushed thinking about living with him, well, not *with* him, but in the same house. The others wouldn't be a problem. I had no emotional ties to anyone other than Jade, and we were used to each other, respected each other's bubble. The rest of the squad? I was sure this would be an adjustment for everyone.

I wandered into the kitchen and looked at all the places possible for forage. The fridge was stocked with an array of food stuffs. I even spotted chocolate hiding in a crisper. I guess we needed to figure out good meals for large groups and a meal cooking rotation. There were enough of us that we could each take a day. Maybe today would be mine. I grabbed a pitcher of filtered water and shut the door, holding up my prize as a question for Holden. He nodded and opened an overhead cabinet which held glasses. Coincidence?

"Have you been here before?"

I have, he continued rummaging, *I helped with the remodel.*

"Oh? Something else you're good at?"

I am, yes. I've done many things in my life. Primals tend to be a little 'jack of all trades' when it comes to physical things. He shrugged.

"So are you a horse trainer? Did we ever establish that? Do you work at the barn?"

His back was to me, so he turned slowly to face me. His eyes bore into mine, so intense. Did he have another way to look? His shoulders were loose and he crossed his arms as he leaned against the counter, the move making his chest and arms bulge.

He was cut. Not near the size of Dane or even Devlin, but chiseled like a statue. Everything about him was rugged from his messed dark hair down to his worn work boots. His smile was warm and knowing when my gaze made it back to his, and I blushed. He chuckled mentally, the sound a pleasing rumble to me, though the only sound others heard was a rush of air escaping through his nose. Did I mention that I loved the fact that I alone could hear his sounds? The voice he would have had—should have had. "Well?"

I work the horses at the barn when I am between cases.

"Between cases? What do you mean?"

My ability makes me a handy undercover agent if needed, he shrugged and stood straight, once again at full height as he walked toward the refrigerator. He continued his thought as he pulled the door open and rummaged for whatever he wanted. *If I'm working on a case for which I need to not be me, occasionally, my time at the barn is much more limited.*

"To what extent?" I never thought about how to gather information other than to glean it mentally.

*Unfortunately, my usefulness is limited to more like surveillance...*he trailed off before gulping and beginning again. *The fact that I cannot speak, limits my effectiveness. I could not do long term and interactive cases, as most, no, all other Primals can speak.*

I hadn't thought of that, but he was right. I remember my thoughts when we first met, the concept of him being physically unable to speak was ludicrous and I kept jumping to the wrong conclusions about what I was hearing. "I'm sorry."

Why?

I looked at him again, now away from the refrigerator but with a host of things removed and sitting on the counter awaiting his ministrations. "I know how hard it is to be different." I tried to pull it off like I didn't care. He didn't believe the front.

Not your fault. His mind was buzzing, running through images like water, scenes where he was looked at with contempt or disdain. All because he was different and couldn't speak. A few lingering scenes caught my attention. There were a group of people, a family, who looked much like him. His family? Should I ask? I really wanted to know but decided today was not the day. I would wait until we were more comfortable with each other, comfortable enough to tell secrets. Lord knew I wasn't ready to spill mine.

I was saved from wanting to pry answers from him by the heavy footsteps and mental ruckus of the others as they descended the stairs, having apparently decided on room designations. The quiet was at once shattered with both actual noise and mental tirades.

This was going to take a lot of getting used to.

Holden continued on his endeavor to create a worthy meal. I felt bad that I hadn't tried, but I just wasn't feeling it today. I wasn't sure I'd be able to come up with anything edible, and I'd rather not have that worry on this first night of forced cohabitation with my team. I pulled my earbuds from my pocket and selected a playlist as I made my way out of the kitchen. The invasion was more than I wanted to endure at the moment, so I wandered toward the front door, remembering the picturesque porch and the chairs settled there.

I escaped the confines of the house just as the horde began inquiring about food and Holden's ability to make it. I probably should have stuck around to interpret but I wanted the quiet. The lull of the breeze and the nature that would envelop me outside. The screen slapped closed behind me and I settled into the white rocking chair off to the right. Closing my eyes, I pulled one earbud from its home letting the insects' song mingle with the lulling piano in my ears and drifted out of consciousness.

The creak of protesting wooden planks had me returning to awareness. Opening my eyes, I squinted into the fiery sunset and the silhouette of a broad man standing shadowed by its orange and pink intensity. The fact that the sun was burning into oblivion for the evening clued me into the fact that I must have dozed off.

The hypnotic sounds of the music in my ear, coupled with the buzzing and chirping of insects and birds was too much for me to combat. Combine that with my mental, and for once- physical depletion, and I had succumbed.

The mental signature of the large shadow pegged him as Commander James. I shielded my eyes and looked into his chiseled features. He looked down at me from the top of the porch steps, having ascended the stairs before alerting me to his presence. "Evening, Commander."

"Evening, Miss Dae," He smirked kindly at me. "How was your nap?"

"Lovely, thank you."

"I'm glad you like it here." He put his hands on his hips and surveyed the surrounding area, closing his eyes and mentally reveling in the peacefulness, much as I had done. I knew I liked him, though I think it was a fairly Primal response to like being out in nature, hearing nothing but what surrounded you, none of which you had a hand in.

"So what brought you back, Commander?"

"Oh, I intended to give you all a bit of time to look around and get acquainted. I always meant to return."

"Do you know this house?" He nodded. "Linens? The beds are bare. I'm sure the kitchen and washrooms are lacking as well. I didn't think to look honestly." I shrugged. I had only been concerned with establishing my claim on the room I wanted, then choosing to escape the ruckus of the entire team crammed into the kitchen.

"C'mon, I'll show you the cleaning and linen closets. There should be enough that everyone has one. We knew we'd have a full house when the squad was approved." He turned from me and continued to the door, waving over his shoulder that I should follow. I did. It wasn't until I entered the house that I registered the heavenly scents of what Holden had obviously conjured up as a meal and the realization that I was famished.

I always ate more than Sages normally did. I assumed due to my Primal genes. The fact that I hadn't eaten since this morning as Holden and I had left for my first day of "training," made me feel like my stomach was going to begin consuming itself in revolt, especially now that I smelled the enticing aroma of pork chops and mashed potatoes.

I swiped my forearm across my mouth to make sure I wasn't drooling, and if I was, to clean up the resulting mess. Commander James walked purposefully into the kitchen, gestured for Holden to follow, then headed to the living area where I stood and the rest of the team lounged in various degrees of activity.

Well, they had been until we walked in. Once Commander James broke the doorway plane, the murmuring and discussion ceased. We all looked upon the commander with curiosity, waiting for whatever he deemed us worthy of discussing.

"Have the arrangements been hammered out?"

The room nodded silently, though a couple furtive looks and puckered brows appeared. Just about everyone shot glares at Steve who just crossed his arms and huffed. He was still pouting about the "accommodations." Spoiled and entitled. I wasn't entirely sure how that happened in a town where money was minimal, but I guess his online shopping abilities were hearty.

Commander James nodded and continued to ignore the heavy silence. "Good, follow me and I will point out all the storage areas and you can begin to settle in." We all filed into a line and trudged after him as he pointed out where necessities were stored. At the end of the tour, we once again congregated in the living room as Holden stole into the kitchen. A moment later, his mental voice reached out to me, letting me know dinner was ready and to move everyone into the dining area.

I relayed the message and made my way in that direction, figuring I could get the table set up for serving, especially since Holden cooked. We would definitely need to make a schedule for meals and chores, because as I looked around at the present company, I knew we would have a fight on our hands about something or other; always. *Ugh.* I really just wanted my own place to come and be alone. To not have to worry about anyone but myself, but it wasn't in the cards just now, and I would need to deal with it. *Hello, headphones.*

Dinner was a quiet affair, mainly due to the fact that Commander James was still present. No one wanted to bicker like children, at least not when the parent was watching. I kept my earbuds in to ignore the mental bellyaching and rambling which was buzzing inside my head. While the others may be enjoying the quiet, it was never truly quiet for me. I ate my meal quickly, as well as a second helping, then scurried away to ready my bed with sheets, and myself with a shower. I really wanted to take my time soaking in a bath, but I knew that was just a dream.

CHAPTER 21

THE MORNING ONCE AGAIN came too early, bringing with it the downside to picking a room on the east side of the house and being unobstructed by trees. The sun's rays beat in through the now cleaned window and danced across my eyelids, clearly laughing at my attempts to hide from their brilliance. I *really* hoped those furnishings came soon, and included drapes.

Supposedly movers would arrive with all our belongings and furniture tomorrow. Couldn't come soon enough. These bright and early mornings made me feel like a vampire. I fought the urge to hiss at the sun and dive into the safety of the shadows hiding in the corners of my room.

I groaned as I once again began my morning routine, though this was the first to be had in my new "home." It was still weird to think of anywhere other than my parents' house, the house I had grown up in, as home. Maybe one day I would feel the term appropriate for this place, but it wasn't today. I loved the old farmhouse and felt the beauty of the place in my bones, but it was not yet home. I needed to work a bit in that direction, maybe once I put some more effort into giving it a bit of a facelift and I could lay claim to its appearance, I would feel more settled.

Oh well, a problem for another day. As for this day, I once again needed to work on my skills and training. I needed to work toward not being a liability to other squad members. Truthfully, it was what we all needed to strive for, though I wasn't sure how many actually would.

I pawed through the small backpack I had brought as an overnight bag and pulled out clothes for the day's activities. As I tugged on my stretchy pants, the others' buzz continued to grow in intensity as they awakened and prepared for the day ahead.

I found my music player sitting atop my cordless charging station where it spent its nights and tucked it into my pants. Plugging myself in again. I breathed out a breath, puffing out my cheeks and soaked in the head bopping tunes wafting to my ears, singing about how the beat makes you move.

"Let's do this."

I proceeded to the end of the hall toward one of the endcap washrooms, every other step creaking across the old wood flooring, only to find the room already occupied. *So it begins.* After finding that the other bathroom was likewise unavailable, I trudged slowly down the stairs and toward the kitchen where I hoped to find some form of sustenance to make my brain and body function for the day ahead. Luckily my healing had kicked in at some point in the last twenty-four hours and I wasn't sore from yesterday's paces. I was ready to improve upon my performance.

The days continued much the same. Every morning we woke and prepared for that day's training. Some days Devlin was our mentor and we were drilled with fitness and strength training, what little most of us could do at this point. Poor Jade was using her inhaler as an extension of her arm, nearly as often as breathing on such days, but she delivered incredible death glares to anyone who tried to tell her to slow down or sit it out. She was just as determined to prove she could hang as I was.

The others had yet to learn that Jade didn't fail. It didn't matter the task, she would not allow herself defeat. It just so happened that until recently, such tasks had been set for her by Sage standards. Standards for which she was more than able to match. These physical trials however, were something else entirely. Her body would revolt one of these times, and I hoped we would get her back from it.

I couldn't lose Jade.

Dane began to work with us at times as well. He wanted us to be conscious of our surroundings, aware of the people and things around us. To feel, see, taste, smell, and hear as much as possible. His lessons were often just as painful as Devlin's. He liked to creep up on us and blare a horn in our ear or shock us if we didn't catch him. One time, we walked straight into a sulfurous cloud as we attempted to track him, not one of the Sage recruits caught it prior to being engulfed in its smelly clutches.

Knowing that our current case involved mental deceit, Jade and I led training on focusing the mind onto something you *knew*, something which brought peace to each individual. We came up with the "happy place" visualization. Much like the cartoon boy who never grew up instructed others to "think happy thoughts," we too envisioned something our soul craved.

Each was different and personal to the user, but its purpose was simple: to ground us. To create something to focus on that could be controlled and hopefully bring back the senses. The key word in there being hopefully.

So we learned. Slowly, but we learned all the same. In the first couple weeks of enforcer training, we heard nothing which gave an indication that our illusionist had struck again, though we couldn't figure out why he wouldn't. He had been successful and extreme in his ministrations prior. I knew he wasn't dormant; it was only a matter of ferreting out what he had done.

Trent was heading up those attempts, reading through all reports and incidents which street enforcers responded to, but we wouldn't know for sure until I was able to sense the mental signatures.

If Trent found an incident or report of something which may have been the work of the illusionist, I was dispatched to investigate. Unfortunately my partner on such forays was Devlin. Holden wasn't happy with that. But with him not able to conduct interviews, he wasn't much more than an extra body in the room that made people uncomfortable or paranoid. Commander James had decreed that his time was better served elsewhere.

It didn't matter that much at this point as we had yet to come across an instance which I was helpful. Devlin still treated me as pretty much useless.

This time we were rolling up to the residence of a Sage who had been assaulted by an NE, both were women. This was different and caught Trent's attention. Most physical altercations involved at least one Primal. Neither Sage nor Non-Enhanced were often found having gone to such

226

extremes. So again, this was an oddity which fell into our realm of suspicion for the illusionist to have been involved in.

Devlin and I meandered up the sidewalk to the small but tidy home, one of many such homes on this street and the surrounding others. The neighborhood was definitely Sage territory and I could feel multiple sets of eyes on our backs as we made our way to the door.

"I always get an itch between my shoulder blades when I have to do home visits to a Sage residence," Devlin mumbled, shuddering from the sensation as he pushed the button for the doorbell.

"Yeah, this is the first time I've felt truly out of place in a neighborhood such as this." Just as I finished my thought, the door opened to expose a small, mousy Sage woman with large dark eyes which were magnified from behind bottle glass eyewear.

"Jessica?" I asked agape. The fact that I now stood in front of the indifferent Sage from the hospital a couple weeks back threw me. I hadn't expected to come across anyone I knew in our search, though I had no idea why it hadn't occurred to me. The fact that she wasn't even an acquaintance, but really just someone I had contact with one time, didn't matter.

It didn't matter that she had not been pleasant at the onset of our search. The fact that she now stood in front of me, with her left arm wrapped in a white plaster cast from thumb to mid-forearm and multiple long scratches marring her left cheek in angry reddish-brown scabs, it hit me. He could affect *anyone*. He, or she, could just have easily targeted my dad or my mom.

"Yes." With that one word, all the haughtiness she had shown at the hospital came flooding into her demeanor. She was not cowering from Devlin or the fact that enforcers were on her stoop.

"Miss Fellers, we are here to discuss the incident which occurred yesterday as you were leaving your workplace."

Nodding once, Jessica opened the door wide enough to allow Devlin and me entry into her home, closing it behind us as we cleared the threshold. Waving us to a small but pristine sitting area to our left, she took a seat on a worn-out armchair, waiting for Devlin and me to find our own.

Apparently there would be no offer of refreshments. I wish I were surprised. Once we were all seated, Jessica proceeded to recite the story of how a woman who was also leaving the hospital suddenly attacked her from behind just as Jessica had reached her vehicle.

I watched the incident play out in Jessica's mind: Her attacker, a woman who was much stronger than she appeared in her compact mom-like packaging, grabbed Jessica's wrist and wrenched hard, blinding pain traveling up Jessica's arm making her hand virtually useless.

As Jessica screamed in pain, she reflexively used her telekinetic ability to throw the woman away from her. The woman was close enough to connect again as she was thrust backward to heavily impact a vehicle in the next row, her fingernails raking deeply across Jessica's left cheek. Sobbing, Jessica ran toward two officers who had noticed the commotion after her scream.

"They ran to apprehend the crazy lady. I didn't look back, just went to intake and tried to be seen immediately." She huffed. "I got out of the waiting room quickly enough, but it still took like thirty minutes before I got my wrist set."

"Did you know the woman? Ever have any interactions with her that you can recall?" Devlin may have been the model of professionalism by all appearances, but mentally he huffed as he slid his eyes my direction. When he remembered who he was stuck with for this interview, he shut down his wandering thoughts, but not before he berated himself for forgetting he was tethered to a telepathic Sage trainee. I had to smile at that, it was fun to ruffle the big man.

"I don't see many people other than those who come through the hospital bruised and bleeding…or those seeking patients. I don't really pay a lot of attention."

It was my turn to snort, drawing a glare from Devlin's pretty face and a confused one from my dear friend Jessica. Apparently she didn't remember me either. All good, I could live with that.

"Was there anything different about that day? Anyone seem upset at you? Any odd interactions?" Devlin stayed on track.

Jessica seemed even more bored, her air of contempt a physical thing that weighed heavily between the three of us. "Odd things?" She tapped her foot.

"Anyone approach you or seem upset after having encountered you?" Devlin tried really hard to keep the annoyed timbre from his voice.

"I dunno," *shrug*, "Some guy asked me out at lunch." She preemptively righted her glasses and fluttered those too big eyes. Color me surprised when she acted as though nothing about the encounter was worth her notice. *Poor schmuck.*

"Did you say yes?" We knew the answer from her body language but needed confirmation. This might be a good lead. The quelling look I received was par for the course. All interactions with Jessica were like pulling teeth, but we needed this lead. As much as we could get. My telepathy might just get this done for us.

"How did the man take it? Did you know him?" I kept my mouth shut and let Dev take the lead, he was the one who knew the routine. I needed to soak up these procedures as much as possible while I still had a mentor.

"I didn't stick around to see how he took it, honestly. My break was over," she spoke as if we were idiots. In fact, her thoughts were saying the word over and over in reference to us.

"Do you know him? Has he approached you before?"

"I don't even remember what he looked like. Wasn't worth my time." Another shrug.

She wasn't lying. Her thoughts didn't show any features, nothing remarkable. Just a white lab coat and dark hair, not nearly as helpful as I had hoped.

Seeing as we had what we could use from her as a witness, we stood and excused ourselves, Devlin exchanging pleasantries as we moved toward the front door.

Just as we stepped back out onto the porch, Jessica voiced the thought that had been niggling at her since seeing me with Devlin on the stoop. "Since when are any other than Primals, enforcers?"

"Thank you for your time, Miss Fellers. We have apprehended and detained the woman who assaulted you, we are heading to her next."

Feeling slighted, Jessica's mental rampage was circled around Primals in general, her bigotry making my temper once again rear its snarly head. "Now, Miss Fellers, it is not very polite, nor *Sage-like* to be so vulgar." Dev actually coughed a laugh at that, though I was sure he'd deny it.

Indignant, Jessica spluttered, "I don't know what you're talking about."

I shrugged, turned from the mousy Sage whose porch steps we still adorned and began my descent to the squad SUV at the curb. I wanted to interview the aggressor. She was the one who could tell us if there was an outside force at play in this incident, though we would still most likely be blind as to the perpetrator.

I reached the imposing vehicle before Devlin, and wrenched the door open with more force than was strictly necessary in my haste. Once I was seated and buckled snugly into the cushioned seat, Devlin made it into the driver's seat. Without looking my way, he asked if I gleaned anything interesting and grabbed the com to Commander James. I relayed the info I got from Jessica, though it wasn't very helpful.

"I'll suggest they send Dane to do a Q&A session at the hospital. Ask about who would have access to the cafeteria. See if we can get Trent to pull up video. Get a picture and name for this mystery scorned lover."

"Smart." I had to give Devlin credit. He wasn't just some hormone addled Neanderthal. He had some sense of pertinent information. Sometimes he even noted things Sages would overlook as unimportant. I hated the idea of admiring him, but I kinda did. *Ugh.* Dev put the com in his pocket after relaying our findings and suggested routes moving forward. Dane and Holden would go to the hospital and try to find

Jessica's less than ideal man. We were closing in, even if it didn't feel like we had anything to go on.

As I mulled over Jessica's comments about her shooting down a suitor, it dawned on me. "Holy crap." He was watching me *at the hospital.* From what Jessica said, he definitely appeared to work there in some capacity.

"What?" Dev seemed annoyed at my outburst. "What are you freaking out about over there?"

"Jessica's story made me realize this guy definitely has an affiliation to the hospital."

"What, why?" His mental state was none too kind toward me at the moment, making me want to take back my nice thoughts about the not being a Neanderthal.

"When he was watching me that night in the hospital parking lo—"

"WHAT?!"

Uh oh. Looks like I may have messed up a smidge. I cautiously looked Devlin's irate direction in the driver's seat. Still feet from me, his presence, and anger swelled to fill the cab.

"Um, the night Rolph Duggan was hit, my telepathy clued me in to his mental signature," I said sheepishly.

Dev had a death grip on the steering wheel, and I feared I'd hear it crack any moment now. "And you didn't feel the need to *tell* anyone about this?" He was running through a litany of curses and fantasies of just what he'd like to do to me in this moment.

I was totally at a loss. It truly hadn't, nothing had come of it, had it? Then I thought back to a few random incidents that occurred after that encounter. Maybe they hadn't been so random after all? I knotted my hands together and looked at my lap to avoid Devlin's stare. For the first time since this journey began for me, I truly felt like a child who knew *nothing*. I would take my licks.

Dev blew out a weighty breath and knocked his head repeatedly against the wheel. "All right. It's done, but dammit Sage, *think*! We could have had this guy already." He took another deep breath before shooting his eyes my direction. At my completely confused look, he dumbed it down, "I could have put Holden on you, followed you. Looked for anything, *anyone*, off. We'll inform the team when we get back to the CP."

I blew out my own breath at his declaration. I could have stopped this? Jessica wouldn't have been hurt, no one else at risk. I was expecting much worse, closer to the pain his mind was conjuring for me, but his words hit just as hard. Everything from here on out which was caused by the illusionist, I could have prevented.

The SUV roared to life, announcing its newly awakened state with audible grumblings as Devlin pulled away from the curb. Next stop: Minefield enforcement holding cells, my first visit.

Within minutes, our silent car ride, or at least our *verbally* silent car ride came to an end as we pulled up at the small station house about a block off of Main. It was a fairly central location which made response time pretty low around Minefield for reported incidents. Now we needed to get to holding and speak to the attacking woman. Was it bad that I hoped she had been tampered with? To me, it meant we only had one psycho to worry about at the moment and not many. It made me feel slightly better to think that. So I took a deep breath, said a silent prayer, and exited the vehicle behind Devlin.

The station house was much different from the command center the team currently inhabited, all desks, gleaming floors and uniformed Primals, the case information tucked safely into manila files instead of on boards for all to see. The smell of body odor and stale coffee mingled in the air.

There were about fifteen people other than Devlin and me, each in various stages of paperwork. The mental voices were many, but quiet as they seemed focused on mundane tasks. Devlin asked a younger Primal male, who looked a bit wet behind the ears and manning the intake area, for Jessica's assailant be brought into Interview Room 1.

A few minutes later, Devlin was ensconced in a rickety plastic chair situated across from a fairly petite and generally unremarkable NE female in a silent standoff. I was again, standing behind a window pane in an adjacent room, listening. She was confused as to why she was being held, why the "child abuser" was nowhere to be found, and what we could want from her.

"Why did you assault Jessica Fellers outside the hospital yesterday evening?"

The woman focused her attention on Devlin, narrowing her eyes in contempt before speaking slowly, as if he were of no consequence. "Is that her name?" She tensed. "She was berating a child, had raised her hand to strike the boy." As per usual when recalling an intense situation, she visualized it again, raising her ire, much as the first assault perpetrator had. But it was perfect. The mental frequency, the imagery, was the work of our illustrious illusionist.

I breathed a small sigh of relief, then instantly felt guilty. I tapped on the glass two times to indicate that I had confirmation of tampering, and

234

Devlin continued his interview by clueing the woman in on the fact that what she saw was fabricated, after which she crumbled into disbelief and began to sob. There was now one more NE in the world who would distrust enhanced. This one was stuck with us in exile.

I left the station with a heavy heart and dragging feet, though I was glad to only have one case at the moment. I hated that we were being given a bad name. There were bad apples everywhere, in every town, and of every race. I couldn't let it get to me, and the ninnies couldn't condemn us all.

That night, my dad surprised me by bringing enough of Mom's homemade meatballs and apple pie for the whole squad. I loved that he came by, that I still had the opportunity to see him outside of work. I missed him, I missed my mother as well, though to a lesser degree which made me sad. I needed to try harder. If I could shield my telepathy from doing its thing so completely, maybe she wouldn't feel as uncomfortable around me, but tonight I wanted to focus on having my father here.

We laughed and ate as a unit, for once forgetting our differences and acting as if we were in fact a team, after of course, I was berated by everyone for not having the mental faculty to think an encounter with our suspect was important information which needed to be shared amidst those attempting to capture him. Their words. After the tongue lashing and notification that Holden would be my ever-changing shadow, it was thankfully dropped and many embarrassing training stories were told, inducing several flushes of embarrassment from each member and guffaws from the others.

At about twenty one hundred hours, aka nine p.m., Dad decided to call it a night and gave me his trademark bear hug as I walked him to the front door.

"Love you, baby girl." He kissed my forehead, gave me a little squeeze and pulled open the door to head into the night. I stepped onto the porch after him, lifting my hand in a farewell wave as I closed my eyes and allowed the night sounds to envelope me. Crickets and bullfrog songs rang through my head and released the last of the day's lingering tension. Tomorrow was Holden's day to impart his wisdom upon me. I couldn't wait.

CHAPTER 22

HOLDEN TOOK HIS TRAINING time at the barn, telling me that understanding body language and communicating with an animal would help me in reading people. While I could read others' minds, their actions were often not telegraphed, so I thought it couldn't hurt. Raven was who he'd always bring out for me to groom and work, but I made sure to still lavish attention on Jasper. I couldn't have my big buddy mad at me.

The first several visits consisted solely of grooming and guiding Raven at a walk from the ground. Next, I was allowed to saddle him and put him through actual work on a long line. It taught me the cues and body language which Raven responded to, as well as what his body did and how his mind reacted; useful for reading body language and consequences, especially from afar. Finally, Holden allowed me into the saddle.

I was so excited, I kissed him before I thought better of it. He smiled triumphantly, and I blushed as I came to the flat of my feet.

"So, uh, yeah. You're going to let me up there today?" I pointed to Raven's back as he stood quietly in the ties awaiting our ministrations. "Like really? I get to drive?"

Well, I'll let you up there, yes, but you're going to be on the lunge line...in the round pen.

"Ugh." I rolled my eyes. The round pen was just that: a circular pen just big enough for the horses to exercise without the human losing control. It had close quarters and ensured that the horse couldn't ignore someone in the center.

The lunge line was like a really long leash. It was insulting. I glared at Holden, showing my displeasure at the thought with my expression; or so I hoped. "I'll give you the round pen, but I don't need the leash." I felt like a child in a tantrum. All I needed was to stomp my feet.

No deal. This is your first time up there, Nat. I won't risk it. I won't risk you. The thought once again set his eyes blazing silver as he looked at me with furrowed brows, determination written across his hardened features, matching his protective thoughts.

"You really don't like that thought do you?" He shook his head slowly, deliberately. "Why? I don't see your eyes change at the thought of anyone else getting hurt. Why me?"

Taking a swaggering step toward me, Holden invaded my bubble of personal space. My chest nearly touching his, I began to labor for breath as I looked into his still blazing eyes, which refused to release me from their hold. His body seemed to swell, to get even taller while we stood in silence.

I care about you, Nat. The others I feel responsible for, but you? You mean more to me. I couldn't bear it if you were hurt. Especially if that hurt was my doing.

"Even if I get hurt, Holden, it wouldn't be your fault. Never *your* fault. My decisions are my own." Then I added deliberately, making sure he could see my conviction, then brought my palm to rest on his solid chest, feeling his heart gallop at our topic of conversation. "I'm not as breakable as I seem." I couldn't tell him the extent the truth of that statement held, not yet, but I wanted him to believe that I could do this, any of it. *All* of it.

We stood in the musty barn, dust floating like butterflies around us in beams of sunlight shooting through the open stall doors. The smell of dirt, sweat, animal, and pine mingled to create the calming scent I always relaxed into while here. I breathed it in, trying not to show just how much I needed him to believe in me. He must have gotten the message because he deflated a bit and looked down at his feet. His hands now rested on his hips—those narrow, glorious hips—as he kicked his boot back and forth through the dirt, a "line in the sand" at his side.

Making a decision, he brought his eyes back to mine, brows furrowed in displeasure. *All right,* he articulated. *I will do my best to allow you to make your own decisions—your own mistakes.* He raised his finger, and an eyebrow at me, clicking his tongue when I attempted to interject, *But if you wish to do anything more than* walk *Raven from his back, you will be on a lunge line today.*

Well, crap. I really thought I had him softening. I felt his conviction, so I knew if I pushed any more, he would just tell me no and be done. I couldn't have that. I needed to get up there. Needed to feel that thousand pound animal underneath me and have faith that our communication was solid, that we would take care of each other. A true partnership. One like the squad needed to embody.

One day, maybe.

Forty-five minutes later, I gingerly dropped from Raven's back and into the dirt of the round pen. A rather large dust cloud wafting up from my not so graceful departure. Raven turned his head toward me and tossed it twice. I think he was happy I was off. Riding the horse was much harder than Holden made it look.

First off, the animal was so big, that every step sent my body into a dip, and my reaction was to grip. Gripping made your body tighten and tip, which in turn severely hindered my base support and ability to influence the horse. Oh, and FYI, gripping makes horses go faster. Learned that as well. Trotting was pretty smooth on Raven until the gripping sped him up, then I went a little tipsy.

I would never admit it to Holden, but I was glad he had a hold of the lunge line today. Raven tolerated me well, but when needed, Holden was there to bring him back. I used and stretched muscles I didn't even know I had, and I knew without a doubt, I would be sore tomorrow. At least until my healing kicked in. It was nice that I didn't have the recovery time the others had, but it was also suspicious. I had taken to attributing it to my Primal heritage, saying that Primals recovered faster, which was true. They didn't need to know that mine was so much more than the standard repair rate.

So far there had been no instances where I really had to explain why one moment there was a wound and the next not. I hoped I could continue with the evasion, but something told me my time was running out. My only hope was that whoever witnessed my ability would keep it in confidence. I didn't need the light shined on me any more than it would be one of these days for working in a physical capacity.

Don't get me wrong, the Sages who knew that my father, and therefore, I, was a hybrid, didn't like me solely for that fact. Mention the mind reading thing and I was a plague, not a gift, so there wasn't much different on that front…but if they figured out I could heal physical ailments faster? I think overzealous Sages, who could be almost psychopathic in their clinical assessments and demeanor, would want to use me as a lab rat. To dissect why I am the way I am, to advance themselves. They wouldn't see the problem with experimenting on me.

So I hid my healing, which was why I had not been allowed to do physical things while a part of the Sage community of Minefield. Now that was shot, and I could only hope that things worked out, that people were better than we gave them credit for.

Holden and I finished cleaning Raven and set him loose in the pasture for the afternoon, where the first thing he did was trot to a big dirt patch near the water trough—and roll. I had learned that horses apparently detested cleanliness. If their stall was clean, it was their cue to urinate or defecate in the middle of said spotlessness, and if you had rinsed them off or given a full-on bath, you could bet it wouldn't be five minutes before they were rolling around in the dirt. Case and point: Raven at that moment.

Crazy creatures.

I turned away as Raven finished his ministrations and ran off farther into the pasture to join the others already happily munching on the grass.

I saw what Holden did at that moment—me. My blondish hair was a mess in its ponytail, cheeks flushed, and blue-green eyes bright. The kicker was the small smile tugging at my lips. I looked happy. I was happy. There was even a dimple.

I liked where I was at in my life for once. I was so glad I had decided to move forward with both the horses and the task force. I'm pretty sure the glow that exuded from me wasn't actually there though. That little detail being only a part of Holden's thoughts.

I looked away, finding a nasty looking smudge of something smeared across my left collar and shoulder. There were little orange chunks clinging to my shirt amidst greenish looking slobber. *Awesome.* I had been inducted into Raven's slobbery affections when I started bringing him carrots. He loved to rub his face on me after I had given him his treats, leaving trails of multi colored, and textured, slime in his wake.

Wanna grab some lunch?

"Sure, where?"

We began a slow stroll toward the barn to continue our clean up, trucking by a couple people on their way to the riding areas. I definitely saw more people now that I wasn't only passing through on my way home in the afternoons. I didn't get many sideways looks either because these people didn't know me, didn't know I was a Sage hybrid. My height kinda ruled me out for the norm, making my time here that much better.

What sounds good? Pizza? Raised eyebrows accompanied the question as he looked down at me. Holden was totally craving pizza, so much so, he was practically salivating.

I chuckled. "Sure, pizza sounds great."

We gathered all the paraphernalia from today's activity. Holden grabbing the grooming box as I cleaned up Raven's "mess" in the aisle.

Reaching the truck, Holden unlocked and opened my door, waving me up into the passenger seat, closing it once I settled. Another new thing, we had an old truck we used now. It was too far to walk from the farmhouse to town in any kind of timely manner, so we had a few older, but reliable vehicles, which were for the partner groups of our team.

This truck was an older model, which had been cast off by its former owner, thus relegating it to Minefield life. That's how we got most our vehicles, especially seeing as we didn't earn money in the amounts the outside world did. So, sometimes people would donate their old vehicles to the programs which provided them for our towns. They weren't usually pretty, and definitely weren't fancy but they worked when needed, and I used it now that I wasn't living within a mile of all my trafficked areas.

As we drove toward Godfather's, a great little pizza place with a very cliché name, I pulled my music player and earbuds from the console and tucked them into my pocket. I wanted to give Holden my attention so I tried not to use the musical escape route around him unless I needed it.

We were becoming more comfortable around each other and having fewer awkwardly heated moments, especially at the farmhouse. The others had stumbled across us gazing at each other, or even kissing, too many times and now we were much more aware, and selective in our isolation. In turn, we had an easier, more fluid relationship. We could be ourselves, the selves that not too many truly saw. It was glorious and made me appreciate him even more.

We exited the truck at the curbside parking in front of the pizzeria. I hopped down from the high vehicle just as Holden rounded the hood and stepped onto the walkway in front of me. He made a gentlemanly sweeping gesture, grandly allowing me to enter before him. I shook my head and chuckled at his antics. "Why, thank you, good sir!"

I secretly loved this playful side of Holden, the one no one took the time to see. I loved that I got to peek behind the curtain, that he felt comfortable enough to let me. I opened the door and breathed in the fragrant aromas which immediately engulfed me: marinara, melted cheese, garlic, rising dough and various meats. *Drool.*

Holden inhaled deeply and closed his eyes, savoring the smells just as I had before putting his hand at the small of my back and walking us farther into heaven. We ordered a large supreme with extra cheese and a basket of garlic knots and topped it off with iced tea. We meandered to a small table in the corner, away from the doors and ovens and found a seat.

The small, red, vinyl-covered chair Holden chose looked to barely hold his weight and creaked ominously as he settled into it. He balanced there for a moment, his arms spread wide, like he was waiting for it to come out from underneath him at any moment. When it held, Holden settled his weight fully, depositing his keys and phone on the small remaining portion of table top before leaning forward on his elbows, his hands clasped one over the other as he watched me with a twinkle in his eye.

"What?" I drew out the word, wary of the look he was giving me. He just smirked and reached forward to take a long pull of his iced tea. I did the same, looking around the restaurant, taking in the ambiance.

This place definitely tried to emulate the things which movies and such showed to be inherently "Italian." I didn't know the owner so I wasn't sure if there were any Italians in their family tree, or even if those stereotypes rang true. That was my major problem with our living arrangements in Minefield; this was it—all we ever knew.

I had never seen an ocean, or even a lake. I didn't know if Italian food was the same in Italy or if what we knew was just some poor imitation of greatness, though I assumed the latter to be true.

There were so many places, so many things that we would never see. I could never experience different accents and cultures or see ancient ruins…tropical paradises were completely out of the question. I had never seen a lion or even a starfish, other than via the internet. What I wouldn't give to see the glistening waters of the open ocean.

We were more ignorant than babes.

I was jolted from my perusal of the red checkered tablecloths and jolly fat guy in an apron and white chef hat—their logo, as our pizza was unceremoniously dropped onto our little table by the rather unenthusiastic girl who delivered it. We thanked her as she wandered behind the counter into the kitchen, receiving no acknowledgement of our gratitude.

Holden dug in with gusto, grabbing the slice which looked to have the heaviest load of toppings and taking a large bite. The funny thing about mental conversations was that you could still hold them while eating. Well, others could. No one heard my thoughts, so I still had to speak. This meant that I did not have the luxury of being understood or even polite by speaking while attempting to chew my cud. So I let Holden talk and relegated myself to answering via head nod.

You did really well today, Nat. You recognized when you were getting unbalanced and corrected. That is very good. That awareness will allow you to make corrections much sooner, keep you from getting hurt. All this while chewing vigorously,

Raven responded fluidly to you. How did it feel for you? Is it what you expected? He once again raised his eyebrows in question, as seemed to be his go to expression when inquiring.

"It was a very weird sensation at first. The dip from side to side was disorienting. I don't know why I wasn't expecting it." I shrugged and picked the onions off my slice of pizza. "It was cool to feel how each thing I did garnered a response from Raven, good or bad." I blushed remembering when I got a little worried and squeezed him. The resulting rush of forward motion was a great reminder of just how much power I was attempting to harness, foolish really.

Holden's thoughts had drifted back to my lesson, his thoughts like a highlight reel of the time we spent with Raven. I blushed again. I looked wrecked, hair flying all directions, cheeks flushed. Many times, I had a pretty intense look of concentration, creases between my eyebrows and biting my lower lip. But again, Holden seemed to still find me attractive. The images were undoubtedly better than real life.

Suddenly, another mental signature broke through my reel, one I hadn't felt in weeks.

Our illusionary.

We were in a corner which was away from the counter where a youngish man stood perusing the menu above the register. I kicked Holden under the table to get his attention. I knew we needed to do something, I just didn't know what yet. I leaned forward, nearly hugging the tabletop in my attempt to be close enough to whisper to Holden.

"The illusionist is here."

Holden cocked his head to the side, a very animal like gesture, as I assumed he listened. He knew better than to turn and look. He trusted that I was sure.

"What do we do?" I was looking over Holden's shoulder to the smaller man still standing at the counter. He was short and thin with thinning dark hair, which didn't match his younger features. The man looked to be maybe late twenties, but it was hard to tell from this angle. All I really saw was a profile.

Sharp would be how I described his features—chin, cheekbones, nose—all seemed thin and pointed. Much like the wicked witch in an old movie I had seen as a child, and I wondered if there were any warts on his face.

I couldn't tell what color his eyes were from where we sat and I really didn't want to draw attention to myself, as I had a feeling he knew who I was and had no way to know if he knew I was enforcing. I remember him watching me outside the hospital, had he seen me with the commander and Holden? Would he recognize Holden now?

I looked back at Holden and gasped, shooting away from the table and back into my chair. He had changed. No longer was the man across from me tall and broad with dark hair and intense blue eyes.

Now there was a man who was much narrower, though he had a rounder face, gray eyes and thin lips. A dusting of light freckles sprinkled his face and reddish blonde hair sat thickly upon his head. It was a bit creepy just how much he could change his appearance. He didn't look like a Primal outright anymore. He was still too tall and...rotund to be a Sage, but he could pull off a ninny with this look. I found this version of

Holden much less appealing, and cringed a bit at the thought. This was so not the time for superficial realizations.

I'm going to send a message to the commander and ask for backup. We don't know why he's here, and right now we have the element of surprise. We don't want to lose it. We don't want him using his ability to cause more harm because of us.

I nodded and tried to nonchalantly hide my face behind Holden while continuing to keep an eye on Mr. Illusionary.

Up at the counter now, giving his order, he was nearly at the edge of my mental range but still came in clearly. Our corner spot was great for privacy, not as great for invading it. He was getting riled up a bit. The girl who served Holden and me was now taking his order with even less enthusiasm than she'd shown us. She wouldn't give Mr. Illusionary the courtesy of direct eye contact, instead talking while looking at the counter or register.

"Excuse me, but can you at least pretend to be interested in my order so I can pretend that when I get it, and it is not correct, that you were not the responsible party for the fumble." There were plenty of insults laced throughout that inquiry but the girl didn't seem to notice.

"Small spinach, tomato, and chicken pizza with extra cheese," the teen drolled in a monotone voice, obviously unconcerned.

"No," he attempted an intimidating growl, "light cheese and extra sauce." Each word was said slowly and individually punctuated, further insulting the girl. Once again, seeming to go straight over her head, or else she was consciously ignoring the jabs at her intelligence. Another Sage trying to make others feel inferior, should have known.

So far, his detrimental illusions, at least the ones we were aware of, had all been aimed at Primals. Except Jessica didn't fit, she was a Sage.

Only way to find out was to get him into custody, which hopefully would be happening any minute now.

Holden looked up, pulling his attention from the com he had been furiously tapping, his back still to the suspect who hadn't so much as glanced our way. *My uncle is rallying the troops. Luckily the others were all at the gym doing drills.* Holden narrowed his eyes as he focused his hearing behind him, without looking back and giving himself away.

I wasn't paying attention to Holden though. Our target's hostility was increasing, which pushed his voice my way. He was thinking about ways to get the girl's attention, though it was no longer about courtesy, or his order. He wanted to once again flex that mental muscle. He was looking for ways to make her hurt herself.

What? Holden apparently picked up on my worry. *What is it?* Every muscle tightened as he stared at me, waiting for me to reveal some horrible truth. Eyes narrowed, he watched me but I was still watching Mr. Illusionary. He definitely meant to "teach her a lesson" but hadn't landed on how just yet, though the scenarios he ran through his head were anything but benign. From handling broken glass unbeknownst to her or having her believe the pizza ovens were closed.

We needed to get to him. He was going to hurt someone again, and I could not just sit here waiting for the green light to move or, more likely, for the Primals on the team to take him down.

What was that?

"Hmmm?" I answered Holden distractedly, still trying to keep my focus on Mr. Baddie.

You mumbled something.

I flicked my gaze briefly to Holden, then back to the counter. The man had moved to the side, closer to Holden and me, but was still watching the server. Plotting, with his back now toward us. I wondered how long it took for him to put an illusion together and project it, hopefully much longer than it would take for my squad-mates to arrive. I must have mumbled my concerns, because Holden once again tried to get me to explain myself.

"He's thinking of harmful illusions to throw at the girl," I said absently as Mr. Baddie's thoughts focused on one illusion and all that he would need to pull into it. He definitely needed time to take in his surroundings: the gleaming silver of the oven, the brick colored tile of the floor, the giant dough mixers against the far wall. Then there was the refrigerator door in the wall opposite the ovens, not to mention the other workers and all the toppings…

I watched as he soaked it all in and began developing his deceit.

"Holden, he's about to make the server girl think the pizza oven is closed, so when she reaches to open it…" I finally gave him my attention. "She'll burn her hand," I whispered harshly, beginning to panic at my forced stasis. My leg was bouncing like it was working the bass drum in a heavy metal song, my only outlet for growing anxiety.

We'll give the team as much time as we can. You let me know when that time runs out.

I nodded vigorously, still bouncing my leg. I chewed my lip as I focused on the man. It had been awhile since I noticed what song rang out among the hidden speakers in the ceiling, or how many other patrons were in the restaurant. Our target had become my only focus.

I narrowed my eyes. "He's about done and seems to be putting the finishing touches on his illusion."

I was marginally aware that Holden was preparing to make a move when the bell on the door rang out, announcing new arrivals. Everyone's attention swung toward the door as several imposing figures in tactical gear entered the restaurant. I deflated, my muscles beginning to uncoil. The team was here.

CHAPTER 23

DANE AND DEVLIN STOOD just inside the door, scanning the interior, two uniformed enforcers filing in behind them. Squished within the horde, nearest Dane and Devlin, were Jade and Steve, looking a bit wild eyed at the situation.

Holden and I stood, our chairs scraping across the linoleum flooring and garnering Baddie's attention momentarily, to which he did a double take when he saw me. The situation registered on his face as well as in his mind.

We were here for him. Somehow we had figured out what he had done and we were here for *him*.

His anxiety began to climb. "He's panicking."

The group which stood by the door began moving into the restaurant. The other patrons scrambling toward the exit as the enforcers moved inward, meals abandoned in favor of vacating the premises. The workers hadn't yet noticed the tension, still toiling away at the orders which had been placed.

The illusionist was looking at the mass group moving to encircle him with growing dread, his mind whirling, but spinning in circles.

He knew he couldn't do a detailed illusion this quickly, or for so many.

That's when everything went black.

One moment I could see. I saw the team encircling our target, saw the panic on said target's face, the sweat on his brow; the desperation in his mind. I saw the team's determination and poise, even Jade and Steve had looked confident. In the next moment, nothing but complete darkness.

Then chaos.

Panicked voices whipped at me from every angle meeting both my ears and my muddled mind. Pans clattered to the ground, chairs scraped as they were bumped by those suddenly in the dark.

Devlin, Holden, and Dane all kept their cool thankfully, and were focusing alternate senses to attempt to overcome their new infirmity. I focused on their low directives. Dane knew the guy's scent and was inching in the direction his nose pointed, or so I assumed based on his comments and Devlin's acknowledgement.

Jade and Steve were pretty panicked, and Jade would be overwhelmed with adrenaline and fear wafting from so many at once. Steve's gift would have been awesome at this moment but without heightened senses to accompany his telekinesis, he wouldn't know where to aim and he wasn't yet strong enough to hold multiples for more than a few moments.

The street team—enforcers who generally only did routine calls in town— who came in behind the team, were not cool. They lashed out, knocking over everything within striking distance and barking out orders to get down. They had drawn their weapons and were blindly waving them, mental voices indicating how close to the edge they were. For supposedly trained first responders, these guys were as bad as the customers.

I moved my attention to Dane. I needed him to make his way to his panicking brethren. Those idiot patrol guys were going to shoot any moment, money said the illusionist wouldn't be the recipient of the bullet.

"Dane, I need you to move to the patrol unit. They're panicking and have itchy trigger fingers." A low curse came from just a few feet away, and a chair skidded as Dane changed course, now tracking the not-too-cool members of the enforcement ranks. Apparently poise under pressure was something they needed to work on.

"Happy place, guys. It's an illusion. You *know* this. Use it to break free," I called as calmly as I could. I couldn't worry about Jade or Steve, they were at least not adding to the mayhem. I couldn't worry about the panic stricken pizzeria employees, not until we were all out of this mess. I noticed that the target's mind was no longer one I heard raised in panic. He was back to being calm, gloating even. Why hadn't he fled?

He wanted to watch what he wrought. He thrived on the panic, the adrenaline, the power.

I knew I could get out of this if I could force myself to think. I couldn't let the panic clawing up my throat win. I knew it was just an illusion, and I could combat that. I stilled and focused inward, trying to block out the surrounding voices. I felt a foreign buzz, a wavelength not my own, humming within my mind. I took deep breaths in my attempts to separate it, to disengage the intrusion from my mind.

Once located, I focused on the fact that I could in fact, see. There was more than blackness around me. There was Holden, Jade, and the rest of the team. There were tables and chairs. There were gaudy cliché Italian furnishings. And suddenly it was true. I saw the chaos which the illusionary wrought. My head was pounding with the internal and external chaos. The panic of those around me. I needed to stop this, I needed to stop *him*.

"Guys, I'm free," I called triumphantly. That seemed to calm Steve, his competitive nature kicking in. Jade would be harder. The Primals on our team all attempted to pull themselves from the dark using the mind tricks we'd been working on in our mental training. I didn't hear the patrol units, and a quick scan showed Dane standing in between two prone and *unconscious* men on the floor among discarded pizza and upturned chairs. Dane's belt was now adorned with two additional weapons.

I spun toward where I last saw our suspect; he wasn't there any longer. Not that I expected him to just stand there, but it would have been nice. I pivoted back and forth, looking. There was too much noise to really pinpoint his mental signature and that confused me. As I came back to the right, facing the storefront window, I was blindsided by a large object which gleamed silver in the sunlight of the window as it fast approached my face.

Pain exploded across my right temple and cheek, whipping my head to the left. I shook off the stinging ache in my face, not allowing the moisture gathering in my eyes to escape. Now was not the time to have my sight obscured. I gained my bearings in time to watch the illusionist book it out the door of the restaurant, the bell dinging merrily as it was jostled.

I had only a moment to decide whether to pursue him or to stay and attempt to stop the havoc. The chaos of the workers' minds which reigned inside my skull, making a pick ax to the eye sound perfectly appealing, hammered home my decision. I needed to worry about my team and the other victims in the restaurant, find out the damage of this little stunt. So instead of heading for the door, I veered toward the counter where this all began.

The once overly stereotypical decor was now strewn about the floor in a manner which resembled the aftermath of a bar fight, or tornado. Tables and chairs were on their sides haphazardly, pizza and drinks splashed violently across the linoleum flooring, very nearly resembling expanding puddles of blood either in color or rate of expansion.

Shaking off the magnitude of the destruction, I found Jade and the rest of the team each working on extracting themselves from the imposed sightlessness. Surprisingly, most of them were successful and had pulled themselves from the hole and were searching for our target.

"He fled a moment ago," I informed them as they cautiously maneuvered around the debris in search. The workers behind the counter had all pretty much adopted a cowering position at various places within the kitchen, but we had one casualty. The girl still burned her hand and still due to an illusion. I had to worry about that in a moment however.

I picked my way to Jade as quickly as I could, "Jade, I'm here," I soothed. When her head whipped in my direction I continued. "I need you to focus on that, on me. I am here."

Jade whimpered slightly, "Nat, I can't hold out much longer. The emotions are crashing me. I'm barely holding on." A tear escaped her eye as she clamped her mouth closed, her limbs shaking from all the emotional buzzing that even I could feel. The pulsing behind my eyes was going to kill me if it went on too much longer so I could totally relate. I needed to take Jade out of this so she could give everyone else an emotional tranquilizer, and we needed to do it fast, before we lost our illusionary.

"Jade, sweetie, I need you to focus on me. Me only." When those gem colored eyes met mine, I gave her my best attempt at a reassuring smile. I tried to be soothing, giving Jade a calm aura to latch onto, maybe act as a grounder, a way to pull out of her head.

"Hey," she said shakily, still affected by the major turmoil which others were embattled in.

I smiled ruefully at her. "There she is." We were the ones more affected by this event, our gifts were like a sponge, soaking up what others flung about. But I needed to push aside my telepathy woes and get this figured out, quickly. "Can you give everyone a bit of calming juju? I know you're still riding their emotions, but we need to pull everyone out of it. I'm thinking our best shot is to make them stop panicking first."

Taking a deep, shaky breath, Jade nodded and closed her eyes. She needed a moment to center herself before she could even think of calming anyone else. Just after, I felt a balm of soothing energy adhere like a second skin to my body.

"Where'd he go, Dane?" I heard Devlin ask.

"He's in a car. Well, Holden's truck, heading toward the fields," Dane relayed.

He must have swiped the keys while he was gloating, Holden had set them on the table when we sat down. Thoughts still hammered at me, but I no longer cared. They didn't puncture my bubble of tranquility. That was a nifty trick. One by one, other minds began to calm as Jade made her way to everyone affected, and together we pulled them out the damaging illusion. It was taking too long and we were now several minutes behind the illusionist.

My sight began to fuzz at the edges, disorienting me yet again, so I moved to sit in the nearest chair, remembering that they were no longer upright only as I began my descent to the floor. With my rear's connection to the sticky floor, the fuzziness began to expand, making me dizzy. "We need to get medics here, check for injured." As my vision tunneled to black, I realized I was going to lose consciousness. I'd have to work on that.

I careened into awareness with the jolting of my prone body. I was being picked up from the floor, completely encased by strong arms under my arms and knees so as to carry me with ease.

"Oh, thank God." Jade breathed as she hung her head and repeated the litany mentally.

I winced as I registered a throbbing across the right side of my face. Bringing up my hand, I poked at the swollen and battered flesh, also finding a largish gash marring my cheek. Man, that was tender.

Don't poke it, Holden scolded as he pulled my hand away and gave it a tender kiss across the knuckles. *We will get you all fixed up once we nail this guy down.* The last of his thought was practically growled. Holden was pissed. I began to sit up but was once again caged by Holden's iron arms.

"I'm all right." It wasn't a total lie. I was starting to feel better, though my face still felt like I had been hit by a cement truck, which reminded me. "What hit me? I swear I feel like it was a bat. It was silver. I remember that much." I opened my jaw, feeling the stiffness and pain all the way past my ear. When I turned my head to look at Holden, I wasn't surprised to see those mercury pools laser focused on me.

Once again, Holden was taking in every detail, cataloging my features, every ailment. I bristled but backed down just as quickly. He was right. I was fragile. This experience only brought that notion screaming into clarity. I was easy to evade, hurt.

You scared me, he said as he gently brushed his knuckles across my unblemished cheek. Everything about Holden had me entranced. His face was so earnest, his brows pinched in remembrance, seeing me unconscious on the floor. His full lips were pursed and strong, angular jaw clenched, making the muscle in his cheek jump. He had felt so helpless, not able to voice any assistance to the team. We couldn't do this now, we had to focus elsewhere.

"It's not your fault, Holden," I assured him. "I knew the risks of this job, remember?" I gave a little shrug. "This was a good experience to serve as a reminder that even Sages can pack a punch." I rubbed my cheek again and noticed the gash was smaller. I held my hand over the wound and darted my eyes back to Holden, then Jade hovering nearby, wondering if they had noticed.

Holden wrapped strong fingers around my wrist, gently pulling the hand away from my face, all while keeping his silver orbs locked on my blue-greens. My eyebrows scrunched upward, and my breathing quickened. *Please don't notice.*

It's smaller, cleaner... Now his brows furrowed, his eyes jumping from my cheek to my eyes and back. *How?*

"Don't say anything, please!" I whispered vehemently. I was becoming frantic, my heart hammering in my chest. I scanned for an escape through the now organized chaos where I could avoid the scrutiny, the questions.

Holden's warm hand once again cradled my cheek, stilling me. *I won't ask now. It is not the time, but I hope you'll tell me when things calm down.* He tried conveying his sincerity, his understanding, through his depthless eyes. I stared back and nodded mutely, worry still rampant in my thoughts, and I'm sure, across my face. And just like that Holden dropped it.

We moved quickly to the squad's mass transport vehicle, Jade ahead of us, continually looking over her shoulder as we hurried along. The van contained the rest of the team who were waiting impatiently for us to get in. Jade beat us and scrambled into the seat farthest to the rear. Holden stepped into the van and ducked inside, never once seeming uncomfortable with my weight as he set me gently on the far side of the bench seat. I blushed at the realization that I hadn't even struggled or protested the infirm treatment.

The moment Holden closed the door Devlin spun the tires in his haste to get moving. It was about this time that I realized the vehicle was equipped with flashing lights and wailing siren, thus marking it as an Enforcement vehicle. How had I not known that before now?

We blew through traffic lights and stop signs like they didn't apply to us, making a few other cars swerve out of our way or lay on their horn. It didn't matter to some that we were chasing a dangerous man, we were just enforcers and thus inferior to them. I would bet all kinds of money that those folks were Sages.

"Where are we going?" I asked dumbly as I finally registered that we were heading out of town. The van's jostling becoming more pronounced, more frequent. Every few moments, Devlin would slow and Dane would stick his head out the window and inhale deeply, much like a dog, then nod and we would continue onward. At one such slowing, I realized there was another vehicle trailing us, the uniformed enforcers made it out of the restaurant, and apparently they didn't want to be left out.

Dane's tracking him. His trail is leading toward the checkpoint. Holden nodded his chin to the windshield of the van; beyond, I could see the razor-wire topped wall looming in the distance.

"Well, that can't be good."

CHAPTER 24

WE CREPT UP TO another vehicle that appeared to have been stopped just before the gates. The older truck Holden and I had been driving earlier in the day, in fact, was idling about thirty feet from the gated checkpoint like a suicide bomber biding its time for destruction. If he was still in the vehicle and the patrol hadn't fired on him, he hadn't done anything threatening. Yet.

I had witnessed what happened when he had time to formulate an illusion, and when he panicked. Did he have enough time to pull one together? We were about to find out. Devlin brought the van to a halt, turning it sideways across the road, with the nose facing left, putting Dane and Holden closest to the target. But I was right behind them.

We were more than twenty feet from the vehicle, so I couldn't read anything from it, the patrolling soldiers along the wall, even further away, were a definite no go. The sound of screeching tires drew attention to the fact that the uniformed enforcers had caught up and were now another unknown to deal with.

"What's the plan guys?" Jade asked, taking the words from my mouth. She seemed calmer now, more determined. Feeding off our seasoned enforcers' adrenaline, maybe?

All the Primals were completely zeroed in on the vehicle ahead of us, sweeping their focus across all our potential foes, there were many. Devlin, being our stealth and tactics guy was not happy about our being out in the open with so much uncertainty. He was scanning for the best places to hole up, places we should get to before things went bad, lower our risks.

"Stay sharp, keep your wits." It didn't take a genius to know that Devlin was only addressing the Sages in the vehicle, though now was not the time to spark an argument.

Of course, Steve had to give him one anyway, smarting off about how we Sages have the brains to think, unlike Primals. Devlin turned an absolutely lethal gaze to him, letting a deep and utterly terrifying sound rumble from his chest. If I hadn't been staring directly at him, I would have sworn the sound had come from some sort of wild animal, the kind we didn't actually have in Minefield. Luckily the effect was enough to shut Steve up, though his mental obnoxiousness continued.

I reached back and popped him upside the head. I was on the receiving end of a decent death glare for it but didn't care. I wasn't in the mood for his superiority complex to bear its ugly face. The van fell silent as we all surveyed the area as well as the situation.

"I would say that our best bet is to rush him before he has time to implement an illusion against us involving those weapons," Devlin jerked his chin toward the guards who each had large semi-automatic weapons within their grasp, "but we've seen what he does when panicked. Imagine what those guards will do when they are."

I scanned the area as Devlin talked out his thought process. There wasn't much around, save for the guard shack, the guards themselves. Their vehicles, a whole lot of reinforcements and an accompanying military base all sprawled in the distance on the far side, even our illusionist wasn't dense enough to attempt to actually get through the gates. The enforcers behind us were getting antsy. They would be a liability; apparently, patrol units weren't nearly as well trained as the Primals on our team.

This area was all farmland, the space we termed "the fields." It was where most of our staples were grown and harvested. It also employed a large number of Primals. On the other side of the wall, the railroad tracks were the only sign of human life within the immediate area. The train rumbled through once a week and only delivered goods to Minefield once a month.

The shack was out of the question as it was too far to reach, much closer to the target as well as the patrol, which could turn on us in a split second without warning. The surrounding fields were dense with corn stalks, it would make good cover if nothing else, but we still needed to formulate a plan to neutralize the threat of the illusionary.

Between us, we could read his mind, change our appearance, read and possibly change his mood, track him, stop him from moving and sneak up on him. Except we couldn't. Because we were in plain view at this point and he had to know we were here. There would be no getting close to him.

The town enforcers tagging along on the chase suddenly pushed open the doors of their vehicle, attention tunneled in on the truck stalled in front of the gates, weapons out. The action was apparently a *go* signal for the illusionist who yelled, "We want out! We're willing to go through you to do it!" He exited the truck making a beeline for the tall concealing plants lining the roadway.

Well crap, I don't know what the illusionist was making them see but it didn't take a genius to know that it put us in the line of fire. Not sure why the bad guy said "we." The border patrol could forcibly stop anyone from leaving Minefield if they did not have the approval to do so, which we didn't, so our being here in itself would make the soldiers…twitchy. We needed to keep the uniformed officers from seeming to rush the exit.

The man hadn't run toward the gate, instead choosing the dense cornfield lining the road. He could blank the stationed guards' vision in a pinch but what good would that do him? Even if he made it past the barrier, there was nowhere to go. Nowhere without putting significant risk to his life, having no access to food, water, or shelter for over a hundred miles in any direction, save for the military installment.

The armed base's sole purpose was keeping us contained. The only way one might squeak by was if it was timed perfectly with the supply train's stop, which it hadn't. The fact that the soldiers didn't track his mad dash, but kept their attention—and guns— trained on all the enforcers, made it clear he was pushing an illusion.

The guards were now on the defensive.

Devlin swore and rolled down his window a few inches, only enough so that he could be heard without completely losing the extra barrier.

"Officers, get back to your vehicle and head back to town. You're not prepared for this fight."

The uniformed enforcers had emerged, tracking our suspect with raised weapons and cautious steps. They moved forward, coming up the side of the van, at least they were aware enough to use our vehicle for cover. Devlin's warning went unheeded. There wasn't much more we could do without inviting hostilities.

We may need to let him go for today, Holden intoned. His thought was valid. There were too many variables. The target was out of my mental range as were the soldiers at the crossover, so I didn't know to what end the soldiers were being manipulated, and if they perceived us as a threat.

"Our best course may just be to concede and regroup. Like I advised our arrogant comrades out there," Devlin mused and tilted his head to indicate the two men still glued to the van's hull. "If they stay there, I can use the van to give them cover to get back to their unit."

That was apparently not in the cards because no sooner had he finished speaking than the uniforms made their move. And all hell broke loose. The rapid *pop, pop, pop* was instantly followed by the shriek of glass shattering as a rear window of our van blew in from gunfire. "Everyone down!" Dane boomed as he launched himself toward Jade and the back of the van, pushing on Holden and myself in his haste.

Devlin tried to get us out of there, but the van sat sideways in the middle of the road, perpendicular to the guards and they had a perfect target. The patrol officers who had been rushing the suspect's vehicle now had nowhere to go. I watched in dawning horror as first one and then the other jerked from impact, more than once, and fell to the road.

Red puddles amassed on the pavement where they lay, their eyes pleading, limbs twitching. My throat closed as I realized we couldn't get to them without risking more of us. Their only hope would be for us to draw fire, and end this quickly. If we called for backup, there would be more of a threat. No one could come to our aid, but maybe we could get a cease-fire called if we could contact Commander James.

We all ducked toward the floor as the van continued to be pelted with bullets, the sound near deafening as the small metal projectiles bit into the steel hide of our enclosure and windows shattered, littering the floor. Our prone bodies sparkled like make-believe creatures I'd read about, not one of us without glass fragments covering our backs.

"Can we get the commander to call the soldiers? Let them know the situation?" I screeched shakily, my face buried in the floor, arms shielding my head and ears. Holden seemed to be doing his best to mimic a human shield, laying most of his large, muscled body atop me. Much as Dane had attempted for Jade. Poor Steve was left to fend for himself.

The van listed heavily to the right, both tires punctured on that side. Devlin floored the now crippled van straight toward the cornfield now directly in front of our vehicle and lurched us into its green depths, the only place that would give us any chance at all to flee the vehicle without bullet holes adorning our bodies. The van was too destroyed to get far, so Devlin guided it as best he could while directing us as well. I vaguely heard Dane relaying info to whom I assumed to be Commander James.

"We need to stay together, these stalks are thick and we could easily get separated. Dane, you need to be point. I need you to track the asshole so we can stop this. Holden, can you bring up the rear?" Holden nodded his agreement, which was apparently the bailout signal. Devlin, Dane and

Holden all thrust open doors and jumped out with weapons raised. Where did Holden get his gun?

There probably was a small arsenal in the back of the van. No telling what the commander had thrown in. We trainees weren't given weapons yet, we hadn't even touched them, so I was glad someone would possibly be able to counter the aggressiveness of the checkpoint soldiers.

We moved to meet on the left side of the van, furthest from our assailants, and allowed for the van to act as a barrier. I never thought I would be so happy to have an older clunker of a vehicle surround me. The only reason we weren't hurt by the bullets was that the van's hide was steel. The only reason it was steel? It was ancient, built before the advent and use of carbon fiber and plastics' extensive use in modern vehicles, and thank God for that. But not having bullet holes didn't mean we had escaped completely unscathed. Each of us now sported a new and wide variety of tiny cuts, thanks to all the window glass we maneuvered over to depart the vehicle.

As I had the thought, I felt the tiny fissures begin to knit themselves together, making my skin the unblemished canvas I'd come to know. My only saving grace was that no-one's attention was on me and that the blood remained, staining my flesh, or I'd be hiding from more people than the soldiers who currently dogged our steps.

The cornstalks squeezed in on us as we stood in silence attempting to read the situation by sound alone. We needed to move. They would come to investigate the van soon, at least some of them. They wouldn't leave the gate unguarded, especially with the perceived threat. And I'd bet money that reinforcements had been called. Damned ninnies. Shoot first and ask questions later seemed to be an acceptable practice here at the gate. Heaven forbid the screwed-up people make it out into the actual world.

Dane's voice snapped my attention to the very real situation in which I currently found myself. "There are two walking toward us," he closed his eyes and after a moment took a deep inhale. "The subject is trying to make it back to the truck. His scent is fearful but moving."

The mental planning that the experienced enforcers ran through was dizzying. Their minds buzzed with so many things I had never considered, the consensus being to move forward without detection. If we could angle toward the illusionist in a direct line and surprise him, we could likely end this fairly quickly, but the dense vegetation that surrounded us, nearly to the point of claustrophobia, would make that difficult.

"Surrender!" a voice commanded. Way closer than any had before, the border guards now nearly upon the van. We needed to move. Now.

"I'll maneuver us into his line, hopefully," Dane intoned.

"Hopefully?" I asked, disbelieving.

He flung an arm out, waving his hand about to indicate the encroaching green stalks, "These have a pretty intense scent of their own," he explained. "I can tell if his scent gets stronger and the general location…" he shrugged helplessly, "it probably won't be perfect."

The silk of the corn heads tickled my exposed skin and tangled in my hair like grasping fingers, as leaves brushed against me from another angle, the sensations nearly overloading my already adrenaline-ridden system. My head screamed from the mental intensity I was amid. If only I could hear anyone else, we would know the state of things. But no, we were isolated in a cornfield amidst acres and acres of the imposing plants. Jade, Steve, and I were nearly swallowed by the tall stalks. We would be lost easily if we were separated. I was now able to read the two soldiers who approached us: shoot to kill. Apparently, they weren't interested in capture.

We were out of time.

CHAPTER 25

I COULDN'T LET US sit around while we were stalked and the offender worked his way to a viable escape. We needed to end this, one way or another.

"The two mobile guards are almost on us. We need to move. Now," I whispered harshly.

Everyone nodded once, almost like it was choreographed, and we slowly but steadily moved in the direction we assumed the wall to be. All the while, trying to employ the stealth Dane and Devlin had drilled into us for weeks.

Dane took point, Devlin behind him, then Jade, Steve, and me. Holden pressed to my back, bringing up the rear. We stayed in a bit of a crouch, which was nearly doubled over for the Primals in the caravan. Luckily, the state of the field, namely in full growth, kept us from making too much noise as we moved forward. The soil was free of leaves, stalks, and general debris which would crunch and snap and expose our position.

My heart continued to pound in my ears, my pulse racing, uncaring of our progress. Jade and Steve were both in the same physical and mental position I was.

Our first real situation. A deadly situation.

The rapid *pop, pop, pop,* of automatic gunfire punctuated my mental point from behind us, the soldier firing randomly, or in our perceived direction. Either way, it kept my pulse beating like a jackhammer.

Slowly, we continued our trek toward where Dane believed our guy to be moving. I had no idea how any of them could utilize their senses in this silk forest. My senses were saturated with the sight and scent of dirt, and the sweet and starchy smell of fresh corn. I normally loved the emanation, but today it seemed cloying, like it was thickening in my throat, keeping me from swallowing effectively. I wasn't sure I'd ever view corn the same way again.

Holden clamped the hem of my shirt, halting me when it tightened and pulled in his hand. In turn, I did the same to Steve in front of me, the action repeating up the chain until all of us were still and crouching, like animals hunting in the swaying stalks.

We're being followed.

Damn. I nodded once to indicate I'd heard, listening with my ability.

I heard two minds behind, but nothing yet in front of us. The men behind us were fewer than twenty feet, while those in front were farther. Not good. I relayed such, in my best whispered voice.

With that, we began moving again, this time a bit more hastily. We weren't making enough progress. Dane cocked his head to the right as he paused to take in the scent he had filtered. "We're getting close," he said lowly.

Our subject. His aroma was strong now, we were almost on him. Within the next couple of shuffled steps forward, I was able to confirm this as his consciousness popped into my head.

"Dane's right, we're nearly on him. He's working to alter his illusion to erase himself and his vehicle from the soldiers' sight. Apparently, this is a bit difficult," I whispered to the enforcers surrounding me. He was working on his getaway. We had one more chance to stop this, to stop him. He was hiding just inside the line of crops creating his illusion.

Now that we were close, Devlin took the lead as the rest of us hung back. We let Stealth do his thing, moving in much the way I had seen leopards stalk their prey in documentaries. We needed surprise on our side, only then could we avoid more mayhem and possible injury…or death. It may have looked like we were just crouching about, but we were all alert, searching our environment for anything amiss, for someone's approach, which was precisely what our target should have been worried about.

A niggling feeling invaded my mind, making me pause.

Devlin, carefully and quietly, made his way toward where our baddie stood within the corn forest. If we hadn't seen him, I would never have known he was there. But that's just it; was it real? That tickle, now that I focused on it, was foreign. It wasn't my thoughts. Once again, the illusionist had infiltrated our minds.

I began moving toward where Devlin quickly approached the target. "Dev, wait, he's—"

Devlin's fist rocketed toward the guy's temple, and continued right through, the momentum nearly felling the massive Primal. The illusion dissipated with the realized apparition.

"Damn it!" Devlin pummeled the ground he knelt upon, his frustration bubbling over. Steve, the idiot, chuckled darkly at Dev's fumble, inciting Jade to elbow him in the gut.

The rest of us warily looked about, trying once again to pinpoint the illusionist. I focused my mind to him again, or tried. He'd moved out of range. Dane was up again. "I'll move behind you, Dane, so I can tell you what I hear. Sound good?"

Dane dipped his chin once, and we all fell into line behind him, hoping his heightened senses could lead us without another false image. The normal teddy bear demeanor the otherwise intimidating enforcer affected was completely absent in this hunt, in its place was a focused and calculated hunter. I didn't hear the two soldiers following us. We must have lost them among the stalks—for now.

Devlin echoed my thought out loud. "Don't trust your eyes. Dane, your nose," then to me, "Nat, your telepathy. These are our guides."

False images kept popping up. He'd be sitting off to our left, then peering out from between the stalks on our right. It seemed as he moved, he pushed out illusions that were stationary decoys. Enough to fool the eyes, at least for a moment. We all trudged by surprisingly quietly, little in the way of unnecessary or snarky comments. Maybe Steve was teachable. After the third dude we came upon, I brushed our target's mind again.

"We're coming up on him."

We slowed, Dane inhaling deeply for confirmation. I kept my mind roving, trying to tune out the determined thoughts of the team. We were almost back to the road and the truck. This was our moment, but it could be tricky. We would be closer to the checkpoint and the border patrol unit. A few more cautious steps and we once again saw a figure standing just inside the crop line. With the knowledge that this was the physical truth, I aimed a question at Steve.

"Hey, can you immobilize him for a few moments so we don't run the risk of him bolting?"

The smirk that spread across Steve's thin face could only be described as sinister. Adjusting his wire frames, he narrowed his eyes and concentrated on the shadowed figure ahead. When Steve gave a decisive nod, we all moved at once, Devlin once again on point. He wanted his redemption.

It wasn't until Devlin was towering over him that the illusionist realized he'd been caught. Dev's crazed smirk and triumphant demeanor had the guy's eyes widening, especially when he realized he couldn't move, thanks to Steve's immobilization.

He opened his mouth to shout, but Dev's fist was there, not giving him the time to do more than squeak his fear. Being that knuckles are mainly skin covered bones, just like the face, the crunching sound of connection was easily audible. I cringed as the illusionary flew backward out of the field and onto the low-cut grass. He didn't move. Devlin's punch had knocked him completely unconscious.

Good.

"You, there! Down on the ground!" The guards near the gate turned in our direction, weapons up and ready. Devlin slowly raised his hands, the gun luckily tucked into its holster at his waist and not in hand. I couldn't imagine that would have gone over well.

He stepped out onto the grass next to the splayed body of our suspect. "I'm an enforcer," he rumbled.

"I said, down on the ground!" the man shouted again, another man slowly crossing to Dev, his gun up and trained on our teammate, finger on the trigger. These guys sure didn't mess around, they'd shoot anyone they deemed a threat.

"Devlin Harlow, part of Commander James's uni–" That's all he got out before he was tackled to the ground. He didn't struggle; just let them roll him onto his stomach and cuff his hands behind him.

"What are you doing here? Is this the other driver?" The soldier peppered Devlin with agitated questions and motioned to the unconscious illusionary. The rest of the team, me included, watched as Devlin was manhandled. Still, he didn't resist, didn't complain. It was definitely not a side of Devlin I was used to seeing. Grass clung to his shirt back and tactical pants, a large clump wedged between his gun and his side.

I hated cowering, but it was the smarter move. We were outmanned and outgunned. If we revealed ourselves as Devlin's companions, tensions would only mount and someone could get hurt. Most likely one of our team. We couldn't risk it.

"Check my back pocket, you'll find my identification and credentials. My badge is on my belt. Did Commander James contact your unit?"

After the soldier divested Devlin of his weapon, he hauled Devlin to his feet, but only with help and cooperation, because let's face it, Dev's a big boy and one ninny was not going to toss him around without his say so. The soldier rifled through Dev's pockets, pulling out his wallet. He flipped it open, read, then looked back at Devlin, reaching forward to push up the hem of his shirt where it now hung loose over his belt. A shiny gold shield at his waistline glinted accusingly in the sunlight.

"Sorry," the soldier mumbled, stepping forward to release Devlin from the handcuffs at his back. "We got a call about your team a few minutes ago."

"What are you doing?" another soldier yelled from his spot by the gate, weapon still up, clearly not understanding why Devlin was being uncuffed and having his weapon returned.

"Thanks, man," Dev said as he brought his hands in front of him and rubbed his wrists, looking down at the unconscious illusionist. "My team is out there." He motioned toward the field where we all crouched like shadows seeking shelter from the light. "We need to get this man into custody. Preferably before he wakes up and I need to knock his ass out again." He gave a wry smile and drew his eyes to our location. "All clear!"

At the call, Dane stood, his head now above the waving stalks, hands up and palms out. The rest of us followed his lead, adopting the same position with our hands, moving cautiously toward Devlin, the soldiers, and the unconscious subject.

The emergence of so many put the rest of the soldiers on edge, their weapons not dropping and minds whirring. They were still unsure of our intentions and weren't going to take chances with any Enhanced, so the weapons stayed raised and ready, their adrenaline high and eyes wary.

"Let's get him cuffed," Devlin said as he moved slowly, deliberately, to our target. Whether the comment was for Dane or Holden, I had no idea. I just knew he wasn't talking to any of the trainees, me included.

CHAPTER 26

THE SUBJECT UNFORTUNATELY DID not, in fact, stay unconscious. Once we had the cuffs on him, Devlin hauled him up and over his shoulder so easily, you would have thought he was hauling potatoes.

He said he didn't want to cradle the man like a damsel in distress, namely because he didn't like him enough to put that kind of care into his transportation. The rough treatment apparently roused our boy, who decided he wanted to struggle. What a futile idea, a Sage attempting to physically maneuver themselves away from a Primal, rather laughable really.

Devlin clamped his arm tighter around Mr. Baddie's legs and grumbled, "Don't. Don't even think about using your illusions right now, Picture Boy." He used his free hand to grab the man's handcuffed wrists and bent at the waist to put the subject to the ground.

The illusionist narrowed his eyes and pursed his lips, a pathetic attempt to stare Dev down. There was zero intimidation in that look, and I couldn't quite keep the chuckle from squeaking out of my pressed lips. Still the typical Sage, assuming a spot of superiority, even when clearly disadvantaged. This one buried his feelings like a champ, only to use them for illusionary fuel.

"If my girl, Nat, over there," he continued, pointing at me, "gives me any indication that you are working on an illusion—" He cocked his head and raised an eyebrow, punctuating his unfinished statement. "Well, then, I'm just going to have to knock you out again. Or maybe I'll let Steve here, seize your muscles. You got a taste of that already. Did you like it?" He shrugged like he couldn't care less if it came to that.

Steve hoped he'd get to. I smirked, but successfully contained my mirth this go around. "Now, unless you want me to call you 'shithead,' you may want to give me your name." Devlin continued.

The illusionary looked slowly around him, taking in the faces of his captors. He sneered when his eyes alighted on Steve.

"Never thought I'd see Alan Davidson's boy playing cops and robbers with a bunch of *Primals*." He practically spit the word. This guy was a real treat, definitely one who felt he was entitled to everything, and that all of those "lesser" than him should move out of his way. Nice.

Wait, Davidson? The douchey politician? The council member? The guy I humiliated on so many levels the last time we met? Well, that explained a lot about Steve. Apparently douchiness and entitlement didn't fall far from the daddy-tree.

Steve never let his arrogant mask falter. In fact, he stood taller, squaring his shoulders. "Father is behind this collaboration. Besides, these enforcers need our help. The aid of those who are more intelligent. I will be a part of cleaning up the filth from Minefield, whether Primal *or* Sage."

I actually wanted to applaud Boat Shoes for the first time since we met for that little soapbox monologue, but again, now was not the time and I made sure not to deviate from my professional façade.

Devlin pushed at the illusionist, making him stumble a few steps away from our circle. "Get moving."

Once back at the main road, we remembered that our van was incapacitated further inside the field, and the only available vehicle which could transport all of us safely was the subject's truck—the truck Holden and I had stowed at the curb of the restaurant. A single cab. Go figure.

My eyes floated to the right and landed on the downed enforcers. Neither was moving, their eyes closed and chests still. The pools of red now darkened to a more inky color as it sat exposed on the bodies as well as the rough, cracked roadway.

Our capture procedure had taken too long to save them. They would not be leaving the wall. Well, they would, but only to find a more permanent resting place. That realization brought us all to a halt around the fallen.

The illusionist had succeeded in bending others to take a life. Two fewer Enhanced in Minefield, all due to a madman's whims. "We need to take these men." I only forced my attention away after I realized moisture was escaping the corner of my eye. This sight, this day, would stay with me forever.

Medics are on the way now that the threat has ended, Holden assured me. *Nat, you should drive. Jade and Steve in the cab with you. The rest of us will file into the bed. We'll hang onto the illusionist.*

"Why us in the cab?"

"You're fragile," Dane answered. Not sure how he knew what I was referring to, but maybe it was just the obvious answer to that question. I glared at him all the same. I was not fragile. But Jade and Steve were. I nodded in agreement and reached for the driver's door of the old truck while the Primal members of our team, plus one captured baddie, piled into the worn bed.

The door creaked loudly as I yanked it open and threw myself inside. I slid open the little center window embedded in the rear panel of glass. I needed to be able to hear everyone clearly. "Back to the CP, or is there somewhere else you want to take him?"

"CP," Dane barked as he slapped the side of the truck bed with his palm, twice. The understood signal for go. "We have more privacy there."

The way he looked at the illusionist when he said this was one of the most ominous things I had ever seen. Our captive seemed to agree, because he nearly pissed himself at Dane's statement. He didn't want to find out what we could do with said privacy. Good, maybe that would make this easier.

I turned the key, which was still in the ignition, and the truck roared to life. Man, we must have been out of it if we hadn't been able to pursue this vehicle immediately. Its loud idling would have made it easily identifiable, not to mention it was one of *our* trucks. Well, I had been temporarily unconscious and was beginning to feel the after effects once again, now that the adrenaline was abating. Speaking of…I reached up and felt for the gash on my cheek. Nothing. Just smooth skin. Tender, but smooth. *Please, don't let them realize it hadn't always been.*

With that last terrifying thought, I gave the posted soldiers a little wave and eased the truck around to head back into town. Steve's and Jade's minds were spinning, reliving everything we had been through in the last hour or so. Had it really only been that long? So much adrenaline and tension. So much fear and uncertainty in such a short amount of time. The minds in the rear of the vehicle were much more subdued. Wary of our captive, but calm.

I tried to focus on the illusionist's mind while not alighting too much on my teammates and still paying attention to the road and everything around it. Needless to say, it was difficult and was pulling my attention in too many ways to be effective in all of them. I decided that I needed to concentrate on two: the illusionary and driving.

Just as we were pulling up to the first stop sign heading back into civilized Minefield, I gleaned that our captive was working on another illusion. "Hold on," I murmured to Jade and Steve. Jade gave me a quick look, then threw her hand out to push against the dashboard murmuring for Steve to *just do it*. Steve rolled his eyes but reached up to grab the handle over the window.

I tapped the brakes to give a quick jolt to all in the truck, a warning, and met Holden's eyes in the rearview mirror. Then I smashed my foot onto the brake, bringing the truck to an abrupt halt. All the Primals in the rear kept their balance and swayed with the motion, their hands against the metal in some fashion. The illusionist on the other hand went tumbling, stopped only when his face met the metal of the truck bed.

He tried to brush the blood running in rivulets down his chin by rubbing it on his shirt. He wailed in agony as his nose also made contact. Seeing as he was still restrained with hands cuffed behind him, he had no way to break his fall to the metal truck bed except with his face. Seeing his ineffectual efforts, nose still gushing blood and dripping onto dirty jeans to mingle with the dirt and grass which also adorned them, he gave up and just glared at me.

Still sitting idly at the stop sign, I turned around in my seat so I could look out the rear window, and made sure he heard me. I wagged my finger, "Uh uh uh, none of that Mr. Baddie." He glared. "I have no problem telling one of the guys to knock you out again, maybe give you a nice shiner to go along with that jaw and nose." I shrugged and gave a false look of sympathy before grinning wickedly and turning to face forward.

CHAPTER 27

THE REST OF THE drive to Sam's, the dual purpose facility acting as both gym and CP, lasted only another few minutes. Though as we drove through Minefield's streets, we received several curious or appalled stares from whoever was out and about. So many questions flitted through minds. It wasn't a stretch for the enforcers to have someone in custody, it was however, for that person to be a Sage. Couple that with the group of Sage in the cab of the truck and we were an enigma for the good people of town.

I don't think our joint task force would be kept secret for much longer. There would be too many questions in need of answers, too many sightings to ignore or brush off. Especially when we continued to investigate in the future. This couldn't be brushed aside as a one-off.

I brought the truck to a stop outside the rear entrance to the gym. Our entrance. The truck bounced as Dane left his seat by launching himself over the side of the truck's bed and landing lithely and silently on the asphalt. He then walked to the rear of the truck to release the tailgate. "I think she improved your look," he snickered at our captive as he reached in and grabbed the illusionist around an arm and pulled.

Our baddie tried to resist, but without his hands and the slickness of the metal, all he succeeded in was making obnoxious squeaking noises as his shoes scrambled for purchase and his dirty pants slid across the ridges. He still refused to talk and determinedly pressed his lips together while shooting daggers at the encroaching Primals.

Devlin and Holden had already left the vehicle. They paused in their trek toward the steel door embedded in the concrete building, giving Dane inquiring glances over their shoulders. Dane didn't need them so they continued on.

I was really missing my earbuds right about now. My head still hurt from the illusionist striking me in the pizza place as well as the residual headache from the cacophony I had heard throughout this afternoon. I had pushed my discomfort to the rear as we faced off with the soldiers at the gate, but now that the adrenaline had worn off, I was really flagging.

It didn't help that I had to use energy in order to heal. I was on the highway to one hell of a headache as I trudged behind the rest of the team, pausing only to enter the security code on the keypad embedded to the right of the door, and entered our domain.

Cool air enveloped me the moment I stepped into the whitewashed hallway. The florescent lighting created odd shadows as I made my way down the short passage to the doors at the far end. Pressing my entrance code, the lights flashed green and the locks disengaged. I pushed into the heart of the information center for our team and headed directly to the large mirrored window along the wall to my left.

I wasn't the only one standing attentively at this location, in fact, most of the team stood like statues, glaring at the captured illusionist. We were all scuffed up and filthy at varying points on our bodies, but we stood enraptured as Commander James began his questions.

"Well, Mr–" Commander James looked down at the table where both men sat and reached out to a smallish black rectangle which sat there. It wasn't until the commander slid it to himself and flipped it open that I realized the item was a wallet. "Cummings." He looked at our newly named subject and laced his fingers together, resting them on his flat belly, then leaned back in his chair and extended his legs—the picture of ease. "Why?"

Mr. Cummings rolled his eyes then also sat back, though his body was nowhere near relaxed. He was so stiff I figured whatever Commander James touched on his person would snap off as if it were plastic. Then again, if the commander wanted to break something on our suspect, it wouldn't matter how loose he was, it would splinter like a dry twig. This physically inferior man couldn't hope to withstand a Primal's strength, let alone compete with it, creating the basis for his lashing out at them with illusions. Or at least that was my theory on his motives from what he was thinking.

Wow, this mind reading thing was actually a handy dandy thing to have at my disposal when it came to the how and why of things in the enforcement world. Who knew?

I quickly refocused on the men in the adjacent room. Commander James was attempting to get information while Mr. Cummings was determined to give none. He didn't know our talents, wasn't aware of how we could manipulate him into telling us the information. I had gathered from my first few weeks' training, that our methods and procedures were wildly different from those of the Non-Enhanced and the outside world.

Out there, a man was innocent until proven guilty. Here, and in all Enhanced communities, we were already deemed guilty—thus the isolation and containment—not to mention we had ways of knowing who was at fault. Our justice was swifter. I mean, out in the world, they don't have telepaths, so they couldn't know for sure if a person was guilty without a confession and statement, not that they'd trust our word if they did have our talents available

Here, if we can get him to think about it, then it becomes my job to write the statement and acknowledgement of guilt. I could be used as a human lie detector, as could Jade. Bonus points for a confession.

Commander James continued his questions in the smaller room, still in repose, though now he was angled forward with his arms draped over his bent and open legs. He looked entreating, like a friend coaxing another to talk about the stupid things they did when they drank the night before. That is, until you noticed the hard glint in his striking eyes or took in his sleek tactical apparel.

"Jerry," Commander James continued conversationally and reached out to grasp Jerry's leg above the knee in a decidedly friendly manner, then casually pulled it back. *Odd...* "Why, man?"

"I have nothing to say and you have no proof." Jerry huffed and sat back defiantly, roughly crossing his arms and tucking his hands under opposite armpits. He looked a mess, still covered in blood from kissing the truck bed, a dramatic purpling bruise swelled on his jaw from Devlin's punch. His clothes were stained with grass and dirt from the resulting meeting with the ground, making them look almost like camouflage.

There was a bloodstained rag on the table in front of him, so apparently Commander James had allowed him to clean himself up before I entered. *Geez, didn't think I was that far behind.*

While Jerry Cummings's mouth said the right thing, his mind skipped back to moments embedded in his mind. Moments which added up to his having a hair trigger when it came to people not reacting to him the way he believed they should have. Like the girl in the restaurant. Like Jessica.

Yeah, they weren't the most respectful, but did they deserve to be maimed? The answer was a resounding *no*. His mind flashed to the Primal man who attacked his neighbor. The man had brushed Jerry aside at the gardens when meeting up with friends playing a Primal game of football.

At The Corner Bean, he'd been told to step aside when he did not have his order readily available. At work, he messed with a coworker's lab results because they had scoffed at his conclusions. Jessica had declined his advances, which confirmed what I had gleaned from her.

It went on. Some were smaller illusions which didn't have far reaching implications, but it seemed as though the Sages didn't have any physical disparity from his attentions, now it was hard to say whether that was due to a subdued vision or the fact that Sages were much less reactive but it didn't matter. He had pictured his targets—his victims—and I had seen the catalyst event for each attack, and some we weren't aware of.

"Your actions today alone, resulted in multiple injuries." Jerry scoffed at the commander's words. "You also caused the deaths of two Minefield enforcers."

The statement had all of us remembering the two overzealous men who lost their lives because they were not trained to deal with and thwart such mental attacks. A weighty knowledge settled across our shoulders as we realized we truly were responsible for the welfare of all those within our confines, and we had failed many today.

We all startled when Trent suddenly crowed in victory. Almost as one, we pivoted to face where he sat at the computer bank, each with a similar look of confusion, if not annoyance. We were all wrapped up in Commander James's questioning of our bad guy and wanted to get back to it. I turned back to the window. I was a primary source of assessing guilt in the non-talkative suspects, but I tried to divide my attention so I could also hear what had Trent riled up.

Commander James was getting nowhere verbally with Mr. Cummings, so he offered to get a water and pushed away from the table. When he entered our space, he growled. It was a sound I was quickly becoming accustomed to, seeing the Primals on the squad all seemed to do it. The commander was still a very formidable and intimidating sight when he was displeased. Looking at me in question, he mentally asked if I'd been successful.

"Yes. I got it. He pictured inciting events after you asked him why. I saw each of our victims, plus more."

Commander James pursed his lips and dipped his chin once, before resting a large hand on my shoulder. "Good job, Nathalee. With your report and hopefully some corroborating evidence," he looked over me at the rest of the team, still huddled around Trent, only now they were all equally as excited as him. "Trent, report!" The order reverberated through my body and off the walls of the room as the commander prowled toward the rest of the team. Commander James stopped as he came up behind Trent's rolling chair and stared at the screen. "Perfect."

Trent's damning information was video feeds. Our town was so heavily monitored, that it was pretty hard to find a place that didn't have some form of surveillance, especially around heavily frequented areas and businesses.

What I had seen in Jerry's mind matched what we found on the feed, and then some. We also found tapes of him at The Corner Bean and our altercations at both the restaurant as well as the containment barrier. Trent copied the evidence as Commander James called his contact within the ninny government with the news.

Within hours, a transport was at the door, ready to take the damaged illusionist off our hands. I wasn't sure how the prison facilities kept their long-term detainees, but I was assured there were measures taken so abilities were not used during the prisoner's stay. The simple way was to sedate the prisoner, making it impossible for their mind, let alone their body, to function. I wasn't thrilled with the means, but what could I do? I was barely eighteen.

It hadn't failed them yet, though Primals seemed to be less affected. I was a little fuzzier on how the Enhanced prisons worked, something about electromagnetic fields that distorted brain waves as well as delivering physical deterrents to inmates. I dunno. I'd make it a point to learn more about "the system" now that we didn't have the lingering threat of the illusionist hanging over our heads, dictating our moves.

To celebrate the success of our first major case, we picked up a ridiculous amount of food from the BBQ place, Smokey Joe's, and traveled by caravan to the farmhouse. With the van out of commission for a bit, this would most likely be how we got around.

I hoped for other drivers' sake that the team didn't have to respond as a whole very often or they would have to deal with each of us doing crazy maneuvers to get around them, especially when they didn't get out of the way. I kind of liked the idea.

We spread the food across the picnic table nestled beneath one of the huge trees that stood as sentry along the sides of the home, and dug in. Seating was crowded, both with food and bodies, but I loved it. This was how we were supposed to be. Laughing and poking fun at each other, but without malice, without bite.

As a team.

I put down my fork and rested my elbows on either side of my still full plate, watching and listening to all the mirth evident in my friends. Yes, friends. I considered all these dysfunctional peeps my friends, and while we may not like everything about one another or get along all the time, we had each other's backs. We had demonstrated that earlier in the day.

It was that teamwork which had allowed us to capture a dangerous and slightly unhinged individual. We would ride the highs and lows of our cases together; the lows of this case would be felt from this day on. We would mourn as a unit and use this experience to keep our vigilance up, a grim reminder of the stakes.

This was the first step toward true cohesiveness, toward freedom. Not just for Minefield, but all Enhanced. We were on our way to proving we could handle our own. Yeah, not all of us were going to get along, abide by the rules or be a good person, but that didn't need to condemn us all. We were no more, or less, dangerous than any other human. We each had the same potential. It was just what we chose to do with it.

I smiled. This was the beginning, and tomorrow was a new day.

For everyone.

One step closer to freedom.

Holden's deep voice reverberated inside my skull, courting my attention. I had a feeling that timbre would always give me a warm and tingly feeling all the way to my toes. His smiling eyes and smooth motions not alerting anyone to the fact he wanted to talk. All it took was a few words to make my mind blank and muscles stiffen. Once again, a deer in headlights.

Doesn't have to be today, he began, never pausing from shoveling the delectable edibles into his mouth. *But I want to know about how you healed so quickly.*

Well, crap.

ACKNOWLEDGEMENTS

There are so many people who helped me along on my crazed journey to make this debut novel a reality. First and foremost to my family for standing with me even when I was completely glued to my computer, blind to the world apart from my stories. They all deserve better, but I thank them for putting up with me. They are my heart.

My first longstanding bookish buddy and all around Superwoman, Heather Renee, I am more than blessed to have you tolerate me. You are the best kind of friend a girl could have and I love you dearly. Don't ever leave me!

Julie Hall is a huge inspiration, both as an author and overall human being. I wanna be like Julie... minus the energy drink addiction. I don't need any more weird ticks. Thank you for always being there to help and making time for little ol' me in the craziness you call life. Amanda is totally lumped in here too. Love you ladies.

C.R. Phoenix, you are a dear and allow me to keep my sanity during all things. You are my rock and sounding board and I'd drown without you.

Lastly, my Enforcers, you guys have been awesome cheerleaders for me and Illusionary and I am humbled by your praise and enthusiasm. I only hope I can continue to make you proud to be called Enforcers.

ABOUT THE AUTHOR

LeAnn Mason is an author of YA/NA Urban Science Fantasy. When she's not writing, she can be found out with her hubby and two munchkins around their Oklahoma home either herding chickens or racing ATVs.

Though currently horseless, she has been riding since her early teen years and adores the giant animals so much that she wrote them into her story. Music is another constant in her life, a literal muse to her writing, so it is no surprise to find it entrenched in the pages as well.

Visit her official website at: leannmason.com or contact her at leann@leannmason.com
Facebook: facebook.com/LeAnnMasonAuthor/
Facebook Fan Group: facebook.com/groups/LeAnnsEnforcers/
Instagram: @leann.mason.author
Twitter: @LeAnnMason01

Made in the USA
Lexington, KY
29 March 2018